Praise for *A Bad Day for Sorry*

"Crime fiction hasn't seen a character as scrappy, mean, and incredibly appealing as Stella in a long time."

—*Entertainment Weekly*

"Markedly original . . . Littlefield uses words, not drawings, but this is as graphic a crime novel as you'll find this side of the thriller subgenre. The story's compelling, the dialogue perfect— and Stella is one of the most memorable characters of this summer or any other."   —Jay Strafford, *Richmond Times-Dispatch*

"An abundance of violence is leavened with humor and heart in this debut novel in what I hope is the start of a new series."

—Hallie Ephron, *The Boston Globe*

"*A Bad Day for Sorry* is another of the year's best debuts, a standout mystery distinguished by its charming protagonist and her compelling voice. We don't get many characters like Stella in mystery fiction, but we should. She's fresh and sassy and an awful lot of fun to read about."

—David J. Montgomery, *Chicago Sun-Times*

"Sophie Littlefield shows considerable skills for delving into the depths of her characters and complex plotting as she disarms the reader. . . . Littlefield's exciting debut should be the start of an even more exciting series."

—Oline Cogdill, *Sun-Sentinel*

A BAD DAY FOR PRETTY

Also by Sophie Littlefield

A Bad Day for Sorry

A BAD DAY FOR PRETTY

A CRIME NOVEL

SOPHIE LITTLEFIELD

Minotaur Books

A Thomas Dunne Book

New York

A THOMAS DUNNE BOOK FOR MINOTAUR BOOKS.
An imprint of St. Martin's Publishing Group.

A BAD DAY FOR PRETTY. Copyright © 2010 by Sophie Littlefield. All rights reserved. Printed in the United States of America. For information, address St. Martin's Press, 175 Fifth Avenue, New York, N.Y. 10010.

www.thomasdunnebooks.com
www.minotaurbooks.com

The Library of Congress has cataloged the hardcover edition as follows:

Littlefield, Sophie.
    A bad day for pretty / Sophie Littlefield.—1st ed.
        p. cm.
    ISBN 978-0-312-55975-5
    1. Middle-aged women—Fiction. 2. Abused women—Fiction.
3. Murder—Investigation—Fiction. 4. Women—Crimes against—Fiction.
5. Missouri—Fiction. I. Title.
    PS3612.I882B32 2010
    813'.6—dc22

                                                            2010008709

ISBN 978-0-312-56047-8 (trade paperback)

First Minotaur Books Paperback Edition: May 2011

10 9 8 7 6 5 4 3 2 1

For T-wa
Never was there a prettier baby

Acknowledgments

I am so very grateful to Toni Plummer, my talented and sharp-eyed editor, and Anne Gardner, who showed me exactly how an ace publicist does her job.

And then there's Barbara: without the guidance of my agent Barbara Poelle, my books would be wan and lesser things. Thank you for steeling my resolve, encouraging my excesses, and finding perfect homes for the stories.

To my friends: Huzzah! My old girls plus the new Pens . . . my poker pals, even those who had the temerity to move away . . . my tour (and scotch) partner . . . my RWA and MWA and SinC friends . . . and Roseann and Cheryl and Jan and the G-F's and P's for sticking with me.

How can I adequately thank you: Bob, kids, Mike and Lisa and Kristen and Maureen—your encouragement and love fuels me.

Prologue

Mama was already down in the cellar with Gracellen and Patches. Gracellen was four years younger than Stella—just a baby, only three—so all she cared about was Mama said they could light candles and make a tent with blankets on the card table. Patches knew something was wrong, though—she whined and paced in circles, her toenails clacking on the floor and her tail between her legs.

Daddy said Stella could stay upstairs for a few more minutes while he and Uncle Horace got ready to go help the trailer park people. It wasn't part of their regular job—Daddy and Uncle Horace were Missouri Highway Patrolmen—but when a tornado came, everybody had to help each other out, 'specially if it was a bad one. And this was going to be the worst one since sixty-one, Daddy said.

The special radio crackled and buzzed in the front room. "Winds up to two hunnert ten," a man's voice drawled.

Outside, the sky was turning green. The little trees the Marshes had planted in their yard next door looked like they wanted to bend over all the way down to the ground. Jamie Marsh's tricycle went driving itself down the driveway sideways, then flipped over onto the lawn, where it sat upside down with the wheels spinning.

Daddy and Uncle Horace were loading the big metal box of first aid stuff into the trunk of Horace's old blue car, along with flashlights and coils of rope. They might have to drive folks from the trailer park over to the high school—that's where the Kiwanis were setting up coffee and sandwiches and cots. Most people would already have drove their-selves, Daddy said, but you never knew when people were going to get stubborn.

Stella stayed on the porch as hail clattered on the roof. A flash of lightning made her jump, and she counted—one one-thousand, two one-thousand, three one-thousand, four—before the thunder exploded like it was right down the street. Stella could feel the crash in the floorboards, up through her feet into the middle of her tummy.

"Now you go on down with Mama and Gracie," Daddy said, climbing back up on the porch for a last kiss on the cheek. Rain dripped from his slicker and his cap, but he didn't seem to care, so Stella decided she wouldn't either, and she didn't wipe away the wet kiss from her cheek. "Be good."

"Bye-bye now, Stella-Bella," Uncle Horace called from the drive, giving her a little salute.

"Come back soon, Daddy," Stella said, her voice small under the sound of the whipping winds. "I'm scared."

"I'll be back before you know it, sweetheart," Daddy said. Behind him, Horace sang the silly song he always sang for her: Stella Stella, Bo-Bella. "But we have to go help these folks first."

"Why do you got to help them?"

Daddy laughed, his smoky voice booming and big. "Why? 'Cause helpin' folks is what men do when they grow up."

Stella shut the front door tight like Daddy said, and ran down the stairs to the cellar, where it was warm and cozy and Mama had a plate of pecan sandies and a cup of Kool-Aid ready for her.

By the next morning, Uncle Horace was dead. A shard of metal window casing broke off one of the trailers in the whipping wind, flew through the air, and pierced his heart.

ONE

· · · · · · · · · ·

This'll put hair on your chest," Sheriff Goat Jones said, handing Stella a little spice jar. His legs were so long that his knees brushed against hers under the old pine table, causing a feathery quiver to flutter through her body.

"Hot . . . pepper flakes," Stella Hardesty read, squinting at the label as she accepted the uncapped jar. Her reading glasses were home on the bedside table. She wasn't planning on needing them tonight. She'd had her eye on the sheriff for just about as long as he'd lived in Prosper, and she figured she had his fine form just about memorized.

"Yeah. Really, go ahead." Goat gestured at the steaming plate of chicken and dumplings, silky sauce pooling next to bright green beans tossed with slivered almonds. "Whenever dinner seems like it needs a little something extra, that does the trick. Gets the eyes to smartin', you know?"

Stella nodded, but she didn't know, not really. Her dead husband, Ollie, had never cooked so much as a can of franks and beans, though he'd spent the twenty-six years of their marriage complaining about *her* cooking. A man in an apron was still a novelty to Stella, but she thought she might be able to get used to it.

Three years, six months, and three days after Ollie died, here she was having dinner with a man who cooked, cleaned, didn't pick his teeth, and had never hit a woman in his life. Things could hardly get any better, so why was she so nervous?

Stella hadn't reached the half-century mark without seeing a little of the world. She had been to Kansas City. She'd eaten in a damn four-star restaurant. She knew which fork to pick up when, and she could fake her way through a wine list, and it had been several decades since she'd felt obliged to leave her plate clean.

But closing her fingers around the little bottle, brushing the sheriff's broad-knuckled, strong fingers with her own, she more or less forgot how to make words into sentences and found herself shaking the jar in rhythm with her own pounding heart, all the while unable to look away from those blue-blue eyes, which even in candlelight spelled *t-r-o-u-b-l-e* in spades.

"Damn, Stella. . . . I guess you like it hot," Goat said, watching the pile of pepper flakes accumulate on top of her chicken.

Stella felt the blood rush to her face and set the jar down on the table with a thud. Goat had been having that effect on her since the first time she laid eyes on him, but the difference nowadays was that instead of giving her a rosy glow, blushing turned the network of scars on her face bright pink.

It had been three months since her last case sent her to the hospital with a couple of bullet wounds and sixty-eight stitches—most of them in her face—but the other guys had fared far worse. Three fewer scumbags polluted Sawyer County, Missouri—four, if you counted the wife-beating husband of Stella's client Chrissy Shaw, who'd practically died of sheer stupidity. Well, that and a Kansas City mobster in a bad mood.

Stella had healed up mostly fine, and even managed to drop fifteen pounds from eating hospital food, and just last week Sheriff Goat Jones had invited her to dinner to celebrate her return to health.

All of which was great. Except for one little tiny problem: though Goat had done some creative fact-spinning on her behalf to ensure that all the potentially incriminating loose ends were tied up after her bloody bout of justice-wreaking, the fact remained that he was a shield-wearing, rights-reading, example-setting enforcer of the law, which put him just about exact opposite Stella where it mattered.

Stella dealt in matters of crime and punishment, too. Only her methods weren't exactly endorsed by the Police Union. Her brand of justice was doled out in secret, in back alleys and secluded shacks, in the dead of night, far away from any citizens who might be startled by the screams of the latest woman-abusing cretin who was having his attitude adjusted.

Because that woman was Stella Hardesty, who'd taken her own husband out with a wrench those three and a half years ago—and who never intended to let another woman get smacked around if she could help it.

And usually, Stella *could* help it. Could help the woman who heard about her in a whispered conversation, who tucked her name away in a far corner of her mind, until the day came when things finally got so bad that there were no other options. When the courts failed, when the restraining order didn't manage to restrain anything, when the man who promised he'd never do it again at ten o'clock forgot his promise by midnight. When a beaten woman finally picked herself up the floor and washed off the blood and took inventory of the latest bruises and something snapped and she decided *this* time was the *last* time—when that day came, she knew where to go, and who to see: Stella was ready for the job.

"So . . ." Goat lowered his fork to his plate and regarded her expectantly.

Stella smiled wildly, casting about for something clever to say. It was ridiculous; never, during the many times their paths had crossed in a professional capacity, had she had any trouble talking to the man. Even when she was trying to keep him from figuring out exactly what the hell she was up to. Which, now that she thought about it, described nearly all their conversations.

"Seems like it's raining even harder," she settled on, immediately regretting it. Jeez—she couldn't come up with anything better than that? They'd already discussed the tornado that had come blowing through town earlier in the day. That had seen them through the appetizer—how she'd heard on the radio on the way over that it was a four on the EF scale, enough to pull up trees and toss around cars. In fact, the announcer reported that the twister had taken out some utility sheds and a snack shack out at the fairgrounds.

They didn't use the EF scale back when she was little. Stella didn't know what the tornado that killed her uncle Horace had been rated. But the memories from that night stayed fresh—the waiting, the sounds of the winds beating at the house above them . . . the terrible heaviness of her father's tread on the stairs when he finally returned.

"You okay there, Dusty?" Goat said, peering at her closely.

Stella took a breath. The memories still made her catch her breath, made her heart beat a little faster.

"I'm fine. Just . . . I wonder if there's gonna be another one coming through."

"Well, there might," Goat said. "They didn't downgrade from the Tornado Warning to a Watch yet—least, not before I turned the scanner off. They got a wall cloud over in Ogden County, looked to be going almost thirty miles an hour northeast. Guy on the radio said they had a report of a waterspout over the lake, down by Calhixie Cove—that was right before you got here."

Stella's eyes flicked over to the scanner on the kitchen counter. It was a sleek, compact thing, a far cry from the clunky NOAA weather radio her daddy owned when she was a little girl. Buster Collier turned it on the minute the sky darkened, and listened to the storm reports like other men followed the Cardinals. How many times had her mother scolded her father to turn off the radio when she put dinner on the table? That was her dad, though—especially after Uncle Horace was killed. It was like he couldn't bear not knowing, like if he turned away from the radio, the storm might rage out of control and snatch away something else dear to him.

Goat's little house was built snug and tight, but she could still hear the winds whistling outside, the crackle of twigs blown up against the windows.

"So another one's coming our way," she said softly. That happened sometimes; they called it a swarm. "I surely don't like tornadoes."

"Is that right? A tough gal like you, Dusty?" Goat's grin quirked up, teasing, but then he seemed to sense her apprehension and the smile faded. He set his fork and knife down and reached across the table for her hand, folding it in his, squeezing gently, and a strange thing happened: on top of the hot-hot gotta-get-me-some-of-that charge that generally accompanied every interaction with Goat, Stella felt something else, an unexpectedly tender something that for some reason caused her eyes to get all teary and her heart to lurch dangerously.

It was almost like . . . like he was offering her *safety*.

And safe was something she'd vowed never to take for granted again, something she had decided she'd rather live without than ever be lulled into a false sense of security. Trust was a door Stella had shut forever.

But Goat's eyes in the candlelight were deep as an indigo ocean, and his fingers stroking hers were warm and strong and rough from hard work. "I mean, just because, you know, they're such a pain . . . ," she stammered. "Power failures and trees getting knocked down and all that, you know?"

"I kind of like tornadoes," Goat said. His voice, always deep and drawly, seemed to have gone a couple notches lower. "All that crazy energy? Like a front-row seat to the end of the world or something."

That's what it had been for Horace, all right. . . . *Daddy's little brother, good with the ladies. They said he was better looking than Daddy, though Stella knew better. Horace loved to tie flies, but*

9

he hated to fish. Came for Sunday suppers, but never quite managed to get up in time for church. Brought Stella licorice and challenged her to watermelon-seed-spitting contests . . .

Stella realized Goat was waiting for her to say something, but nothing came to mind. Hell, she was quite a head case tonight. She'd thought about canceling, but she'd been looking forward to tonight—so she snapped off the radio once they announced the twister had blazed its path through town without injuring anyone, then gritted her teeth and driven over in the pouring rain, trying to keep her heartbeat under control.

Still, maybe a date was a bad idea. Her body might have recovered from the whole killing-spree thing, but it looked like her emotions might need a little more time in the airing cupboard before she took them on the road.

She hadn't thought about Uncle Horace in years. And what was with the tears? She'd survived worse—way worse than a wayward little memory—without cracking like this. It was downright embarrassing.

Goat's dining room suddenly seemed a little too small. She blinked a couple times and pulled her hand away from under Goat's. Maybe she did want him bad, but she didn't need his pity, or sympathy, or whatever the hell it was that was causing him to turn on the charm.

He sighed and tapped his fingers on the table. "Look, Dusty, you know what you need?"

Stella shook her head, helping herself to an oversize sip from her wine glass.

"You need a little meat on those bones. You're looking awful skinny. Come on, now, try the chicken. It was my mom's recipe."

Stella couldn't help it—she sat up a little straighter and inhaled a nice big breath that set off her bosoms to their best advantage. *Skinny* wasn't a word she'd heard directed her way in a long time. Even shed of those fifteen hospital pounds, she was still on the generous side of womanly.

Well—some fellas liked that.

Maybe it would be possible to get this evening back on track after all. She gave Goat her best there's-more-of-me-where-this-comes-from smile. "Why, thank you, Goat."

"So—come on, just a bite." Goat's grin tilted to one side of that broad, sexy mouth.

"Um." Stella picked up her knife and fork and carefully cut a dainty bite of chicken and slipped it in her mouth. Immediately a capsaicin-packing burst of heat rocketed across her lips and tongue, and Stella flapped her hands and mewled in pain, swallowing the mouthful and praying that it wouldn't set her gut on fire. She grabbed her water glass and took a powerful swig, letting the water overflow out the corners of her lips and down her cheeks.

When she finally opened her eyes, gasping for breath, she saw that Goat was laughing.

He was covering it up pretty well, trying to keep a serious expression on his face, but his muscular shoulders were quaking with mirth, and his eyes were all crinkly with amusement.

"Darlin', a little dab of that hot pepper'll probably do the trick next time," he finally said.

Stella glared and finished off her water. She set the glass down hard on Goat's dining room table, making the candles jump and skitter in their brass holders. "I'll try to remember that."

"You've got a . . ." Goat reached out and carefully brushed

at her lower lip, his fingertip caressing the tender spot above her chin in a way that caused a little shiver to shoot up from her toes to somewhere along her spine, leaving sparklers lit up all along the way. "A flake, I think."

He showed her the tip of his finger, and sure enough there was a tiny little speck of pepper stuck to it. Stella picked up her napkin and dabbed daintily at her mouth.

"Oh," she said. "Thanks."

She set her napkin back on her lap and Goat kept his gaze fixed on her face and damn if she didn't find herself staring back, and then a few seconds or maybe it was a few hours went by, Stella couldn't be sure, and he slowly reached for her hand again, right there on the smooth pine surface of the dining room table, and this time Stella let him, and she had time to remark to herself on just how big Goat's hand was compared to hers as he ran his thumb slowly over the sensitive skin on the inside of her wrist—and then the doorbell rang.

Stella blinked.

It rang again, three quick blasts, and Goat released her hand and she managed, barely, not to cuss out loud.

"Excuse me," he said softly, and pushed his chair back. At least the man had the decency to sound disappointed.

He unfolded himself from the table, all six-foot-four of hard-muscled law enforcement pride of Sawyer County, and as he went to the door, Stella took the opportunity to scrape as much of the hot pepper off her chicken as she could, burying it in a little pool of sauce with her fork.

The ringing had turned to pounding by the time Goat got the door opened, and the rush of the wind and rain splatting against the house drowned out whatever the visitor had to say, though Stella could make out a high and rather desperate-sounding voice.

Stella turned in her chair just in time to see Goat stagger back and send the door banging against the wall.

"What the hell are you doing here, Brandy?" he demanded.

A generous five feet of womanly curves clattered into the house on ridiculously high heels and stood shaking a fuchsia umbrella out on the hardwood floor, touching bloodred-tipped fingers to a complicated platinum-blonde updo.

"I declare, Goat Jones," she said. "That's a fine way to greet your wife."

TWO

. . . .

Your *wife*?" Stella demanded, pushing back her chair and standing in order to view the full measure of this disturbing turn of events.

Goat's gaze flicked from one woman to the other and back. He retreated from the front door, still holding a kitchen towel, which he waved in front of him like a matador confronting an angry bull.

"Uh, Stella, this is my ex-wife, Brandy Truax—"

"Not quite, babycakes," the petite party-crasher said. She finished her hair-fluffing with a final pat or two and tugged at the bottom hem of her snug knit skirt. There wasn't quite enough skirt to go around, and Brandy's straightening efforts revealed a band of skin around her midriff. Her sweater was knit of thick pink yarn and might have kept her warm and toasty, except for the fact that it seemed to have been designed for a five-year-old and didn't begin to cover the top half of a decidedly grown-up and almost certainly fake set of breasts. With her skyscraping platform shoes and her top-heavy mass of curls and her sparkly makeup and extra-long lashes, Brandy looked like she'd been hanging around Dolly Parton long enough to pick up some fashion tips. "You never quite got around to signing the documents, remember?"

"Me?" Goat paused midshuffle. "It was *you* that wouldn't sign, remember? I just paid that shyster Gordy Gates another six hundred bucks to drive the latest copy over to you back in January. He said you told him you needed to talk to your astrologer and figure out the right moon phase for signing, or some such load of crap."

Brandy sighed dramatically and set her purse, a large gold oblong clutch tricked out with studs and metal trim, down on the table with a thunk. She didn't seem to notice or care that she had nearly knocked over the bottle of wine from which Stella had consumed a mere half glass—a show of temperance that now seemed like it might have been wasted.

"You, me, does it really matter who it was?" Brandy asked no one in particular. "I swear, that's what got us in trouble in the first place, Goat, all that finger-pointin'. Never does a bit of good, if you ask me."

Stella made tracks for her own purse, a considerably more subdued number that she'd stowed carefully next to the front door along with her umbrella, which had mostly dried in the hour that she'd been at Goat's. "My, my, look at the time," she murmured. "Just delightful to meet you, Brandy, but tomorrow's a work day, and, well, you know how these things go."

"Oh, hell, Dusty—" Goat gave his own chair an angry shove, clacking it against the table. "No need to go off all half-cocked like this. Lemme just figure out what Brandy here needs and send her on her way and we can get back where we were."

"I really don't——," Stella began. All the lovely shivery feelings from earlier in the evening were gone, as though the heavy cloud of perfume that Brandy brought in the door with her had doused the sparks that had been sparkling between Stella and the sheriff for months. Years, even.

Stella had become a bit of an expert in relationships, seeing as she was a member of the marital counseling profession, loosely speaking. At least, she did a lot of listening when women showed up at her door, looking to become members of the not-going-to-take-it-anymore club. Working with her clients took compassion and reasoning skills and coaching and encouraging and a heap of intuition and enough optimism for two, since generally the ladies didn't bring much of that with them.

Over the years, Stella had learned a thing or two about what could go wrong in the marital union—and she'd never seen a lingering-spouse situation that turned out anything but messy. She'd assumed, along with everyone else in Prosper, that Goat's marriage was a clean kill. Learning that it had popped up from the grave was not encouraging. Men whose baggage contained undead relationships were to be avoided.

There was the player, the man who'd tell you his marriage had been over for years, even while his wedding ring was cooling in his wallet. Well, Goat wasn't one of those, Stella was sure, since she'd seen for herself that he'd been decidedly single for the three years since he moved to Prosper to head up the sheriff's department. So single, in fact, that he'd felt free to show a number of the local ladies a nice time—or so the gossip went.

Then there were the never-quite-split ones. That's what this situation looked like it might turn out to be.

Last January, Nora Romero had hired Stella to do some

heavy-duty explaining to her boyfriend, Nick, that it was not okay to use her credit card to pay for long-distance conversations with special ladies on the other end of 900 numbers, but while Stella was doing her due diligence, she discovered that there was another mad-as-hell gal over in Brisbane, Ohio, who just happened to still be married to Nick and wondered if Stella could get him to pay back the $2,300 he'd run up on *her* credit card, making long-distance friends before he skipped town.

Not that she expected Goat was spending his public servant's salary on heavy breathers whose pictures appeared in the back of men's magazines. For one thing, he wouldn't have to. She wasn't the only filly in town who'd taken a shine to the man; it seemed that tall, sexy, righteous men in uniform were in short supply.

But that little crush, or whatever it was, needed to be laid to rest. Stella had entirely too much drama in her life already without getting dragged into a tug-of-war with a damp sexpot with questionable fashion sense and very poor timing.

"I need to run by the shop," she said. Besides her unofficial side business, Stella ran the sewing machine repair and supply shop she'd inherited from Ollie. "Make sure everything's okay."

"You already checked," Goat protested. He had called and offered to help her nail plywood over the windows before the tornado went through, but Stella turned him down, since they were predicting the storm would stay south of Prosper. Later, when darkness arrived earlier than usual and Ted Krass over at the Live Super Doppler One Thousand Weather Center got on the radio to announce that the funnel cloud had traced a route through the fairgrounds and skipped across Broadway before heading out the west side of town, she made a couple of calls to make sure the shop was still standing.

But she knew from experience that once her luck turned, it tended to stay turned. "I need to check again," she said, adding a little ice to her voice. "Sometimes trouble comes along when you're least expecting it."

Goat followed her to the door and reached out like he was going to grab her arm. Stella stepped neatly out of the way; her physical therapist had recently added some tai chi moves to her daily workouts, which really boosted her agility.

"At least let me follow you over," Goat said. "It could be dangerous out there."

"Hey!" Brandy hollered. She set her fists on her curvy hips and pushed out her glossy bottom lip in an impressive pout. "Hello! What am I, chopped liver?"

"No, you're not," Goat said impatiently, "but far as I can tell, you're warm and nearly dry and fixing to plant your butt in my house, and that makes you accounted for in my book, while Stella here seems hell-bent on going looking for trouble."

"Is she your girlfriend?"

Stella felt her face flush even as Goat stammered out several rounds of we're-not-this-isn't-I-don't equivocating. At least he didn't say no, exactly. But he sure wasn't saying yes either.

His wife, or ex, or whatever the hell she was, was plenty short on manners, talking about Stella like she wasn't even in the room. But she had Goat's ticket: the question stopped him in his tracks and reduced him to a gibbering idiot.

While Brandy drilled him with a gaze that could light fires, Stella made it to the door and twisted the knob. Immediately the force of the wind and rain blasted it practically out of her hand; it was as though the storm wanted to come on in and witness Stella's humiliation for itself. An icy draft of rainwater hit Stella sidelong in the face and sluiced down her neck, ruining, no doubt, her only 100 percent silk top.

"All righty then," she called, and slipped out into the storm, yanking the door shut behind her with a mighty effort.

Then she waited on the porch, not even bothering to open her umbrella, since it would have immediately been blown inside out in the wind, and gave Goat a count of ten to come after her.

Make that a count of fifteen . . . twenty.

Hell.

She bolted for her trusty green Jeep Liberty and practically threw herself into the driver's seat, slamming the door shut behind her. She shook the water off her head, splatting droplets all over the car's interior, and jammed the key in the ignition. Without bothering to check what she might run over, she hit the gas hard and backed around in a tight arc before reversing and aiming the wheel toward the lane. In the pitch-black night, with rain slamming down in sheets, it was more of a guess than a certainty, her headlights picking out an undistinguished stretch of mud ahead. Her tires spun for a few seconds in the flooded gravel drive before finally catching with a vengeance.

Hurtling over the uneven road, bouncing around in the Jeep gave Stella a small measure of calm.

Once she was back on the main road, she eased up on the gas a little. Grudgingly, she snapped on her seat belt—no sense giving Goat's ex the satisfaction of a gory death if she got in an accident tonight—and hit the CD PLAY button. Emmylou's voice blasted into the car, in the middle of the song Stella'd been playing at a high volume as she drove over earlier.

I want a high-powered love
got to have intensity

Well, that was when she'd thought the evening might end up with her getting a little something more than a friendly handshake. Stella snapped the sound system off with a sharp jab.

Damn.

It was one thing to carry a torch for a man you couldn't—shouldn't—ever have. It was quite another to accept his dinner invitation and let all those wouldn't-it-be-nices start turning into hopes and plans and, when you got it especially bad, a *future*. Start believing in your own luck, and soon you were having high-minded ideas about how you might tickle fate with a whispered suggestion and a lucky roll of the dice.

Stella had shaved her legs . . . and not just the calves and knees, but her thighs, too, an extra effort she hadn't made in ages. Yesterday she'd suffered the indignity of a bikini wax down at Hair Lines, which entailed not just memorable pain but also Pearl, the aesthetician, whistling through her teeth and remarking, "Guess it's been a while since you got the lawnmower out of the shed, ain't it, Stella?"

Stella had recently patched things up with her daughter Noelle after being estranged for a few years. Noelle just happened to be in the beauty business herself, and agreed to make the half-hour drive over from her house this afternoon to touch up Stella's color and tame her brows. It helped that Noelle didn't have a washing machine at her house; Stella got to see

20

her daughter at least once a week these days, when Noelle brought her brimming laundry baskets over.

Stella ran a hand through her rain-ruined hairdo, which Noelle had fussed over for what seemed like hours, dyeing it back to what the two of them remembered her natural shade to be before all that unwelcome gray showed up, and then adding a crazy halo of tinfoil highlights and lowlights. While they sat around waiting for all that beauty to take effect, Noelle painted Stella's nails a shade called Tokyo Rose and came at the Goat question from every direction she could think of.

Stella was proud of her girl—relentless and nosy, just like her mama. But Stella didn't give up much, nonetheless.

Which was a good thing, considering how it turned out. Next week, when Noelle came in the door with her laundry, Stella would breezily claim that she and Goat had a perfectly nice time, but the romantic attraction fizzled out and they decided to just be friends. Maybe Noelle would let it drop without a big third degree.

Yeah. Right.

Stella turned onto the old ranch road and was headed back toward town when her cell phone rang, scaring her half to death. Todd Groffe, her thirteen-year-old neighbor, had updated her ringtone again, and it sounded like a man being castrated while someone played the *White Album* backwards at 66 rpm.

"What, what, *what?*" she demanded as she fumbled for the answer button and nearly hit a cat bolting across the street in the downpour despite having reduced her speed to a mere fifteen miles per hour, the little Jeep buffeted about in the near-horizontal rain and shrieking wind.

"Phones are out."

"Well, speak of the devil, you little monster," Stella grumbled. "I was just thinking about how dang much I hate that—that *thing* you put on my phone."

"What—The Thermals?" Todd's adolescent voice cracked with incredulity. "Stella, they're fuckin' *genius,* man!"

"Watch your mouth. And I want my old ring tone back, hear?"

Todd's snort of disgust came across loud and clear. "Mom says tell you the power's out over on Hickory and they say it'll prob'ly go out here too and do you got candles and shit or are you staying over at your friend's. What friend's house are you at, anyway?"

Stella could hear Todd's mother, Sherilee, in the background, hollering at Todd to watch his mouth, but with less conviction than Stella, probably because his six-year-old sisters were screaming at the tops of their lungs. Damn. Stella had forgotten she told Sherilee about the date. Or dinner, or whatever the hell it was.

For a woman whose business relied on a level of discretion matched only in the bowels of the Pentagon, Stella had sure managed to shoot her mouth off enough to guarantee herself a whole mess of regret.

"Tell your mother," she said icily, "that dinner was fine, but I am looking forward to spending the rest of the evening *alone.*"

"Whatever—why don't you tell her yourself. I ain't your goddamn message service."

"Fine. I will. Put her on. I'm sure she'll be glad to hear about that math test you left at my house the other day."

Silence.

Stella regularly called the boy's bluff, but he never seemed to tire of trying to sneak one past her. "What I thought," she said. "Okay, so whose message service are you now?"

Todd hung up before Stella could mess with him any further, and she added a note to her mental to-do list—thrash that boy within an inch of his life—before tapping the brakes and bringing her speed down barely above a crawl.

She switched on the radio and fiddled with it until she managed to get KKRN News Radio, home of the Live Super Doppler One Thousand, in addition to being the hotbed of everything newsworthy in Korn Kountry.

". . . tracked west of Sedalia, winds at two hundred—"

So the second twister had materialized after all. Two hundred miles an hour—that was no autumn rain shower. This was turning out to be a hell of a weather event, to quote one of Ted Krass's most favored turns of phrase.

"Several sightings have been reported along the border of Sawyer and Latham counties. The storm is moving north-northwest at speeds approaching thirty-three miles per hour and has taken a route south of Fairfax and through north central Prosper. Damage estimates are not known at this time. . . ."

Stella's heart did a little stop-start.

The north end of town was where Hardesty Sewing Machine Repair & Sales was located. More important, it was where Chrissy Shaw and her two-year-old son, Tucker, lived.

Stella veered into the turn lane and took a sharp right onto Broadway, the fastest route to the middle of town. She was more than a little worried about Chrissy. Tucker had been kidnapped a few months back by his worse-than-deadbeat step-father, who'd hoped to trade him for favors from the Kansas

City organized crime cartel, but got himself shot dead and stuffed into a Rubbermaid storage bin instead.

Chrissy hadn't wasted too much time mourning her dead ex, but helping Stella get the boy back had gotten *her* shot, too, more seriously than Stella, who'd suffered a hit to the stomach that miraculously managed to avoid destroying anything critical, and a mostly superficial shoulder wound. Chrissy, still recovering from the bullet that tore up a lung and damaged her heart, was helping out part-time in the sewing machine shop while she followed the program of rest and therapy that would restore her to full health. While the sessions were coming along well, and the doctors had declared the girl stronger and more determined than any patient in their collective memory, Stella didn't want Chrissy to have to worry about blown-in windows or trees falling down on the house.

Well—*house* wasn't exactly the right word. Stella burned rubber the rest of the way to the parking lot that Hardesty Sewing Machine Sales & Repair shared with the China Paradise restaurant. Roseann Lau, China Paradise's grumpy owner and cook, had invested in an apartment building a while back and moved into its ground-floor rooms, adding "ill-humored landlady" to her résumé and leaving the diminutive apartment at the back of the restaurant empty until Chrissy moved in.

It had been simple enough to set up a plywood ramp to the back door while Chrissy was still in a wheelchair, and now that the girl was up and about, she had begun scouring off the decade's worth of grease and smoke that had wafted from the front restaurant back to the little apartment.

As Stella turned down Third Street toward the shop, she was relieved to see there was still power in the neighborhood.

Felled branches and uprooted bushes and all manner of debris littered the streets, but so far she'd seen only a few upended trees and none, thankfully, blocked traffic. By morning, judging from the looks of this storm, there would be crews out with chain saws and chains, dragging off chopped-up tree trunks; pickups with ropes tied to their hitches extracting evergreens from picture windows; folks with their sleeves rolled up, hauling junk out of caved-in garages and sheds.

She was relieved to see that nothing worse had happened. It wasn't rational, but tornadoes always left her unsettled and anxious, the memories from the past lodged somewhere deep where time couldn't erase them.

Stella's sister Gracellen had called Stella shortly after she and her husband moved to California years ago. "Stella," she exclaimed, "they get a little three-point earthquake out here and they act like it's the end of the world. When somebody's china falls off the shelf, it makes the evening news!"

Stella shared her sister's astonishment. Sure, the west coast occasionally had a genuine earthquake disaster, like Loma Prieta in '89. But Stella and her classmates hadn't spent their elementary school careers huddling in the school basement during tornado drills for nothing: a single Midwestern tornado season could kill more folks than several decades of earthquakes along the west coast.

In the news, they were just numbers. Three dead in eastern Ohio. Four killed in flash floods along the Mississippi.

In '66, the tornadoes took a single victim, but Stella hadn't forgotten.

She rounded the corner into the parking lot, and there, in all its squat cinder block glory, was Hardesty Sewing Machine

Sales & Repair. China Paradise was still standing as well, though the Dumpster behind the restaurant had tipped over and garbage had blown across the lot. A broken umbrella, spines snapped and bent, was splayed against the wheels of Chrissy's old, beat-up Celica. Stella pulled in next to it and cut the engine, and rolled her window down far enough to peer out.

A light burned in the living room of Chrissy's apartment. Stella couldn't make out any movement behind the sheer curtains, and she debated whether or not to bother the girl. If Chrissy and Tucker had managed to get to sleep during the storm, it might be better to let them catch up on their rest. On the other hand, if Stella went home now, she would be up all night worrying.

Go on a vengeance quest with a person, stand shoulder to shoulder battling the bad guys, go down fighting while she loses consciousness at your side—experiences like those tended to bring you mighty close to a person. And her towheaded sideways-grinning new-tooth-drooling brat, too, for that matter.

Before Stella could make up her mind whether to stay or go, the door to the apartment was flung open and Chrissy Shaw stood with her arms folded across her chest, blond curls springing out crazily around her china-pale face, lacy pink camisole incongruously pretty over baggy gray sweats with PROSPER H. S. PANTHERS printed down the leg.

"Get on in here, Stella, 'fore you drown your badass self!"

Stella hesitated, her face pelted by stinging bullets of rain. "You sure you're up for company, sugar?"

"You ain't hardly company," Chrissy said, rolling her eyes.

"And I ain't puttin' on any fuss for you neither. You can fetch your own durn beer and fix your own sandwich, but I sure would like you to get on in here and explain what you're doin' at my house 'stead of gettin' yourself properly laid by that law-man of yours."

THREE

. . . .

Sheriff Goat Jones leaned in close and brushed his damp, incredibly smooth-shaved cheek against Stella's.

"Mmm, hmm," she purred. "That's the way I like it."

But then for some reason he took one of his size 13, shined-up black service shoes and toed her right in the painful part of her bum hip. Even as he ran his silky-smooth cheek along the top of her nose, he dug harder at the poor worn-down joint.

Then he kicked her.

"Damn it, Goat!" Stella yelped, and opened her eyes.

She found herself staring into two very large, unblinking pale blue eyes set into a cherubic little face with a drool-dampened chin.

Before she could react, Tucker leaned in close and put his forehead flat on her face and mumbled something that sounded like *Sow*. He hadn't managed *Stella* yet—he was sticking to one-syllable words for the moment.

As charmed as she was to find Chrissy's little boy trying to scramble up onto the couch with her, Stella was disappointed to discover that the whole Goat thing had been a dreamy illusion.

She looked down and confirmed that it hadn't been Goat's shoe at all that was causing searing pain up and down her leg, but Tucker's overlarge toy truck, which he'd somehow managed to haul up and drop on top of her, despite the fact that it was nearly as big as he was. The sharp edge of the yellow metal truck bed poked painfully into her flesh, even through the pile of blankets and quilts that Chrissy had dug out of the closet for her last night.

"Hey, little T, how are you, precious?" Stella said, yawning and setting the truck on the floor. She scooped the boy up for a snuggle. "Listen, let's just forget that whole 'damn it' thing. Sometimes Auntie Stella says bad words by accident. But that doesn't mean you have to."

She slowly eased up to a sitting position as Tucker wiggled out of her arms and disappeared under the blankets. She tried to work the stiffness from her neck and back with a series of shoulder rolls, which caused some suspicious popping noises. She was too old to be sleeping on couches. After last night's tossing and turning, she'd probably have to put in some time later on her own firm Sealy Posturepedic to catch up on her rest—if her house was still standing. At least there probably wouldn't be any customers in desperate need of sewing machine oil or dressmaker's chalk today; the Home Depot was likely to be the only store in town experiencing a run on supplies.

"Sow . . . Sow." Tucker popped his head out from the covers, his grin sprouting dimples.

"Oh, so there you are, you li'l nubbin," Chrissy exclaimed, coming around the corner holding two big mugs of coffee. As she set the mugs down and scooped up her giggling boy, Stella's phone, which had slipped out of her purse and lay on the floor beside the couch, started up its terrible racket.

Tucker's little face screwed up, and he looked like he was getting ready to wail.

"Aw, now, give it a few years," Stella said, seizing at the thing and stabbing the ANSWER button. "When you're a big boy, you'll think that's the music of the heavens. Probably be skate-boarding holes in my driveway, too. Y'ello?"

The voice on the other end launched into a stream of sobbing and run-together words, and Stella sat up a little straighter. A work call, then. Dang—she needed her reading glasses, which were undoubtedly back home on the kitchen table, and her notebook, which was still in the Jeep where she'd left it when she washed up last night with the storm. Speaking of which: Stella glanced out the single window in the apartment's narrow little living room and saw cerulean skies dotted with a smattering of cotton-ball clouds.

Wasn't that just always the way? Her daddy used to say that the day after a tornado brought the sun running to make up for lost time, and today certainly seemed to prove the rule. Golden September sunlight streamed through the glass and sparkled up the surfaces of the room's simple furnishings, glinting off Tucker's and Chrissy's matching white-blond curly mop tops.

Well, lovely as the new day might be, her caller evidently had more pressing concerns on her mind.

"Now slow down, hon," Stella said soothingly, thinking back over her most recent clients, trying to figure out who might have met with some new and upsetting type of setback. The thing was, there hadn't really been much in the way of new jobs lately. With Stella out of commission for a few months, her side business had gone into a holding pattern. Ladies who'd been working up to the idea of taking decisive action against their no-good, wife-smacking, covenant-breaking mates had heard about Stella's misfortune—everyone in town knew that Stella wasn't in any kind of shape to be winding up the justice machine—and had no choice but to dial back their determination for the moment.

When you were a beat-up wife, suffering in silence was generally a familiar strategy. Stella had done it herself plenty often before she'd finally snapped and taken Ollie out. The thing about a mean and hateful man was that he'd keep. Wasn't like, if the gals had to wait a few more weeks for Stella to get back in full fighting form before they could embark on their quests for vengeance, these crappy husbands were going to go transforming themselves overnight into doting soul mates. No, these guys pretty much stayed true to type, never varying much from their agenda of hurtin' unless some sort of major upset came along to knock them off their sorry feet.

"Honey, who is this now?" Stella asked, cradling the phone close against her ear so the wailing voice wouldn't carry. It was instinctive, trying to shield little Tucker from this sad aspect of her business.

"It's Neb," the voice wailed. "I mean this is Donna, Donna Donovan—"

"Donna!" Stella exclaimed. "What in heaven's name—? Did Neb do something—?"

"No, no, he hasn't done anything," Donna interrupted. "Don't think that for a minute. But we need you. *He* needs you. Can you get on over to the fairgrounds fast?"

"Has something happened to Neb?" Stella asked.

Nebuchadnezzar Donovan was the lone exception on the roster of men who'd been on the receiving end of Stella's professional attentions—the one man whom she considered to be fully rehabilitated after what had turned out to be a fairly brief probation.

Of course, he hadn't been a typical parolee, either. Neb wasn't guilty of smacking Donna, his bride of twenty-five years, but his sudden and nearly devastating conversion to cultlike religious fundamentalism a little over a year ago had made Donna desperate enough to hire Stella to talk some sense into him.

"Nothin's happened yet," Donna said, her voice taut with worry, "but Sheriff Jones came by around six and picked Neb up and said something had come up down at the demolition derby track at the fairgrounds, that he needed Neb's help with. After a while when he didn't come home, I got worried and I called him but he had his phone off, 'cept around seven thirty here comes a call from the sheriff's phone—I got that caller ID—and Neb tells me Goat's only let 'im have the one phone call to let me know not to wait breakfast for him, so I says is something wrong and Neb says no in a way that makes me pretty sure he means yes, you know? Something is *definitely* wrong over there, Stella."

"Okay," Stella said, thinking fast and rubbing sleep out of her eyes. Chrissy was in the apartment's minuscule kitchen breaking eggs into a bowl, and Tucker had wandered off carrying one of the hot pink rubber clogs Stella kicked off the night before.

One of the little-known facts about Neb Donovan was that

he'd battled an OxyContin addiction. This was before his whole come-to-Jesus phase and after an especially bad, prolonged battle with a disk in Neb's back that slipped far enough to send him into a world of exquisite hurt, the kind that required frightening quantities of pain medication to be tipped down his throat like so many Nerds candies. His back healed, but by then Neb had developed an unseemly fondness for the little yellow pills.

Neb had done most of his Oxy-popping out at the track, a convenient location, since he was the year-round maintenance man at the fairgrounds.

"Has he been at the track working this week?" Stella asked. With the Sawyer County Fair only weeks away, Neb's job would be kicking into high gear, getting everything ready for the thousands of visitors who would come from all over the state to converge on Prosper, champing at the bit for a full day of corn dogs and midway rides and prizewinning pickles and hogs.

"Oh my, yes. But them organizers got him hopping around busier than a tick on a cat's back, with their last-minute schedule changes and what-all, he ain't come home on time in weeks, I swear they have no idea what it takes to . . ." Donna's voice trailed off, and Stella heard her sniffle.

"Donna? You okay, honey?"

"Do you—?" Donna coughed gently and cleared her throat a couple of times until she got herself under control. "Do you think he might be into the Oxy again?"

"I don't think so," Stella said, but in truth she had no idea. Oxy was a deadly habit, cheap and available enough out in the sticks that rural folks could develop a troublesome taste for it.

And besides, it wasn't really sheriff department business to round up unfortunate junkies—unless they'd done some sort of additional crime-committing while they were high as a kite. "Do you want to meet me at the track and we can see if we can talk to Neb in private and find out what's going on?"

"I don't want to go over there," Donna said quickly. "How's that gonna look—like I'm checking up on him. If they don't already think he's using again, they will then. If *you* go, it can be like, you know, you just heard about the fuss and were curious and what-all."

"Okay, give me ten minutes to get myself put together here, and I'll head over and see what I can find out."

"Oh, would you?" The relief in Donna's voice was palpable.

Stella promised again and hung up, then heaved a huge sigh. "Chrissy, that was Donna Donovan. The sheriff's hauled Neb out of bed and got him over at the fairgrounds and won't let him go home. I'm sure it's nothing, but Donna's fit to be tied and I told her I'd run over there and check on things. I don't suppose you could fry me up something in the next two minutes, do you? Oh, and can I borrow your toothbrush?"

"That's disgusting," Chrissy said as Stella folded the quilts and blankets and stacked them in a pile at the end of the couch. "But I suppose you ain't got a lot of choice 'less you want to breathe dragon breath on that man of yours. Which I don't guess is gonna help you get laid. But what do I get outta fixin' your breakfast, I'd like to know?"

Stella ducked into the little bathroom but left the door ajar. The apartment was so small that she could keep talking to Chrissy in the other room without raising her voice. "How about, I don't know, a fifty-thousand-dollar signing bonus if you come work for me full-time?"

Chrissy snorted with laughter. "No chance, you ain't got that kind of money. Besides, I ain't goin' criminal, not with this boy to raise up all by myself. I'm perfectly happy running the sewin' shop and you can carry on all your lawbreakin' high jinks without me."

Stella grinned to herself as she finished brushing her teeth and splashed some cold water on her face. It was funny how much she'd come to rely on Chrissy, and not just to take over part of the workload.

She opened the medicine cabinet and helped herself to Chrissy's hairbrush.

"Yes, you can use my makeup," Chrissy called. "Seein' as you're going to be visiting with your boyfriend an' all. Just go easy on the blush—you always put on too much and then you end up looking like a old tramp."

Stella, who'd already picked up a Maybelline quad eye shadow in fetching shades of gold and pink and burgundy, frowned at her reflection. "He's not my boyfriend," she muttered. Not her *anything,* now that his wife or ex or whatever the heck she was had shown up. Visions of Brandy's casual little wave as Stella let herself out—flicking hair spray–stiffened waves of blond hair over her shoulder and mouthing *buh-bye, now* with a pout that had to have been collagen-assisted—caused a heartburn-like pain to lodge in her chest.

Stella jammed the eye shadow quad back onto the crowded shelf and slammed the cabinet shut. "And if I want to look like a tramp, why I'd just like to see anyone try to stop me."

The judicious silence that followed suggested that Chrissy had decided to keep her opinion to herself, a rare enough event. Hell, Stella hadn't meant to snap at her—but that comment had stung. Since she and Noelle had resumed cordial relations, Stella asked her daughter for help in the personal-grooming department, and she thought she had been making progress. Still, cosmetics—an industry she had supported as enthusiastically as anyone in her younger years—had certainly changed in the last decade or so while her attention had been elsewhere, and reentry was proving a little more difficult than she'd expected.

She left the bathroom, pointedly ignoring her reflection. "Can I borrow a T-shirt or something?"

"Yeah, whatever you can find in the dresser."

Stella sorted through stacks of neatly folded tops until she found one with a minimum of embellishment—a pink T-shirt that was mostly plain besides a dainty little drawstring neck. Stella slipped it on and wadded her old one into a ball, then shoved it in her purse.

Chrissy popped out of the little kitchen, holding a paper plate.

"This here can be yours," she said, "but not unless you let me get them Comcast guys out to the shop. I cain't stand that connection speed no more, Stella. It's slower'n molasses in January."

"Fine, whatever." Secretly Stella was pleased to see Chrissy developing a talent for the computer. It would certainly be nice to get the record-keeping out of the shoe boxes and entered into some sort of orderly system. And set up online ordering for the stock. And half a dozen other tasks she hadn't had time for since the justice-delivering business ramped up. "Get the damn cable."

Chrissy smirked and handed Stella over the plate. A buttery fried egg cuddled up next to a couple of slices of toasted Wonder Bread that had been spread with grape jelly.

"Now, how am I supposed to eat this in the car?" Stella demanded.

Chrissy frowned. "Well, if you don't like it, I guess you can just leave it here, Miss Picky-Pants."

"Can't you just roll it up into a tortilla or something?"

Chrissy sighed and took the plate to the counter. In seconds she handed it back, stacked into a sandwich, the egg purplish amid the jelly. She reached for a box of baby wipes, yanked out a couple, and handed them over, too.

"Here. So's you can clean up after. Now go catch bad guys," she said.

"Will do." Stella bent to kiss the top of Tucker's little head. "I got to go, Tucker. Can I have my shoe back now?"

"Sow. Sow." Tucker hugged the shoe tight and ran to the corner of the kitchen, pushing his little body into the lazy susan.

By the time she got out to the Jeep, Stella realized she felt worse about taking her shoe back from the little guy, who was now sobbing inconsolably on the kitchen floor, than she had the last time she had pounded some wife-beating creep within an inch of his sorry life.

FOUR

· · · · · · · · · · ·

When Stella reached Prosper's two-block downtown, the tornado's path of destruction became obvious—it had wended its merry way right across Broadway, taking out a little drive-through latte hut on the southwest corner of Poplar that Stella had never cared for anyway. Waiting in a line of cars for a cup of coffee—it struck Stella as inviting one of the more uncivilized tentacles of big-city living to reach down and take root with its greedy corporate suckers. To see it reduced to a roofless pile of timber was a guilty pleasure.

But Stella was sad to see that the ten-foot-tall fiberglass bucket of paint that had graced the roof of Myle's Paint and Wallpaper since Stella was a girl lay in pieces in the parking lot across the street. How many times had she admired its faded kitschy glory over the years, a beacon above the rest of the downtown? A streetlight had crashed down on top of a newish Accord, shattering the windshield and making it unlikely that anyone over three feet tall would be comfortable in the passenger seat. Everywhere, trash fluttered lazily in the gutters and pools of water left from the storm steamed in the unseasonably warm, bright morning sun.

Stella waved to the folks she saw out with brooms and mops and trash bags. Most waved back with expressions of reasonably good spirits. That's how it was, after a twister; as long as it wasn't *your* picket fence that lay in a pile of splintered lumber, or your neighbor's doghouse that got uprooted and set down on top of *your* prize rosebushes, there was almost a festival air about the day after, everyone out counting their blessings and cleaning up the aftermath.

Though Stella was never able to join in. She remembered the sound of her mother's muffled sobs on the beautiful clear morning following the tornado that took Uncle Horace. She remembered her father standing on the corner of the porch staring out at the field, not even seeing the snapped stalks, wearing the same clothes he'd worn the night before to go help folks, his hands trembling at his sides.

She snapped on the radio, still set to KKRN from last night. Don Stetson—morning DJ—was plodding through the news at a considerably heartier clip than his weather-predicting colleague Ted Krass had managed even in the thick of the storm.

"—west side of town," he was saying. "Particularly over to Calhixie Elementary and down to the fairgrounds. Little tykes are in for a surprise when they go out for recess and find out their playground's no more'n a big old crater, heh, heh, guess it's going to be a little extra serving of the three *R*'s for the kids until they get that sorted out. Readin', 'ritin', 'rithmatic, that's what it takes these, days, don't it? Back to the basics, is what

39

our country needs. Gonna compete on a global level, why you got to start right here at home. Is what I always say."

Stella snorted. Don Stetson, whose real name was Don Butts, had repeated the seventh grade a couple of times when basic algebra couldn't seem to get a foothold anywhere in his young mind—and then he'd tried his hand at personal investment counseling up in Independence before being asked to leave after directing his few clients' investments into a shady fund repped by a lovely, curvy former Miss Iowa. Luckily his uncle owned KKRN and saw fit to give the disgraced financier a fresh start.

That was as good a use for the news media as any, Stella figured—employment of last resort for the unemployable.

"Now over to the fairgrounds we got reports that the New Century Pavilion's lost a bunch of shingles off the east-facing half of its roof," Don continued with an audible shuffling of papers. "But the big news is at the demolition derby track. Seems the snack shack's blowed clean over, from what our, uh, reporter in the field has to tell us. Fact, there's a po-lice presence there right now." There was another shuffling sound and then a faint wet plop that suggested Don had taken a little break to discreetly spit out his chew. "Now at the Freshway, somebody left a crate of melons, word is they were watermelons but that's not entirely clear at this juncture, out where the twister—"

Stella snapped the radio off. Well, hell, odds were that Goat's borrowing of Neb was no more than a bit of conscientious attention to the damaged Prosper infrastructure. If Neb had just seen fit to mention the snack shack's demise to Donna and reassure her that the only business they were conducting was of the now-what'll-we-do-for-hot-dogs variety, Stella might still be back in that cozy nest of blankets, watching Sponge-Bob with Tucker. Just like a man to leave out the key details—even the good ones were often beset by flaws that seemed endemic to the male half of the population.

Still, she was more than halfway to the fairgrounds, and Stella figured she might as well check things out. She went to work on her egg-and-jelly sandwich—which was actually less terrible than she expected—and picked up her pace as she hit the long open stretch on Clayton Road. That she was driving roughly parallel to the meandering trail the twister had taken was occasionally evident when she spotted an uprooted and tossed section of fencing or tree with its roots in the air, but thankfully this part of its journey, at any rate, had gone mostly overland through soybean and corn fields, leaving farmhouses and barns and silos and trucks sitting in pretty much the same spots they occupied before the storm.

As Stella came up on the fairgrounds, she could see what Don had been talking about; the big New Century Pavilion, a giant shedlike structure erected in honor of the arrival of the twenty-first century, had divested itself of at least a third of its roof, as though it had indulged in a powerful sneeze. Shingles lay on the ground like sprinkles on a cupcake, and here and there the sun shone through the top of the building.

The big steel gates at the front of the grassy parking field had been left open, and Stella drove over fresh ruts, following the trail to where Goat had parked his department-issue Charger up near the front of the field. *SAWYER COUNTY SHERIFF DEPART-MENT* was stenciled on the side of the car in spiffy right-tilting lettering, in an all-business font that implied a law enforcement team that brooked no nonsense.

Parked next to Goat's car was Prosper's other departmental patrol vehicle, a slightly less-well-cared-for version used by Ian and Mike, Goat's deputies.

Stella was a little surprised to see that the whole crew had turned out for the occasion. A single blown-over structure, even one as beloved as the snack shack, didn't seem to justify the presence of more than one small-town lawman.

The only other car on the lot was Neb's pickup, a well-kept two-tone Dodge whose rear was festooned with several varieties of looped-ribbon magnets that showed his support for OUR TROOPS and, if Stella recalled her earnest-cause-affiliation colors properly, breast cancer and colon cancer and Alzheimer's disease, and—somewhat surprisingly—gay pride.

But as Stella got out of the Jeep and shook a pang out of her bum hip, another vehicle drove down the grassy lot at a spirited clip, jouncing across the uneven ground with a breezy disregard for the strain the terrain put on the shocks and, presumably, the passengers inside. Even from a distance, Stella could make out the custom aluminum enclosure welded on the back, and a frisson of anxiety zipped along her nerve endings: the thing was a tricked-out Ford F-Series in the navy blue favored by the Sawyer County mobile crime scene unit, a heavily customized roving lab dedicated to studying and sorting out the bouts of mayhem the residents of rural central Missouri occasionally wreaked upon each other.

The truck's presence did not bode well.

Stella had seen this vehicle once or twice before, but generally its arrival prompted her departure. It wasn't the sort of thing a perpetrator of violent crime generally likes to see around the same town where said criminal made a habit of hiding her evidence.

Generally, the crime scene bunch stayed close to their home base in Fayette, but they were always happy to oblige when the county's outposts needed the kind of crime-solving firepower that a sleepy community like Prosper couldn't justify.

To wit: homicide. Yep, it generally meant that some schmo was having a very bad day when the Fayette crew blew into town. Showing up here at the fairgrounds meant bad news for the victim of whatever crime had merited a call to the county seat.

Stella walked a little faster as the vehicle did a precise, sweeping three-point turn and parked nose-to-nose with Goat's vehicle. If she had to, she'd pretend not to hear if anyone called out a greeting, in case they decided to ask what she was doing here, but Stella didn't want to give anyone reason to stop her from seeing Neb.

By the time she crossed the landscaped berm separating the lot from the back side of the aluminum bleachers that stretched out along the sides of the track, Stella was practically jogging. Before the unfortunate series of events that had landed her in the hospital, Stella was in the habit of taking several six- to ten-mile runs every week, alternating her pavement pounding with extended bouts with the Bowflex machine she'd taken over after Ollie's passing. Her injuries had forced her to temporarily lay off the high-impact components of her regime, but her physical therapist had her doing yoga, a surprisingly pleasant discovery. In fact, after a couple months of hard work, Stella found that the various poses had toned entire stretches of flesh she'd long ago written off to permanent squishiness.

Still, she missed the running, the mind-clearing benefits of loping along through quiet dawns with only her own thoughts for company. Now it felt good to stretch her legs, and as she rounded the end of the bleachers, she sped up to a full-scale run.

She came to the enormous open track, the earth damp and frothed by the storm, and glanced over at the other side. What she saw brought her to a skidding halt, her feet in her rubber clogs flopping hard against the concrete walk.

The other set of bleachers hadn't disappeared, but it looked as though the twister had yanked it out of the ground, crunched it up in its whirling jaws, decided it didn't care for the taste of aluminum, and rudely spit it back out.

The damaged frame had collapsed a good twenty feet to the left of where it once stood, the supports sticking out at odd angles like some fourth-grader's toothpick-and-glue model of the Saint Louis arch that had been jumped on by a pesky little brother with a grudge.

Behind the ruined bleachers, where the snack shack had hunkered along with a scattering of picnic tables, was a pile of rubble and a small knot of people. Swaths of white-painted wood siding lay scattered like torn cardboard. Broken chunks of the Formica counter were half-submerged in mud and debris. A few long two-by-sixes lay at the edge of the mess, almost as though they'd been stacked there by some particularly ambitious citizen who even now was getting started on repairs.

Here and there were scattered bits and pieces of the shack's contents. The popcorn machine, its glass in broken shards, lay upended twenty feet away. Waxed paper soda cups were everywhere, almost like giant confetti playfully sprinkled by the departing storm. The sign, which used to read CANDY NACHOS SOFT DRINKS ICE CREAM had disappeared except for a jagged section that read simply DY NACH, a phrase that struck Stella, in her dazed state, as vaguely Germanic.

Clustered around the foundation were Goat—looking smart in his yellow department-issue windbreaker and pressed khakis, a pair of worn hiking boots his only concession to the conditions—and his deputies, and Neb Donovan.

Neb and Mike Scholl sat on an overturned cabinet that served as a makeshift bench. Their expressions were hangdog, their complexions on the gray side of pale, and their clothes were streaked with dirt. They had the air of a couple of fraternity boys who'd come home from a drunken evening only to find themselves locked out, and woken up hungover after a few hours' sleep in the bushes.

At least, Stella thought, Neb couldn't be guilty of anything too egregious, since the members of the Prosper Sheriff's department were paying him little mind.

Ian had his hands jammed into the pockets of his own windbreaker, which was not an official part of the uniform but rather an ancient-looking gold varsity letter jacket with black sleeves and an embroidered Missouri University Tiger.

Goat was talking into his cell phone and staring into what looked like a sizable hole in the shack's foundation. Stella was confused by the hole, because even a three-point tornado like the prior afternoon's wouldn't be able to dig up solid concrete. As she got closer, however, she realized that the hole was the result of one of the structure's steel girders being ripped out of the foundation. When the shack blew over, the force of the building being wrenched free had caused the post to come out, cracking and bursting the concrete into which it had been set. Clots of concrete still clung to its base, giving it the look of an upended tree with its roots exposed.

Goat turned toward Stella when she was twenty feet away, and his expression did a funny little presto-change-o. He'd had the focused grimace he tended to get whenever events presented him with a problem he couldn't immediately fix. It made him look smart. And dedicated. In a hot, don't-mess-with-me kind of way.

Stella, who had spent the last few years avoiding encounters with Goat in anything that might be considered a professional capacity, had nonetheless been desperate enough to ask for his help several times. There was the time one of her clients went missing, and Stella got the Sheriff's department to join in the cross-county hunt. Just a few months earlier, she asked for Goat's help when Tucker was taken. And it was Goat who she called just before she passed out from blood loss when things went seriously south.

Still, it was a delicate thing, bringing in the law when you were working at what technically might be described as cross purposes. Stella preferred to view their efforts as complementary—the yin and yang of holistic justice. But sticklers might have a little trouble with the differences in their methods.

For instance, while Stella and Chrissy had been fighting the ugly underbelly of the mob presence in rural central Missouri, circumstances necessitated a certain amount of unregistered firearms and illegal searching and breaking and entering. Goat and his deputies, on the other hand, focused on the standard above-board chores like interviewing persons of interest and canvassing neighborhoods for witnesses and collecting evidence.

It all worked out, in the end. Stella wasn't great with details. And paperwork? Forget it. So it was all to the good that while she was helping the bad guys reap what they'd sown, there were other folks focused on keeping the evidentiary trail pristine.

When Goat was on the job, the closer he got to the source of the wrongdoing, the more his loose-limbed, easygoing charm got smartened up and turned into a dangerous-edged determination that, no matter how many times Stella tried to deny it, gave her a knockdown thrill. While on the case, Sheriff Goat Jones was a tall-standing, oath-upholding, brook-no-nonsense embodiment of the long arm of Missouri law.

And all wrapped up in those snug-fitting khakis and mirrored sunglasses, to boot.

Stella noted the way Goat held the phone to his ear: his muscular arm, bent at the elbow, positively strained against the sleeve, which had evidently not been tailored for a man who enjoyed kayaking around the Ozarks every chance he got, building up big rock-hard biceps. And those trousers—ordered extra-long, no doubt, for Goat's lanky build—she appreciated the sharp knife-edge crease and the smart, tailored cuffs, but what she really dug was the excellent view of his nice, tight rear whenever he turned away from her. There was every reason to believe that his butt—legs, too—were every bit as well-maintained as those arms.

The only problem was—as she'd discovered last night—the

goods on display weren't actually available. No, they were pre-owned; and if Brandy wasn't spinning tall tales, still off the table by reason of a previous legally binding situation.

Stella's cheeks flamed at the thought. She felt betrayed. Or, at the very least, bamboozled and underinformed. She didn't care to be taken advantage of on a good day, but when she'd squeezed her midsection into an uncomfortable girdle—more specifically, a Spanx Hide & Sleek Hi-Rise Panty with Thong Back—when she'd endured her daughter's sinus-searing, scalp-burning, double-process hair color—when she'd popped open a brand-new tube of Maybelline Great Lash Mascara in Blackest Black—well, on such a day she found it particularly galling.

While Stella covered the last of the distance to the little group gathered around the wreckage of the snack shack, her emotions running their complicated gauntlet, Goat flipped his phone shut and slipped it back into the holster on his broad, shiny black belt. Neb looked up at Stella, but barely seemed to register her presence—if he recognized her at all, it wasn't clear from his unfocused gaze. Mike gave her a weak little wave.

Only Ian managed much of a greeting. "Mornin', Miz Hardesty," he said, touching the brim of his black-and-yellow Sawyer County Sheriff's Department baseball cap, which Stella happened to know was not a bona fide part of the uniform, but a freebie the department had made up several years back when Sheriff Burt Knoll was still alive. Sheriff Knoll had gone in for swag in a big way, especially at Christmastime, when the town's most upstanding citizens, as well as a few of his favorite reformed criminals, received an ashtray or a pen or some other useful item with the department logo embroidered, emblazoned, or otherwise affixed to it.

"Good morning, Ian. Mike. Neb." She nodded to each man in turn. Then she turned and faced Goat, forcing her gaze up as far as his chin. "Goat."

"What are you doing here, Stella?" he demanded.

Well, so much for worrying about letting the man down easy. There was about as much warmth in Goat's voice as in a freezer-burned Eggo waffle. Still, it was Stella's job—since she was present on behalf of Neb—to play it cool.

"Well, I heard on the radio that the shack blew over, yesterday when I was—" *On my way to your place,* Stella had been about to say. "—when I was out," she amended. "Didn't have much going on this morning so I thought I'd come and see if I could lend a hand."

"Is that right. What were you thinking to do, stitch it back together with your sewing machine? Maybe donate a big hank of yarn to tie the bleachers up with?"

Stella blinked. If there had been any doubt as to his mood, the way his brows knit together as he fixed her with an extra-searing stare, sparks practically flying from those ice-blue eyes, even paler than usual under the bright September sky, laid it to rest.

The man was not one bit happy with her.

Well, what the fuck? Hadn't *he* been the one to unleash an unreported spouse right in the middle of what had the potential to be a pretty damn romantic dinner? Hadn't he been the one to have married a brassy-haired, big-titted, vavoom-hipped, gap-toothed man-stealing kind of woman in the first place?

That thought ratcheted through Stella's brain so quickly and unexpectedly that she found her bottom lip was hanging open without a single thought to justify putting into words. She hadn't realized how much Brandy's big entrance last night had upset her until just this moment, when the woman's parting grin intruded on her vision like a big stop sign while the clouds gathered on Goat's sharp-planed features. He made mad look good, she had to admit; there was something about that generous mouth set in a firm line above that equally firm jaw that gave her an extra shiver even as she felt her back go up defensively.

Well, hell. Goat Jones might be hot, but Stella Hardesty didn't put up with unprovoked meanness from anyone. Never again would she volunteer for the receiving end of a man's bad mood. Not even Viggo Mortensen could treat her like this—on a morning when not only had she done nothing wrong, but also hadn't managed a single cup of coffee—and get away with it.

"I'm sure I could come up with something," she said, meeting Goat's scowl dead-on with her own, "I'm finding I can do just about anything on my own as good as it can be done by committee. Especially these days, when you never know what-all you're gonna get when you go bringing in outside help."

Goat opened his mouth to respond, then closed it again. Noises behind Stella let her know why—she turned and saw that the crime scene unit had arrived. There were two men and a woman, the men dressed in navy long-sleeved shirts that would soon be much too hot as the sun rose in the sky. The woman strode quickly in the lead and the men struggled to keep up, dragging their gear in wheeled duffles. One of the men had a serious-looking camera slung around his neck. The overall effect was of badly dressed tourists who'd accidentally become separated from their tour group and were racing to make it back to the harbor before the cruise ship departed without them.

"Sheriff," the woman said, nodding at the group. "Good to see you again. So where's this mummy you all turned up?"

FIVE

. . . .

Stella blinked in the bright sun of the storm-scoured morning and gave the woman from the crime scene unit her full attention. A little taller than Stella's five feet six inches, the gal was as thin and leathery as a strip of beef jerky, and dressed in an overlarge wrinkled pale pink canvas blazer that looked like it used to be white until it had a laundry accident. She looked like she'd busted plenty of balls in her day, and Stella figured they ought to get along fine, except the woman was staring at her like the remains of a bug squashed on her shoe. Stella squinted at the laminated ID on a chain around her neck, and made out the Detective insignia. DETECTIVE SIMMONS.

"Mummy?" Stella asked politely.

"Who's she?" Simmons replied, poking out her chin in Stella's direction.

Goat squared his shoulders and, ignoring the question, stepped forward and offered his hand. Simmons met him head-on with a strong grip of her own. "Daphne," he said. "It's been too long." Then he shook with the other two men, murmuring a polite greeting.

Stella figured he was hesitating his way out of having to introduce her, so she stepped right in behind him and did her own shaking and helloing. "I'm Stella Hardesty," she said, "very dear friend of Neb here."

Simmons's handshake was unenthusiastic, and Stella quickly passed to the two men, leaning in to read the lettering on their gold name tag pins. "Officer Hewson," she said. "Officer Long."

"It's just Harvey and Chuck, ma'am," the shorter one said.

"Well, and you can call me Stella," she said smoothly, stepping between the techs and their boss. A quick glance at Neb revealed that he hadn't shifted from his spot, and he wasn't looking any less likely to hurl. If anything, he looked even more uneasy. She gave him a quick glare, a get-your-shit-together kind of look, but if he got her meaning, he didn't show it.

"It's just terrible, all this devastation and destruction," she continued, wondering if she could distract them long enough to pluck Neb out of his makeshift seat and get him home. As curious as she was to see what the mummy was all about, Stella's first duty was to remove Neb from this atmosphere of unbridled suspicion. The equation that was forming in her mind was not to her liking. Presence of sheriff plus visiting crime-scene-solvers plus some sort of mummified body plus pale and quaking civilian on overturned cabinet did not, in her professional experience, bode well for the civilian.

Besides, whenever Stella was faced with a new and unknown enforcer of the law, caution was her byword. Especially when one of her clients was involved; then she became as protective as a feral cat when a chicken hawk gets between her and her kittens. And while Neb wasn't a typical client, she'd grown fond of the man, and she wasn't about to let anyone ride roughshod over him.

"It sure is good of you all to come all the way down to Prosper, but didn't you all have any twisters of your own?" she said, taking two little steps to the right in order to block Simmons's view of Neb. At the same time, she craned her neck toward the fissure that snaked through the concrete foundation. It widened to a debris-littered hole where the girder had ripped clear of its mooring.

She saw a flash of blue—a bright, clear blue as though the sky over Prosper were being reflected in a mirror. She edged closer, stutter-stepping along in her clogs as discreetly as possible, knowing that any minute Goat or Detective Daphne Simmons was liable to yank her back.

The blue was some sort of fabric, maybe a tarp or sheet. Dusty with concrete, it appeared to be stuck to some of the larger chunks, and in other places had pulled free from the wreckage. It was draped over a body-shaped lump, and Stella peered at the ends, trying to determine which way was up, and if any details—body parts, for example—were poking out where she could see them.

"Ma'am, this is an official investigation," Simmons said with about as much warmth as a ham hock in a meat locker. "Kindly back away from—"

"Holy fuck," Stella exclaimed, because a final few shuffling sidesteps brought her close enough to get a full-on view of the near end of the lump, where the sheet had been pulled away—

—revealing the vaguely facelike gray stretched mask of horror nestled in the blue folds with its protruding cheekbones and jaw wrapped in leathery skin and its stringy crumbling eyes and its horrible stained-tooth grin and freakishly preserved wig of perky blond hair in a cut that belonged on a housewife from a Kansas City suburb, not this Halloween nightmare—

—and then Goat's hand closed on her arm and gave her a good solid yank, dragging her back away from the hole. Instinctively, Stella wrenched away from him, but there was more power in Goat's one-handed grip than Stella managed to churn up in a week's worth of workouts on the Bowflex, and she was helpless to go any direction but the one Goat had picked out for her, which, as it turned out, was back toward Neb's cabinet.

Goat gave her a not-ungentle shove, which caused her ass end to make solid contact with the plywood surface, right next to Neb. It didn't hurt anything other than her pride, and Stella considered jumping up and objecting, but one look at Goat's face convinced her that this was one of those times that came along occasionally where every word you uttered dug you a little deeper into a mess of your own making.

The mummified body in its blue shroud provided enough of a distraction for the visiting crime-fighters that they forgot Stella for a moment, crowding around the remains of the shack's foundation and making all kinds of appreciative sounds.

Stella tuned them out for a moment and turned to Neb. "That what I think it is?"

"Yeah, Stella, if what you're thinkin' about is a nasty-lookin' old rotted human body that's been layin' under my shack for three years," he said glumly. "I think I'm gonna puke again."

"Who is it?"

"I b'lieve that's what they're all trying to figure out." Neb took a much-folded, none-too-fresh-looking handkerchief out of his pocket and wiped it across his face. The day was headed toward the hot side of warm, but the faint sheen on Neb's pallid skin appeared to be a product of nerves and nausea.

"Seems to me they might want to figure out who was here pouring that concrete," Stella remarked, thinking back to three years ago, a time when she had been distracted from the town's goings-on by what turned out to be a steady ramp-up to and subsequent sorting-out after her bout of murderous husband-eliminating rage.

"Well, now, Goat already done that first thing," Neb said. "He's a sharp-enough one, I'd guess."

"No kidding?" Stella maneuvered her butt on the hard surface of their makeshift seat, trying to find a position that was a little easier on her hip and hoping to avoid splinters. "Well, who is it?"

Neb watched her attempts to get comfortable with sympathy as he stuffed his handkerchief back into the pocket of his drawstring lounging trousers.

"Funny enough," he said in a tone that indicated any humor involved had long since frittered itself away, "that would be me."

Donna Donovan liked strawberries. A *lot*. The plague started in her front yard, where a large wooden strawberry that Neb had cut out with his scroll saw was nailed to a stake driven into a nest of sprawling pink impatiens. *The Donovan's* was painted on it in a curlicue-style script, the overzealous and not strictly accurate apostrophe taking the form of a little green leaf on a tendril that twirled down from the cap of leaves on top.

Stella passed by the sign and headed up to the door, which featured a wreath of plastic greenery and fuzzy faux strawberries, but she didn't have time to knock before Donna herself flung the door open and swept Stella into the house, nearly tripping over a large yellow cat.

"Oh, Stella, I don't know what I'm going to *do* I'm so upset," she said. "I can't bear to call Bobby and Luther—why, this would just break their hearts."

Donna and Neb's grown sons had left Prosper for more exotic locales: Bobby was studying forestry in Minnesota, and Luther was managing a sports bar in Saint Louis. Back in Neb's drug-fancying days, and later when Stella was saving him from the lure of the straight and narrow path, Donna had insisted on keeping the boys in the dark. She didn't want to worry her darlings, even though they were well into their twenties now.

"Mmm-hmm," Stella said noncommittally. Considering her track record with her own daughter, who had gone more than three years without speaking to Stella at all, she had a hard-and-fast rule against handing out parenting advice. If someone had come up with the one true way to get the job done right, Stella sure hadn't heard about it.

She evidently wasn't following Donna through the tidy split-level house fast enough, because Donna slipped her hand into Stella's and tugged, dragging her into the kitchen and nudging her toward a chair. The chair's pad was waffle cotton stitched into a strawberry shape. As Stella sat herself down, setting her notebook and pen on the table, she noted that little had changed in the kitchen since her last visit: a wallpaper border of teapots and strawberry runners still graced the top of the red-painted cabinets. A row of porcelain canisters shaped like berry baskets lined the countertops. The theme played out on the red teapot on the stove, the tea towels hung on hooks, the tiles on the backsplash, and the ruffly curtains in the window. Even the magnets on the fridge were shaped like plump little berries.

Stella thought an hour in the kitchen would make her vomit, but she kept her opinion to herself.

"So what have they done with him?" Donna said, plopping into a chair across from Stella. She slid a platter of sliced coffee cake toward herself and started pinching off little pea-sized crumbs and nibbling at them. Stella was quite familiar with this coping technique, which basically entailed eating enough food for a large family in increments so small that it hardly seemed likely they could possibly contain any calories, and she helped herself to the other end of the cake.

"Well, now, Donna, it's all just information-gathering for now," she said. "I expect the sheriff'll give me a call just as soon as they're ready to release Neb. I asked him to, as a courtesy, you know."

"Why didn't you stay there with him? He needs someone on his side," Donna fretted. A smudge of jam traced the corner of her mouth, and a hank of hair had escaped its barrette and hung over her cheek, clues that she was falling apart. Donna never, ever looked anything but her finest unless her world was well and truly crashing in on itself.

She was one of those ladies who took seriously her mother's admonishment to offer her best side to the world. Her hair was always done, her makeup carefully applied, and her clothes neat and pressed. For a bit of individual flair, Donna favored bright-colored separates that molded themselves to her curvy shape and generally found some creative way to let a bit of undergarment show, either at her cleavage or up the slit of her skirt or peeking out over her low waistband in the back. Thongs had been a happy discovery for Donna. She'd amassed a wardrobe of lingerie in every color, so the peep show was always nicely coordinated.

But today she had on a lavender knit jacket over a stretched and gapping lime green camisole with plain beige bra straps showing. Her gray sweatpants came all the way up to her belly button and hinted at nothing more than a possible call to get on the StairMaster a bit more often. In short, she looked a mess.

"Now, Donna," Stella said gently, opening her notebook. It was a fresh one from the stack Stella kept in her hall closet. Every case got a new notebook, purchased in bulk from the Wal-Mart sale bins, and this one featured Wow! Wow! Wubzy! at the Wuzzleburg Celebration. Stella didn't know much about Wubbzy other than he was shaped like a yellow nine-volt battery with a snout, and she doubted kids found him all that entertaining, despite the fact that big lettering down the side declared him *ABSO-HULA-LUTELY HYSTERICAL*—she wouldn't have been surprised to learn that his creators had been impaired by OxyContin abuse themselves. "You know I'd be there if I could, but you need to remember I'm just a civilian. Those folks being down from Fayette and all, Sheriff's got to clamp down on procedures. That's how they do."

Donna paled even further. "But, Stella," she said hoarsely, her voice barely above a whisper, "you've got to make them understand it's not the way it looks. Do you think I ought to call Priscilla?"

Priscilla, Donna's attorney niece, had just passed the bar exam over the summer and joined up as a junior associate at a firm in Joplin. Stella wasn't convinced the girl was really the best choice to defend her uncle, if it came to that.

"Let's not get ahead of ourselves," Stella said cautiously, "but if we decide . . . down the road . . . well, I have some names we could consider. You know, since Priscilla's probably so busy getting settled in her new job and all."

"Oh, but no one can defend a person like family, Stella," Donna said. " 'Cause she would *know* he's innocent."

"Uh, yeah." Stella figured a change of conversation might be in order. "Tell me again about the snack shack. Help me out with a time line here."

As Neb had explained before Goat gave Stella the heave-ho, and Donna confirmed on the phone as Stella drove over to the Donovans' house, he had indeed been a key player in the construction of the snack shack, but he had no memory of wrapping up any blond ladies in blue sheets and laying them out in the framed-out foundation before backing up the concrete mixer and covering up the whole mess with a fresh batch of Ready Mix.

"Why, you remember," Donna said. "It was after they re-did the track. Got one season into it and everyone was so dang parched during the demolition derby. Don't you recall? There was practically a riot in the stands when the Optimists ran out of lemonade."

"I'm kind of fuzzy about the details," Stella said. "I was, ah, having some drama in my own personal life back then."

Donna looked at her blankly; then comprehension lit up her gaze. "Oh," she said. "That was when, uh, Ollie died."

A faint blush crept across her cheeks. Everyone in Prosper knew the official version of Ollie's death, of course; how the old sheriff—Burt Knoll, Goat's predecessor—answered a call from a neighbor worried about strange sounds coming from the Hardesty home, and discovered Ollie's forehead caved in and Stella sitting on the floor next to him, holding a wrench.

Everyone knew, too, how the judge had folks lined up out the door of his office wanting to offer up accounts of Ollie smacking or threatening or being just plain unconscionably mean to his wife at some point in their twenty-six-year marriage.

But naturally enough, no one really talked about it after Stella's acquittal. She herself didn't remember the details of that day for several months, and by then a little seed of an idea had begun to germinate in her mind, a growing conviction that no woman should have to put up with abuse by her husband or boyfriend, and—to Stella's surprise—that she might just have a calling to help put a stop to it. After all, she already had one notch in her belt, so to speak.

As all this remembering and realizing and deciding was going on, Stella maintained a very tenuous hold on the finer details of her life. Other than getting herself up in the morning and back to bed at night, she pretty much ignored the rest of the world and let it take care of itself.

"So," she said now, "why don't you pretend I wasn't around back then. Like I was off visiting my sister in California or something. Tell me everything."

Donna took a deep breath and a fortifying lump of coffee

cake. "Well, now, Neb's back went out January of that year . . . and he had his surgery in February, and the rehab and all went good 'cept for by then he'd got a taste for that poison, only course I didn't know it. That whole summer was—well, you know. What with them pills and all."

"A haze," Stella suggested.

"You might say. Now, that was Howell's last year before he retired, so Neb was still the assistant groundskeeper."

Howell Laurey used to be the head caretaker, an ancient grizzled man who'd been running the place since the '80s, less effectively every year, until they'd finally hired Neb to pick up the slack while Howell wheezed toward his twenty years and full retirement benefits. Stella vaguely recalled how the landscaping overgrew its bounds toward the end of Howell's tenure, how the buildings sprang leaks and paint peeled and fences went unmended, while Howell doddered painfully around with the assistance of a cane as gnarled as he was.

"Howell and Neb did a half-ass job right up through fair time," Donna continued, "and the town got some complaints. Porta-potties not getting emptied, gates not opened on time, trash around the midway, like that. But the thing people complained about most wasn't even their fault—everyone wanted better food at the track now that it was all spiffed up."

"It wasn't great before," Stella said, remembering the old structure, a carportlike shed with rough wooden shelves, from which the Sunrise Optimist Club sold Hostess Fruit Pies and bags of chips and sodas and lemonade.

"Yeah. So they got plans for the new shack, got all the supplies ordered, and Neb got to work on it."

"How did he manage?" Stella asked. "With his, you know, troubles."

"You'd be surprised," Donna said. "That Oxy is evil. It makes you feel so good, you got your energy, you feel like you can do anything. 'Specially once he started railing it."

"Railing?"

"You grate the coating off them little pills . . . grind 'em up, and bam—there you go. Folks get where they don't want to wait for the time-release."

Stella grimaced. There was a reason she stuck with her pal Johnnie Walker Black. A little discretion, a responsible use policy, as it were, and she managed just fine. "Where was he getting it?"

Donna picked up a pink paper napkin and tore it in half, slowly. Then she tore it again. "Got into the retirement money," she muttered. "There's folks out there that'll sell you anything. I didn't know for a long time. Cain't believe it now, but Neb was just so good at hiding it. And you know, that Oxy, you can cover it up. Not forever, but for a while there at the start of it, Neb just seemed kinda extra energetic, and then he'd go and sleep for twelve hours and wake up feeling like he had the flu."

"Well, sure, honey," Stella said soothingly. "Nobody would ever have guessed. Don't you feel bad about it."

"Do you know," Donna said softly, fixing Stella with wide, troubled green eyes, "for a while I thought he might be having an affair. They say a new woman can perk a man right up, make him care about things he hasn't cared about in years. Time I . . . time I . . ."

Donna's voice wobbled with stored-up tears, and Stella gently pressed her own pink paper napkin into Donna's free hand. "It's okay."

Donna cleared her throat. "Time I found out it was just, you know, drugs, I was so relieved it wasn't a woman, I could have cried."

"Of course you were relieved," Stella said. "Listen, I wonder . . . would you have Neb's doctor's number handy? I might give him a call."

"Why, sure, if you think it would help. You think maybe Dr. Herman could tell the sheriff and them that Neb was too bad hurt to have done that concrete pouring?"

"Oh—was he?"

"Well, no, not really, 'cause the doctor said he could go back to all his regular activities a few months after the surgery." Donna chewed her lip. "But maybe if you explained how *important* it was . . ."

"Donna," Stella chided, "doctors got a code of *ethics*. They can't be lying like that, even for a good cause."

"Oh. Oh, well." Donna got up and fetched a little berry-printed address book from a shelf above a tidy desk in the corner of the kitchen. She slipped on a pair of reading glasses and ran a chewed-on fingernail down the *H* page until she found the number, then copied it onto a piece of pink notepaper.

"Thanks," Stella said, and tucked it into her pocket. "Now, back to the snack shack . . ."

"Yes," Donna said. "Right." She blew her nose daintily on a tissue plucked from a strawberry-printed box cover on the counter, and cleared her throat. "Neb always has loved building things. Even being high, he liked getting out there and working on it."

"Was Howell helping out?"

"Yes—yes he was, but he didn't do much other than set his bottom on a barrel and tell the other fellas what to do."

"Who else do you mean, when you say 'other fellas'?"

"Well, they had that boy Cory Layfield helping out, remember, his uncle was—"

"Layfield, Layfield," Stella interrupted. The name was familiar.

"Yes, his uncle had shingles. Or something like that. Cory came down from Rolla to help out when he was sick, and while he was here, he picked up a little work around town. Nice boy. We had him out to dinner once or twice."

"Well, we got to figure Howell didn't go abducting and murdering any ladies, don't you think?"

"I can't see as the old guy had that kind of pep in him," Donna agreed.

"And Neb didn't do it." Stella kept her professional skepticism out of her voice. There was more looking into the man to be done, but Donna didn't need to know that.

"He certainly did *not*," Donna huffed, as if reading Stella's mind.

"Well, you know what that says to me . . . could be Cory Layfield isn't quite so nice a boy as you think he is."

SIX

. . . .

Stella pulled slowly into her driveway, noting the piles of downed branches lying around her yard. A few were sizable, entire limbs ripped from the sweetgum trees that shaded her house and the red oaks lining the street. Now there was a calorie-blasting few hours waiting to happen. She'd have to see if old Mr. Bayer across the street would let her borrow the chain saw to cut up the biggest branches.

One of the ceramic flowerpots that flanked the front door lay on its side, cracked and shattered, clots of dirt and broken geraniums spilling out onto the walk. A four-foot section of gutter had come loose from the roof and hung, swaying gently, clumps of damp leaves stuck to its sides.

Stella opened the garage door with the remote and navigated carefully between the yard tools and other clutter stacked along the sides, turning off the ignition when she hit the tennis ball suspended from the ceiling.

She let herself in the door to the house, and was hit with the stench of garbage. She entered the kitchen and saw that the floor was littered with the contents of the trash: coffee grounds were scattered in a three-yard radius, orange peels were tossed everywhere, papers fluttered in the breeze from the outside. A package of stale bread had been torn open, but only crumbs remained. Yogurt containers, takeout boxes, Lean Cuisine packaging, clots of cold spaghetti . . . all had been dragged around the kitchen, globs of gunk of unknown provenance smeared on every surface.

A rhythmic thumping sound came from under the kitchen table.

Stella picked her way carefully across the floor to investigate. Crouching down and pushing one of the dinette chairs out of the way, she saw a medium-sized white-and-black dog lying on its back, eyes rolling back in its head, tongue hanging out of its mouth and tail wagging so hard, it smacked against the table leg. Incriminating bits of food were stuck to its snout.

"Shit," Stella breathed softly. "Who the fuck are you?"

At the sound of her voice, the dog's tail-whapping sped up to a frantic pace and it nudged closer to her with a lavish waggle of its hind legs. Then it rolled to its stomach, looked up at her with wide eyes the color of root beer, and flattened itself as low as it could, chin flat on the floor, and whined.

That tail never stopped wagging.

Stella noticed another smell in the olfactory stew and glanced around for its source . . . ah, there, over by the fridge— evidently the dog couldn't wait to get outside to relieve itself.

Stella hauled herself up off the floor with effort and threw her keys on the table. Only then did she spot the note. Written in a juvenile scrawl in maroon marker on a torn envelope were these words:

Her name is Roxy, she like's scrambled eggs
Don't tell mom she's here!!!!!!!!

"Figures," Stella muttered. She recognized the handwriting—it belonged to Todd Groffe. The boy knew where her spare key was, and while she couldn't be sure why he'd sicced this small canine vessel of destruction on her, she was willing to guess.

The dog had the look of a runaway. Stomach slightly caved in, it hadn't eaten in a while—hence its zeal with the trash, perhaps—but there were signs that until recently it had been a cared-for dog, a pet. Its coat was smooth, without burrs or scabs; its ears hadn't been torn or chewed in a fight. It had no collar, no tags, but Stella felt sure it had belonged to someone not long ago.

She. *She* had belonged to someone. Stella sighed and knelt back down next to the dog, and laid a hand on her back, where a trio of large black spots made a sort of saddle design. Her fur was agreeably soft, and Stella gave in and petted her, tracing the black-speckled sides and stomach with her fingers, smoothing back the cockeyed, soft triangular ears, the dog rolling her eyes and grinning in ecstasy and whining happily.

Much as she hated to admit it, Roxy seemed like a nice dog, with the sweet temperament of an animal at the passive end of the spectrum. She didn't act like a dog that had been abused—kicked or hit or worse. What she had, instead, was that love-me-please-please-please eagerness that seemed born into a pup every other litter or so, the boundless trust and friendliness that in the right house made a perfect child's pet, a loyal dog that would allow itself to be pawed and gnawed and dressed in doll's clothes.

In the wrong house, this sort of dog seemed to invite abuse. Much like some women—the sweet, naïve ones—when they got together with a man whose evil streak was of the vicious woman-hurting sort, it seemed like they couldn't do anything to prevent the meanness heaped on them. Stella hated that, hated the way the innocent sometimes drew fury to themselves like flies to honey.

But no one had done this dog wrong. How she had come to be in Todd's company was a mystery, but the reason she was now boarding at Stella's was not: Sherilee was allergic. Not the-occasional-sneeze allergic, but red-eyed, mucousy, hive-raising, miserable allergic. Stella had seen the evidence herself on the prior occasions that Todd tried to smuggle animals into the house: the kitten in his closet, the guinea pig he brought home from school after forging a note in his mother's hand explaining to his teacher that the Groffes would be delighted to care for the classroom pet, Peanut, over spring break.

Peanut had spent spring break at Stella's, instead, and Todd had spent it grounded.

But the dog was a whole new level of bold disregard for his mother's comfort and respiratory health. Stella wondered where Todd could possibly have hidden her—and what he'd told Sherilee when Roxy was discovered. Sherilee would never have allowed her son to dump the dog on Stella; that must have been a covert op.

"Don't get too comfortable," Stella said. "And—and you're in big trouble. Big, *big* trouble." She debated locking the dog in the bathroom while she cleaned the kitchen, but with her luck, Roxy's tanks wouldn't be empty, and she'd end up with a puddle on the bath mat.

Stella glanced at the clock. Nearly nine. After the visit to Donna Donovan, she'd put in a full day with Roseann Lau cleaning up from the storm around the parking lot and the restaurant and shop, and helping Capper Tackett across the street board up the front window of Tackett Stamp & Coin, which had been shattered by an errant hubcap sent hurtling its way by the previous day's winds. It was likely to be a few days before the glass repairman would be available.

Once the window had been secured and the street restored to order, Stella called over to Dr. Herman's office and finessed an appointment with him for the next day. All it took was pretending that she was Mrs. Donovan, and that her husband was curled up on the floor in a rictus of pain; she expressed her fears that Neb had somehow massacred another disk in his back, and assured the receptionist that she'd alternate heat and cold to give her poor husband a measure of comfort.

Then she and Chrissy and Roseann and Capper and a few other Third Street merchants had dinner at China Paradise. Roseann, grumpy as ever, threw in a free order of steamed dumplings. Tucker ate most of them before the party broke up so he could have his bath.

Now it was time for Stella's standing appointment with Johnnie Walker Black, maybe a nice hot shower, and then bed; she was exhausted. She didn't have the energy for this mess.

Damn dog. She looked for kitchen twine in the cupboard, didn't find any, and finally turned up a couple of extension cords. She tied one around Roxy's neck in a square knot and looped the other around to make a sort of leash and set out the back door.

"This ain't no walk," Stella said as Roxy bounded ahead of her, delighted to be outside, straining on the extension cord. "This is just once around the backyard to pee."

Roxy, though, had other ideas; she stopped to sniff at every rock, plant, fallen leaf, stick, and hole in the yard. Her white-whiskered black snout sniffed delicately, but when something interested her, she pawed and scratched with abandon, the low whine in the back of her throat expressing pure interest and delight.

Stella realized she was letting the dog lead her around. "That's enough," she snapped, and yanked on the cord, dragging Roxy back toward the house. She debated tying the dog up to the back porch, but the cords' knots didn't look like they'd hold. "Look here. You can come back in, but you're sleeping in the garage tonight."

Roxy gave her a quizzical look, the whiskers on one side of her face tilting up curiously, and sat still while Stella untied her in the kitchen. When Stella got a broom and dustpan, Roxy's jaunty expression deflated and she slunk to the corner of the room, where she lay on her belly and rested her chin on her paws. She tracked Stella's every move, her long-lashed eyes mournful and, if such a thing were possible, apologetic.

"Don't give me that look," Stella grumbled, but once she had the floor swept and the trash rebagged and hauled out to the garbage cans in the garage, she gave the dog another look, hands on hips.

Sighing, she wet a washcloth and dabbed a bit of her good lavender-scented liquid hand soap on it. "Hell," she sighed, "if we're going to hang out, you got to keep up your end. No need to look low-class just 'cause you've traveled a rough road . . . know what I mean?"

She gently sudsed up the dog's snout, then washed the grime off her paws and legs and a few spots here and there where bits of pasta sauce were stuck to her fur. She rinsed the washcloth and carefully dabbed the soap away from the dog's soft coat, finishing up with a fluffing from a fresh dishcloth. She surveyed her handiwork, Roxy regarding her solemnly in return.

Then Roxy picked up her paw, deliberately, almost delicately, and laid it on Stella's forearm—and Stella knew she was done for.

"Shit," she said. "I don't need a dog. I don't *want* a dog. You got owners already, don't you? Some nice family somewhere?"

There was a noise behind her, the door from the garage opening, and a gentle cough. Roxy tensed up and started making a low rumble in her throat, and the fur stood up along her back. Stella whirled around, and found herself staring at the woman who'd interrupted her evening with Goat Jones.

"Brandy," she said. "Did you miss out on the knocking lessons when you were a kid?"

"Oh, excuse me," the woman said. This evening she was wearing a shimmering red pantsuit, a whole lot of ruching in the jacket making it fit as close as if she'd wrapped herself up in red florist foil. "I saw the lights on, and the door to the garage was open—"

"That's because I was taking out the trash," Stella said, emphasizing that last word.

Trash. It was on the tip of her tongue to describe the teased-

and-sprayed high-heel-teetering woman in front of her, but Stella was uncomfortably aware that she was in range of breaking one of her own rules, and that was a place where she'd sworn off loitering.

There were plenty of men in the world who were ready to call decent women terrible things: whores, sluts, skanks. Why was it that the insult that came first to some men's mind when describing a woman had to do with their willingness to give up exactly what these same men spent most of their waking hours trying to get their nasty hands on?

Stella recalled something a client had once said, once she'd shed herself of a boyfriend whose jealousy took the form of choking her half to death when she put on a short skirt and high heels to go dancing: some men get agitated by women who look like they can make their own fun. And now Stella was dangerously close to being guilty of the same thing.

If she was really honest with herself, if she looked past the eye shadow with glints of glitter, and the out-to-there stick-on lashes, and the ankle bracelet with the giant Diamonique sparkler, what she was looking at was no more or less than another woman with a claim on the man she wanted.

And she was jealous.

Fuck. Sometimes when she had these mental dialogues with herself, Stella hated being right.

"You got a little . . . somethin' . . . um . . ." Brandy reached out a sharp pokey fingernail and dabbed at Stella's cheek. Roxy stood up, head lowered, her throaty growl escalating into a lip-curling snarl. Stella laid a hand on the dog's back and shushed her; to her amazement, Roxy settled down.

"Sit," Stella said experimentally.

Roxy sat. She didn't look happy—she looked like she wanted to take a bite out of Brandy's plump calf—but she sat.

"My dog doesn't like it when folks get in my personal space," Stella said coolly.

Brandy shrugged. "Well, I'm not fond of dogs myself, so I imagine we'll just both stay out of each other's way." She held her finger up, and they both examined it: a bit of dried parsley, perhaps. Or worse, considering the muck Stella'd been cleaning up.

Stella stared down at herself: sweatpants grubby at the knees from scrubbing the floor, smudges on the pink T-shirt she'd borrowed from Chrissy. And the smell coming off her wasn't the freshest, either; she'd never managed a shower, given that she'd gone from Chrissy's to the track to working around the shop to Roxy's squalor.

"It's been a long day," she said. "Look, I need a drink. I can drink alone, or I can pour us both one and we can sit down and get to know each other properly."

Brandy hesitated for a moment, then set her purse—a boxy red patent job this time—down on the kitchen table. "I suppose I might have just a bit of something."

Stella pointed to the corner of the kitchen. "Git on over there," she told Roxy.

Nothing happened; Roxy glanced at Stella, then went back to snarling at their guest.

"She ain't trained," Brandy observed.

"Yes, she is. She's just—very protective. Excuse me a moment."

Stella got a couple of old towels out of the linen closet and made a nest in the corner of the kitchen. Roxy stayed where she was, sitting and glaring at Brandy the whole time.

"Now, lie down," Stella said firmly. Roxy sighed, then trotted over to the towels, made a few pawing circles, and collapsed in a heap, batting her tail a few times in appreciation. Stella got a couple of tumblers from the shelf, and her bottle of Johnnie.

"Ice?" she asked after pouring her own straight.

"Yes, please."

Stella fetched a few cubes from the freezer without comment, though she didn't think much of anyone who needed to tinker with a good honest belt. She poured a slug over the ice and handed it over.

Brandy looked at it dubiously. "When I said 'just a bit,' I was being, you know, polite."

Stella raised an eyebrow and set the glass back on the counter, then poured slowly until Brandy said, "That'll do it, I guess."

The tumbler was nearly full.

They sat at the table, Stella sinking into her chair with a sigh, the day's tension seeping out of her muscles, her feet grateful not to be bearing her weight after hours of trudging and cleaning up debris and hauling trash. At the end of the day, especially one like today, she felt the ghost of her bullet wounds, a slight throbbing in her gut where one bullet had nicked her spleen, and an ache in her shoulder where the other had passed clean through. But worse was the fatigue, a weariness that emanated from her feet up through her legs and clear out to the end of her fingers. She planned to overcome it—Stella Hardesty *would* come back 100 percent, and that was a fucking promise, if only to herself—but she wasn't quite there yet.

She took a sip and let the whiskey burn its familiar soothing path down her throat.

Brandy tossed back a healthy gulp of her own and regarded Stella through narrowed eyelids. "So, Stella," she said, licking her plump, shiny red lips. "Let's talk about my husband."

Stella blinked. "Ex, is what I believe you mean to say. Least that's the story he's been telling around town ever since he got here."

Brandy smiled, a not-particularly-nice smile that didn't do much to warm up her icy green eyes. "Oh, now," she said. "You know how men are. Sometimes they need a little time to cool off. After, you know, a misunderstanding."

"Three *years*? Must have been a hell of a misunderstanding. What happened, one of you in the habit of speaking in tongues or something?"

"I prefer not to discuss the specifics of our relationship," Brandy said delicately. She took another healthy gulp; the level in her glass was getting low. Stella automatically reached for the Johnnie. She'd been to Costco, and there were a couple more fresh soldiers up in the pantry, so there was little chance of running out—and her mama had raised her to be gracious to even the most unwelcome guest.

"Seems to me that it was news to Goat that y'all still had one," she said, topping off Brandy's drink. "Relationship, that is."

"Hmmph," Brandy said, making the syllable sound both patronizing and mirthful. *Oh, silly you.* "What we had—*have*— is special. It can stand tests that might kill other folks' marriages."

"Oh?" Stella didn't bother to mask her skepticism; she'd seen her share of dead marriages herself—and helped kill a few more.

"Goat has to go out and *prove* himself, now and again," Brandy explained. "He's a warrior. That's why he's drawn to keepin' the peace and bustin' heads and all that. I read a book about it, how men have to be in touch with their inner vanquisher. The masculine side needs to conquer. But when he comes home, what he needs is a soft place to land . . . a *feminine* side. His other half."

She pointed to herself as illustration; her feminine side, apparently, was located somewhere in the vicinity of her silicone-assisted breasts, which today had been molded into a pair of conical-shaped cups, à la Madonna in the '80s. Not a bad look, Stella had to admit, grudgingly.

"Seems to me he's done okay with just his male half, here, for a while. Any particular reason you've picked now to go worrying about him?"

Brandy blinked and for just a moment something flashed across her eyes—something dark and out of place on her gaudy, confident features. "It's time to mend fences," she muttered. "My horoscope said so."

"Yeah? Which one would that be? *Cosmo, Woman's World? Star?* 'Cause I got to tell you, sometimes I get an inconsistent read from them. You know? Like one of them tells you a windfall's coming your way and the other one says it's time to pinch your pennies. . . . I mean, seems like it could make a person kind of schizophrenic, counting on them for direction."

Brandy frowned. She considered Stella for a moment, and then she picked up her glass and nearly drained it again. When she set it down, her expression had settled into equal parts crafty and curious.

"Okay, sister," she said. "Let's cut to the chase. I don't know what you think you have going on with Goat, but I can give you one real good reason to back off."

"Yeah? What's that?"

"Does the name Loriann Portera ring a bell?"

Loriann had been a client a little over a year ago. She'd hired Stella to convince her husband that it would be easier to move out of the state—after deeding her the house—than to keep getting drunk every Friday and Saturday night and taking all his disappointments out on her.

"Loriann and I got to be friendly last year at the gym," Brandy continued. "She told me all about how *convincing* you could be. And I'm glad you were able to help her, I really am, only some folks might not approve of your methods. 'Specially law enforcement folks. You see what I'm sayin'?"

"No one's going to believe a crazy story like that," Stella said quickly, but inside she felt a little blip of panic. She had always known this day would come, when someone would find out what she did, someone who wouldn't honor the delicate web of secrecy that allowed her to keep helping people.

"Oh, I think they might," Brandy said calmly. "I asked around. Seems like Loriann ain't the only gal you been working with. All's it would take is for someone to open up an investigation, start handing out subpoenas and lie detector tests and all that kind of business. I mean, it could get real complicated, real quick. I'd just hate for that to happen, especially 'cause— and Stella, you got to understand I'm on your side here. I totally get that there's women need to go your route to get justice. And I want you to be able to keep takin' care of 'em. Only, you got to see I have a need here, too."

"Yeah? What's that?" Stella demanded.

"What I need is for you to stay the hell away from my man."

Stella regarded Brandy through narrowed eyes and tried to judge exactly how serious the woman was. Something still was not sitting right with her. She could certainly sympathize with Brandy's desire to get her hands on her own ex—what red-blooded woman could resist a man like Goat?—but there was something the gal wasn't telling her. And if Brandy was going to come at the discussion in a shifty-type way, Stella figured she was allowed a little truth-skirting, too.

"Okay," she said, crossing her fingers under the table. "Fine. What exactly are your terms?"

"Here's how it's gonna be," Brandy said. "You walk away from whatever you got—or *imagine* you got—going with my husband. You need to consider him off-limits. He ain't yours to date. Or, or *flirt* with even. Or whatever else kind of ideas you got."

"Well, I can't hardly avoid talking to him," Stella hedged. "It's a small town and all, plus we got us a friendly relationship."

"Just how friendly are we talking? You slept with him?"

"Not yet."

"Kissed him?"

Stella felt a flush creeping from her chest, up her neck, into her cheeks. "None of your damn business," she said.

"You said—"

"Okay. Fine. No. I mean yes. Once." Which was almost true: she hadn't ever kissed Goat, but at one point when she was slipping into a narcotic haze the day after the surgery that removed the bullet from her gut, she felt his lips brush her forehead before he left her hospital room.

"Huh. I'll take that as a no."

"You can take that as a—"

"Calm down, Stella, you don't need to be like that. We're working together here, right?"

Yeah . . . though Stella also wanted to get laid again before she was dead. And doable single men in her age bracket weren't exactly thick on the ground. And as much as she'd been ready to scratch Goat off her to-do list the night before, having Brandy calling the shots irked her.

"Whatever," she sighed. "Look, I can't promise I won't talk to Goat. But I promise I'll keep our conversation all business. And you keep your damn mouth shut about *my* business."

"Fine."

"Why do you care all of a sudden, anyway?" Stella asked, genuinely curious. "Seems like if you wanted your man back, letting him off the leash for three years is a funny way to show it."

Brandy took a healthy swig of her drink, shuddering slightly as it went down. "I got out of a long-term relationship not too long ago," she said. "It didn't end real good. It unfortunately reminded me how rare a good man is. You know?"

Stella knew, though she didn't care to commiserate on the subject. "Look, this has been a real fun visit and all, but I'm done in."

"Yeah, you look it."

Stella fumed. "So what I'm sayin' is, you may want to just collect your things and head on back to Goat's guest room."

"What makes you think I'm staying in the *guest* room?"

"You saying you aren't?"

The two women glared at each other, until finally Brandy blinked first. *Damn right,* Stella couldn't help thinking, *he's keeping your high-maintenance ass on ice.* She felt a little of the tension in her chest dissipate.

"The situation at Goat's is fluid," Brandy snipped, slurring her words.

"You sure you're okay to drive?" Stella asked, thinking: *lightweight.*

"Why? Are you inviting me to spend the night here? Like a sleepover, just us girls?"

"On second thought," Stella snapped, "I'm sure you're fine." She picked up Brandy's keys from where she'd tossed them. The keychain was attached to a little plastic rectangle that read IF YOU'RE RICH, I'M SINGLE.

Brandy scraped her chair back and stood up unsteadily. "Well, if I get in a wreck or something, I guess they'll know who to blame," she sighed.

"Who, me?" Stella demanded. "Or Johnnie Walker here? I don't think so, honey. 'Cause let me tell you, when you go around pointing fingers of blame for messin' up your life, nine times out of ten you'll find you're pointing right back at your own bad self."

SEVEN

· · · · · · · · · · ·

S tella was out of the house the next morning by nine. It
had taken a little extra time to get ready, because she
was in the unaccustomed position of planning to use her
feminine wiles to get some information.

And the information-giving-up target of her plan was Goat,
which added a layer of ambivalence to the proceedings. She'd
promised Brandy she'd stick to business with the man—but
there didn't seem to be any reason not to try to tilt the encounter in her favor. She hadn't promised not to look and smell irresistible while they were doing said business.

After trying on four outfits, Stella finally settled on a skirt
that had last fit when the elder Bush was still in office and
which, if she stared at her backside in the mirror at precisely
the right angle, gave her ass kind of a sassy Tina Turner shape—
more generous, certainly, but still curvy and high.

Makeup had been another minefield; with her head full of
Noelle's counsel from her last visit—"Matte's so last season,
Mom"—she gouged a fresh track in an old bronze eye shadow

and dusted up her lids, adding a bit of Avon Glimmerstick eyeliner in Majestic Plum. It was quite a challenge: she had to wear her reading glasses to see well enough to work, but then it became doubly difficult to get the makeup brush where it was going. It was like trying to sew on a button through a layer of Jell-O.

Perfume, at least, was easy. She gave herself a generous spritzing of White Diamonds, which always made her feel flat-out sex-goddess hot.

On her way to the shop—a quick stop to make sure Chrissy was set for the day—Stella carefully ate her way around the edges of two Pop-Tarts, avoiding the jammy middles where all the calories were clustered, and taking dainty bites so as not to mar her lipstick. Beauty was a hell of a taskmaster.

The shop was empty, except for Tucker, who was seated cross-legged on a big floor cloth stenciled with railroads, a much-chewed Thomas the Tank Engine in his drooly fist.

"Sow!" he exclaimed, waving the toy train in the air.

"Hi, punkin," Stella said, bending down for a knee-creaking embrace. "Where's your mama?"

"Down here," came Chrissy's muffled voice from beneath the computer desk Stella had set up adjacent to the counter where the cash register sat. "Stella, you ever hear of a damn fire code? You got about fifty cords all pluggin' into each other and no surge protector—why, I'm surprised that storm didn't blow this place outta the ground."

"I've been meaning—"

"You've been meaning to do a lot a things, but none of 'em's done theirself, I notice. So I'm taking care of this for you."

She backed out from under the desk, trailing a power cord

so fresh and new, it still kinked where it had been folded. It was connected to a little black blinking plastic box.

"What's that—a bomb? You fixing to blow up the place and start over?"

Chrissy sighed with a full measure of drama. "This here's a wireless router, Stella," she said. "The Comcast fella dropped it off for me this mornin' 'long with a couple a surge protectors so you don't go blowing us up to kingdom come. I had him charge your Visa."

Stella put out a hand to help Chrissy up, noting that the girl was getting a little more limber every day, hardly hesitating at all anymore when she bent at the waist. "What'd that cost me? And how'd you get him here when all kinds of folks were probably lined up for service, I wonder?"

"The receipt's in the drawer," Chrissy said, straightening her clothes and dusting off her knees. "And he was tryin' to git in my pants, I reckon."

"No shit? Well, see if he'll give you free lessons, then."

Chrissy fixed her with a disdainful glare. "I don't need no lessons. I read that manual, come with it. Done set it up myself. Now we'll just power back up and see—"

She toed the power strip's switch and stepped back, hands on hips. Together, they watched the Mac—only a year old, a splurge after Stella received a handsome bonus from a client whose husband had been siphoning money into a variety of secret investments that came to light following a hunting accident that left him with a bullet in his butt—whirr to life, the router signaling furiously.

Suddenly a full-screen image of a hard-muscled, deep-tanned, dew-dotted male torso, the nether regions tucked into a rather tiny thong that was by no means adequate for the job, flashed onto the Mac.

"Oh, dear," Chrissy said. "That darn Brody Jenner. Stella, you would not b'lieve what-all you can find on that TMZ website. It's positively distracting."

"Hmm," Stella murmured.

A sprinkling of icons blipped into place, and Chrissy clicked on one that looked like a button inscribed with a gold *W.*

"Check *this,*" she said proudly. The *World of Warcraft* portal popped up on-screen, an impressive stone arch guarded by cloaked red-eyed giants. In short order, there were a variety of trolls and thugs whacking each other with broadaxes and clubs.

"Neat-o," Stella said. "Look, you want to really make yourself useful around here, why don't you see if you can hack into the Show Me Five Paydown and transfer some of the cash from those state lottery crooks over into my account."

Her finances, she suspected, were a little dire, since she hadn't brought in any extra sideline money in recent months, and Hardesty Sewing Machine Shop & Repair had been closed while she and Chrissy recuperated. Stella was paying the most urgent bills as they came in, but she'd been afraid to check the balances in her accounts.

She owned a book by Suze Orman. That was a start, anyway. In the one chapter Stella'd read, Suze had made the point that it was kind of dumb for women to bury their heads in the sand and let money issues get the upper hand. Well, that Suze was a smart one, all right, and just as soon as Stella got an evening free . . . or hell froze over . . . she intended to see what else the woman had to say.

"You sayin' the lottery folks is crooks?" Chrissy demanded, so incredulous she let a hairy dude with hooves and horns club her character into a bloody pulp.

"Well, if you believe that taking money from poor folks and handing it over to bloated government agencies makes a person a crook, then, yeah, I guess I do," Stella said.

"Stella Hardesty," Chrissy breathed, her voice nearly quaking with conviction. "It is the God-given right of every citizen of our nation to gamble. You take away a person's gambling rights—why, it's gonna be our right to bear arms comin' close behind."

"Chrissy—," Stella started. Political discussions with the girl, she'd learned, were the sort of activity that required an erasure of all the basic tenets she'd long assumed right-thinking people shared. Growing up in a family of six children on hardscrabble acreage without enough resources to support all those folks comfortably—Chrissy's early training focused on a special family blend of ingenuity and bootstrap opportunism that reflected nearly unplumbable depths of skepticism and idealism. She wasn't dumb—far from it—and she wasn't always wrong, either, but adjusting to Chrissy's world in preparation for a serious discussion required a nearly Zen-like realignment of her preconceptions that Stella simply did not, at the moment, have time for.

"Honey. Let's table this particular discussion, okay? I just wanted to see if you were all set for the day before I headed out."

"Well, all right." Chrissy turned her attention back to the screen. Her character, a horned, tusked creature in a leather bikini, picked up a spiked throwing disk and let it fly. "Nailed you, you speckle-assed little yammer."

"I hope the customers don't cut in on your playtime too much."

"Aw, hush, Stella, I just got this set up for Todd."

The boy biked over to the shop a few days a week, when he couldn't find anything better to do; Stella figured that playing on a computer in her shop probably beat smoking weed with the deadbeats down behind the Arco while he waited for his mom to come home from work.

Recently, though—as Todd approached his fourteenth birthday—she suspected the boy had another reason to be visiting the shop: a bit of a crush on Chrissy.

"Now, you watch his tender little heart," she warned. "Won't do to go breakin' it before he's even had a chance to kiss a girl."

"Oh, now," Chrissy said. "Boys used to fall in love with me all the time, and it ain't never killed any of 'em."

Stella resisted pointing out that one, at least—her ex, Roy Dean—lay dead in the town cemetery. After all, it wasn't really accurate to say that a broken heart had led to the man's death sentence at the hands of the Mafia.

"Anything you want me to look up for you while you're gone?" Chrissy continued, shutting down the game.

"Thought you weren't interested in my side business," Stella retorted. "You know, you wanted to keep your knickers pristine and all."

"Yeah? Well, not to complain or anything, but I've just about sucked all the joy outta stocking thread as I think I possibly can. I need a challenge."

"A challenge," Stella repeated. "Okay."

She took a pen and a note from the cube on the counter—it read SHE WHO DIES WITH THE MOST FABRIC WINS—and scribbled out a note:

Cory Layfield
Background
Priors—associations, juvenile records, ???

"Here," she said, handing it over. "See if you can, I don't know, Google all this or whatever. I got a recent address and I imagine I'll just work from there unless you come up with something better."

"Boy howdy," Chrissy said, taking the note and slipping it under the keyboard. "That ain't much of a challenge."

"Well, don't get too excited, you're not going to find anything but junk."

"What's that supposed to mean?"

"Nothing, it's just that if you want to get anything besides a zillion pointless hits, you have to know what you're doing."

Too late Stella realized her error: Without meaning to, she'd implied that Chrissy did not, in fact, know what she was doing; and if there was one thing she'd learned in their young partnership, it was that Chrissy Shaw had had about as much being dismissed, marginalized, ignored, put down and left for stupid as she was planning to take. Stella began edging away from the counter, toward the door, taking her purse with her—a quick retreat was always the best option when Chrissy was provoked.

"I didn't mean—"

"Fuck that!" Chrissy exclaimed, her cornflower-blue eyes snapping, her generous gloss-sticky lips thinning to a hard line. "I *know* what I'm doing, all right. I'm workin' for shit wages for a woman with no more education than *I* got. And if any provin' needs done, I reckon you'll be eatin' those words for dinner, so I wouldn't go around callin' me no kinda—"

"Sorry, sorry, sorry," Stella called hurriedly as she backed out the door. As she practically ran for the Jeep, she remembered a truth she'd picked up in recent years, something she really ought to have put on a sign and hung up out front:

The less a woman has to lose, the quicker you better get out of her way.

Stella knocked sharply on Goat's office door for the second time. His office had a very large window—on account of the sheriff's offices being housed in what was once a Hardee's restaurant, with the kitchen now converted to records storage and a supply closet and a conference room, and the staff offices carved from what used to be the dining room.

A spanking-new Hardee's had been built out State Road Nine in the mid-'90s, where traffic from the interstate was more likely to find it, but Stella had eaten in the old one often enough in her younger days that she still got a flashback every time she opened the double glass doors from the parking lot, one of the building's features that had gone unmodified. She could almost smell the char on the charbroiled burgers.

The big windows had been covered with mini-blinds in a pinkish shade of mauve to match the industrial carpeting and wallpaper from the remodel, but Stella had learned that crouching down at the right angle from a vantage point in the shrubbery gave a person a pretty clear view of the goings-on inside, so she knew that Goat was at his desk. Besides, Irene Dorsey, the departmental receptionist and records officer, stage-whispered, *"He's hiding,"* with a theatrical nod in the direction of the sheriff's office.

Stella could feel Irene's curious gaze on her as she waited impatiently for Goat to give up the ruse. Irene was a holdover from Sheriff Burt Knoll's administration, but she'd made the transition to the new sheriff with ease. It wasn't hard to do— her working style of listening attentively and then doing things exactly as she damn well pleased went equally unchallenged by both administrations.

Goat was no dummy. Sheriff Knoll hadn't been either. Both knew better than to go trying to fix something that wasn't broke, and Irene—with her sharp memory undiminished by age, her unyielding loyalty to the long arm of the law, and her matronly scent of rose water and Jean Naté dusting powder— worked plenty well just the way she was.

"He's been hiding since that crew took the body and high-tailed it back up to Fayette yesterday," Irene clarified in a slightly louder whisper. "That Detective Simmons says she's coming on back in her own car this afternoon, and Goat don't want nothing to do with her."

Stella turned away from the sheriff's door and considered Irene thoughtfully. Seventy if she was a day, Irene seemed to think she had the entire town fooled about her age due to her zealous if not entirely professional home hair coloring. Her thin strands were dyed a relentless black, and not only did she keep up with the roots, but she often ended up dyeing the skin that encroached on her hairline, too, giving her a special-effects horror movie effect—as though she was wearing a gray latex skullcap with a wig attached.

Irene was holding a copy of *In Touch* out as far as her arms extended in front of her, peering over the tops of a pair of coral pink–framed reading glasses. She licked her thumb, then her forefinger, before turning a page.

"So . . . what do you think of those folks from up in Fayette, anyway?" Stella asked Irene.

"Well, now, they been here before. Once in 2000, once a few years before that." If Irene had an opinion on the subject, it wasn't forthcoming.

"Murders?" Stella asked. While her own interest in deadly crime hadn't really gotten jump-started that far back, she thought she'd remember the violent spilling of blood of one of her fellow citizens.

"Hmm, not so much," Irene said. "In 2000, remember that coot fell off his dingy and drowned in the strip pits, and then the next week them kids were ditching for senior week and one a them got fished out—"

"Tragic," Stella murmured, because she did remember that one, a skinny kid who'd been something of a local sensation on the track team.

"Yes, but remember Sheriff Knoll got it in his head it was a serial killer at work. Drowndin folks." She shook her head incredulously. "I coulda told Burt it wasn't nothin' of the sort, but you remember how he got. Them crazy theories of his.

Anyway, they sent that bunch down from Fayette back then and they poked around a little and come up with the bodies' blood alcohol levels and whatnot and finally everyone was satisfied it wasn't nothing but stupid at work."

"Well, what about the other time? Before that one?"

"You remember that whole Trusty Carmichael thing. . . ."

"Oh, that." Trusty Carmichael went a little nuts one summer after his wife of thirty years left him to go up to Saint Louis and enter a convent. He grew convinced that God was performing blood sacrifices on the picnic table in his backyard, but it turned out that the blood came from his own chickens, which he killed off over the course of a few weeks, chopping one up every time he got too despondent over Mrs. Carmichael's defection to the holy side. "Least that probably didn't take them a whole long time to figure out."

"Not with the feathers and all, no."

"Guess we just don't have a whole lot of mayhem around here," Stella mused, reflecting on the locations where she'd done some of her messier work. Generally it took just a bucket of rags and some Windex or Soft Scrub to clean up after even the most spirited discussion with one of her parolees, as she wasn't spilling murderous amounts of blood—just enough to do the trick, that was the rule.

Not for the first time, she flashed a quick prayerful thank-you up to the Big Guy for helping keep hid what she'd hid in the first place—the not-so-accidental nature of the string of accidents that had befallen the worst offenders of devil-baiting hatefulness against their women.

"No, ma'am," Irene said serenely. "And that's how we like it."

"So what's Goat got against Simmons?"

Irene laid down her magazine and beckoned Stella conspiratorially. "Now, you didn't hear this from me," she said, "but I believe that woman has designs on him. I heard her asking him to have dinner with her today when she was getting ready to leave last night. Seein' as how she'd be all by her little lonesome out at the Heritage House Motel and didn't have any idea where to get a decent meal. It was quite a sight to see, Stella, that woman carrying on. She don't have, you know, the equipment for it."

To Stella's startled amusement, Irene slipped her hands under her bosom and gave herself a brief little lift-and-display.

"Irene!" Stella said, blushing. "Not every man's a tit man, you know."

"Well, now, honey—it ain't just that. She's got that nasty smoker voice and she bites her nails and she don't have hardly any tush on her at all. And she's not particularly friendly . . . to me, anyway. Called me 'Miz Percy' twice, even though I corrected her the first time, and it's spelt out right here, *D-o-r-s-e-y,* plain as day." Irene tapped her engraved gold nameplate for emphasis.

"Why, that's terrible," Stella murmured. She didn't have any particular ill feelings for Simmons, but it was clear that the woman wasn't all that smart if she'd missed out on the number one rule of getting on in the workplace: Make friends from the bottom up.

It wasn't such a difficult lesson as far as Stella could see—why folks ever figured to get anywhere if they couldn't be bothered to spare a kind word for the people who did all the work. If you woke up with the flu and wanted to be squeezed in with the doctor, why, you'd better darn well be sweet to the scheduler. If your cable TV went on the fritz, hollerin' at the customer service gal wasn't going to get you anything but transferred to the wrong department.

And if you wanted to make time with the sheriff, you had darn well better play nice with Irene.

"I just call it like I see it," Irene said primly, returning to her *In Touch*.

"Well . . . I do hate to miss him," Stella sighed, turning as if to go. "Seein' as I was going to go pick up some Pokey Pot sandwiches and I know how fond of them he is."

In truth, it was Irene who favored the barbecue joint on the other end of town, a place that simmered its pork shoulder Carolina style until it was reduced to tender, vinegary shreds and tucked it into soft white rolls baked fresh every morning. Irene, who had to man the desk through the lunch hour, usually had to make do with whatever she brought from home.

"Oh, I'd hate for Goat to miss out," Irene said, snatching up the phone hastily. "Plus I wouldn't mind one a them myself."

Stella tried to keep from smirking as Irene stabbed at the button on the intercom. "I know you're in there, Goat Jones," she said, "and if you don't haul your ass out here this instant, I'm gonna shred up your *This Old House* magazine what just come in with the mail."

She replaced the receiver with a satisfied little smile, adding "He sure does love that magazine," just as Goat's door burst open and he stood there, six feet four lanky inches in a tan polyester uniform, glowering at the pair of them.

"Women," he said with venom. "God's sent me a plague of

women, when all I'm trying to do is mind my own business. And every one of y'all bent on causing me pain."

"Nothin' you ain't got comin, I'm sure," Irene murmured, focusing on her celebrity gossip while Stella tried to look innocent, a trick she'd been polishing for quite some time.

EIGHT

. . . .

Stella nibbled at a french fry, watching Goat try to eat his fast-falling-apart sandwich. Between the dripping sauce and the overstuffing that had gone into his Pokey Pot Junior, more of the sandwich was landing on the plate than was making it to his mouth.

Stella, who had a couple decades of Pokey Pot experience, had long ago developed a two-pronged approach to their sandwiches: Eat enough of the middle with a fork to ensure that when you picked up the remainder, the innards would stay put.

The other key was to order the Pokey Pot Baby. It was a rare person who could polish off a Junior at lunch—and Stella knew only a handful of people who'd ever made their way through a Big Pig. Nonetheless, a greasy paper sack holding a Big Pig, its top folded down several times and stapled, sat next to her on the table, a reward for Irene, who had come through for Stella in the clutch.

"I hear you have a date tonight," Stella couldn't resist saying.

Goat swallowed hard and dabbed at his mouth with a paper

napkin, then took a long drink of sweet tea. "Ain't a date," he managed to get out.

Stella shrugged. "Oh . . . a *professional* thing, then."

Goat didn't say anything. He frowned and glowered at the table. Stella couldn't help noticing that frowning lined up all the hard planes in his face in a breathtaking display of masculinity.

"Uh, probably having to do with that dead gal," she went on. "You all figure out who she is yet?"

Goat flicked a glance at her, just long enough for Stella to read the blip of intrigue there. "You know I ain't gonna talk to you 'bout that, Stella."

"Oh," Stella said, keeping her expression neutral. "Only reason I ask, is, maybe it would give us something to help convince you Neb didn't have anything to do with it."

Goat snorted. "That's not my concern. Way we see it, Neb's sitting on a whole lot of trouble right now. Your boy wasn't exactly an altar boy back in the day. Fact is, he got him a taste for that hillbilly heroin. We know all about it, Stella, and that Oxy's one expensive damn habit, the kind that might inspire a man to take what ain't his in order to pay for it. I'll tell you what, once we confirm who that woman is, it's only gonna look worse for Neb."

"Confirm—like you got an idea already?"

"I didn't say that." Goat's glare got stonier, and he gave his plate a desultory shove, sending it to the middle of the table with the four different kinds of hot sauce.

"Well, it's pretty clear you do. Got something on her to make the ID, did she? One of those clever crime scene types figure it out?" Wallet, keys, medical bracelet—there were a lot of possibilities, Stella reflected, especially since the body had been wearing clothes, which implied pockets, with opportunities for personal belongings you didn't tend to have on a naked dead person. "How you do the ident on a mummy, anyway? Do the fingerprints even work?"

Goat ignored the question as he got his wallet out and started peeling off money for a tip. Stella watched with secret admiration. Not too many folks put money on the Formica tables at Pokey Pot's, probably because they had to do all the work themselves, from waiting around for their food to show up in the pass-through to the kitchen, to busing their own tables. It was local courtesy to take an extra Wet-Nap from the basket and give the table a once-over for the benefit of the next diners to happen along, but that was about the extent of the diner's obligation.

A man who tipped generously was likely to be considerate in other ways as well—that was Stella's theory. Ollie had been a first-class skinflint; she'd once seen him pocket the tips from the tables they passed on their way out of Denny's. If Stella was ever to get hold of a new man, picking someone as far opposite of her dead ex as possible seemed like a good start.

"Tell you what," Stella said, reining in her rogue thoughts and trying a new tactic. "How about I spring for some cobbler, okay? We can split it."

Without waiting for an answer, she slid off her chair and went back up to the counter, and ordered a big piece with ice cream, two spoons.

Back at the table, Goat looked unaccountably glum.

"So," Stella said, taking a big bite of the gooey cinnamon-flecked apples, catching a glob of ice cream in her spoon. "You all are thinking this was like a robbery gone bad, then. This mystery gal was loaded, so whoever it was held her up and then, what, shot her? Hit her on the head? Stabbed her?"

"I didn't say that." Goat ogled the dessert between them.

"Couldn't they figure it out with all that fancy equipment they dragged down here? Hell, they looked like a bunch of Amway salesmen, Goat. 'Cept for that Detective Simmons—I notice she lets the other folks do her heavy lifting."

"Daphne's good," Goat said through clenched teeth. "She's fast-trackin' it up there. They say she's got a shot at sheriff when Stanislas steps down."

The truth was that while everyone called Goat Sheriff, and Burt Knoll before him, they and the chief gunslingers at the other three branch offices, in Fairfax and Harrisonville and Quail Valley, were all *undersheriffs*. They all reported, on paper, up to Dimmit Stanislas, the top Sheriff of Sawyer County, who these days spent most of his time ignoring his doctor's orders after his second stroke and smoking his way to an involuntary retirement, the kind that requires you to haul around your own oxygen.

"Hmm . . . that would make her your boss, wouldn't it?"

If it was possible for Goat's eyebrows to lower any farther, for his scowl to deepen, that did the trick.

An unpleasant thought occurred to Stella. "Hey, you don't have a problem working for a woman, do you? 'Cause I got to tell you—"

Goat slapped the table so fast and so unexpectedly that Stella jumped. "*No,* Stella, I ain't got any problems with women, except for the fact that all of you chose the same damn moment to visit all manner of torture on me."

He looked so miserable that Stella felt a little sorry for him.

"We were having a perfectly nice dinner," he said, picking up steam. "Least I thought we were—and then you go storming outta there like—like I tried to feed you cat food or something and then Brandy—hell, that woman can make me crazy in a New York minute and why she's moved her ass into my house, when last I heard she hates my guts—well, that's a mystery right there, and then I got Daphne Simmons across the conference table telling us how the team's gonna do this and we're gonna do that and all of a sudden her hand's on my knee squeezing like she thinks I got the evidence stashed in my pants—"

He clamped his mouth shut and blushed a deep shade of cherry red. Stella didn't know whether to laugh or apologize, but one thing was clear: The man had been pushed to his limits.

"Oh, dear," she said. "Well, I can't help you much with your ex, but tell you what, why don't you hunt up the Sawyer County Services employment manual, and see what-all it has to say about sexual harassment, because if I'm not mistaken, no still means no."

"Forget it . . . ," Goat said darkly. "It's nothing I can't handle."

"What's that supposed to mean?"

"It means I think I can keep my pants on without your help, Dusty. Okay? So let it drop."

He was embarrassed, and he was irritated, and he looked like he might be ready to bite her head off—but the bottom line was that he wasn't buying what Daphne Simmons was selling. Stella had to chew on the inside of her cheek to keep from grinning.

Instead, she gave the cobbler a nudge in his direction. Men—they never seemed to appreciate the problem-solving powers of sweet buttery carbs. "Pick up your spoon," she said. "We'll figure this mess out. Meanwhile, you might as well keep your strength up."

After lunch, Stella headed over to Fairfax, a fifteen-minute drive that took twice that today when she got stuck behind a horse trailer. Pulling into town was not so different from pulling into Prosper, except everything was just a little neater, a little fresher, a little more spit-shined. The new medical complex they built out by Fairfax Municipal Hospital had a lot to do with that—now the county's doctors and nurses and lawyers were mostly concentrated in one place, with a whole new crop of specialists in residence to drive their fancy foreign cars around and fix a host of medical problems that had previously gone untended or patched up as well as the local internist could manage. Stella didn't have any solutions for the national health care crisis, but she figured she and her insurance carrier were doing their part by keeping her medical team occupied and paid during her recovery; she and Chrissy had become quite familiar with the maze of offices as they visited their surgeons and physical therapists and cardiologists and orthopedists and an oral surgeon to reconstruct Chrissy's busted teeth and even a dermatologist, who was doing her best to help Stella's scars fade into oblivion with a variety of expensive treatments.

Stella navigated the rows in the parking lot, looking for a spot with a little extra room on the sides. The spaces were so damn narrow—and she couldn't stand the thought of some rehab patient in a cast lumbering out of the passenger seat and whacking the door into the Jeep's green paint. Finally she found a spot between a brand-new Prius and a well-maintained Lexus.

She found Dr. Herman's office without any trouble in one of the many wings in the cluster of buildings. There was nothing special about it. A quick glance showed the usual spread of magazines and tired silk flower arrangements. Someone had stapled paper leaves and pumpkins onto a bulletin board covered with a variety of forms and announcements.

Stella checked in with the pleasant-enough receptionist, saying that Neb was in the men's room and, given his terrible pain, might be just a minute or two, but that was fine because as his wife, she needed just a second of the doctor's time to speak privately with him concerning the safety of certain sexual practices for a man with a disk surgery on his record. That got her a quick pink-faced "all righty, then," and Stella picked up a copy of *Working Mother* magazine and started flipping the pages.

Every doctor's office she'd been in during the last decade, she reflected, had copies of that damn magazine, and as Stella waited for Dr. Herman, she started a low burn.

She had technically been working for only three years, if you didn't count the occasional hours she put in helping Ollie in the shop. In general, her departed husband preferred to run the shop by himself, so Stella had raised their daughter Noelle, and then when Noelle left the nest, turned her attentions to the community, participating in every church committee and neighborhood watch and fire department bake sale and Prosper Pride Day and garden club beautification project and on and on and on.

In all those years, Stella didn't recall a giant surfeit of empty hours. From the early years of waking with the baby all night and running the house all day, through the seasons of church fund-raisers and campaigning for school funding and doing the books for the shop and running elderly neighbors to the grocery, Stella figured she went to bed just as tuckered every night as her office-working sisters. Glancing up at the gal behind the desk, who was peering at a monitor and tapping at a keyboard from a comfortable chair, she didn't guess there was much point to trying to guess who was more done in at the end of the day: the desk jockeys or the carpool drivers and candy stripers.

On the other hand, a visitor from another planet, picking up *Working Mother* and glancing through the ads, might guess there was a strong correlation between receiving a paycheck and a bursting need for Botox and Gas-X and luxury sedans and quick-dry nail polish. If that celestial visitor scanned an article or two, she'd be scratching her Martian head and wondering why the female backbone of the white-collar workforce was so all-fired obsessed with composting their coffee grounds and visiting the national parks and navigating sibling rivalry.

Someone would have to take that Martian gal out for a stiff drink and explain that a whole lot of folks, *Working Mother* among them, got their jollies and made their money from dividing the sisterhood, from making them figure one bunch had a leg up on the other. And that pissed Stella off plenty. She tossed the magazine back on top of the pile, just as a petite gal popped her head out the door and smiled.

"Come on back, dear," she said with a voice like honey, even though she had at best half a dozen years on Stella, and all her annoyance retreated back down to its usual low simmer.

She followed the gal, admiring her scrubs, which were decorated with scarecrows and burnt-orange piping, down a hall to the door at the end. It was opened a crack, and she stepped deferentially aside, gesturing like Vanna White, and said, "Go on in, hon."

Stella shouldered her way in and leaned across the big walnut desk for a handshake. "Stella Hardesty," she said. "Pleased to meet you."

Dr. Theodore Herman raised his ass off his chair a foot or so and shook her hand. He was a pleasant-looking man, if a little too smooth-edged for Stella's taste. His white coat was crisp and pressed, his steel-gray hair was perfectly styled, and his teeth were as white as a dinner plate—but his hand when they shook was cool and surprisingly squishy.

Not at all like Goat's. The sensation of his hand surrounding hers the other night popped into Stella's mind, the warmth of his rough-callused skin, the pressure of his strong fingers as they teased at her palm.

Stella realized that Dr. Herman was staring at her expectantly. Oops.

"Oh, uh . . . excuse me—," she stammered. "Could you repeat that?"

Dr. Herman raised his eyebrows but gave her a brief, chilly smile and said, "I was just saying that I was under the impression that Mrs. Donovan was bringing Neb in."

"Oh, that," Stella said, pouring on her most winning smile.

"I'm sorry for the misunderstanding. What I said was that I am here, ah, in the capacity of, to help Donna and Neb. He's come under attention of the, uh, certain legal agencies and I am, as their representative, that is to say, in an effort to clear up this little misunderstanding—"

Dr. Herman raised a well-manicured hand to stop her. "I'm sorry, I'm afraid I don't completely understand. Is Neb in legal trouble?"

Stella arranged her features in what she hoped was a thoughtful, intelligent frown. "As ridiculous as this is—and I'm quite certain it's nothing but a series of misunderstandings—it appears he may be a suspect in a possible murder."

At this, Dr. Herman's eyes widened in surprise. "Not that body they found out at the fairgrounds?"

Stella dipped her chin and stared at a gold pen lying at a precise angle on Dr. Herman's desk blotter. "I'm afraid I'm not at liberty to say," she said softly.

"Are you . . . a detective?"

Stella was not, in fact, until just that moment, when it occurred to her that the position might have certain advantages. "Private, yes," she said, nodding and thinking her strategy ahead. "I would be happy to get my identification from the car, if you like—under the new codes we are required to keep a copy in the car and I haven't quite adjusted to—"

"No, no, that won't be necessary," Dr. Herman said, "as long as you keep your questions general. As I'm sure you know, I cannot comment on any specifics of Mr. Donovan's care, or any patient, for that matter, without a more compelling legal basis." He relaxed back in his chair and smiled blandly.

"That oughtta work," Stella said. "Here's the thing. I know that Neb battled a powerful OxyContin addiction following his treatment, and I—"

"Hold on, there," Dr. Herman said, raising his hand again. He sure did seem to like using hand signals to direct the flow of his conversations. "I can't confirm that, as it has to do with the specifics of a patient's care."

Stella blew out a breath, frustrated, and thought of another angle to come at things. "Well, how about this," she said. "If a person is addicted to OxyContin, I mean they got it bad, popping them things for breakfast, lunch, and dinner . . . is it possible they could do something, like a violent act, and not remember it?"

The question seemed to take Dr. Herman by surprise. He regarded Stella thoughtfully, and then his gaze drifted up near the ceiling for a few moments while he tented his fingers and swung his chair in a small, lazy arc for a bit.

"OxyContin is a derivative of heroin, as you may be aware," he finally said.

"Yeah, I know. They call it the hillbilly heroin and all that."

"And as such, like heroin and, for that matter, all narcotics, an excessive dosage can cause a benumbing or deadening effect. Which makes it effective as a pain treatment, of course."

"Huh." Stella fought the urge to roll her eyes at the doc's long-windedness. She'd seen this happen often enough with her own physicians that she knew it was easier to just let him run his course than to try to hustle things along.

"Now, of course, the effect of any narcotic—or actually we prefer the more precise term opioid—on an individual depends on the dose and the route of administration, and what other medications he might be taking, and several other factors. And some of the potential side effects are contradictory, like drowsiness and sleeplessness, for instance, or constipation and diarrhea."

"No kidding. But as for remembering—"

"There's some evidence that short-term memory may be impaired in some patients in some situations. Perhaps you've heard people under the influence of psychotropic substances claim a certain clarity of thinking, a so-called mind-blowing experience—"

"No, not personally," Stella said hastily. "But I've, you know, heard stories."

"Yes, well. Frequently what is experienced as a heightened sensitivity to one's surroundings is actually accompanied by lowered awareness of events and the passage of time. In addition, normal behavioral checks and balances, which are quite complex in terms of brain chemistry but might be summarized in lay terms as inhibitions and social filters, do not function normally in these conditions."

"So you're saying that a fella could get himself high as a kite and—well, let's just come up with a for instance. Could he get in an argument with someone, and—in a fit of violence, uncharacteristic violence, as this hypothetical fella generally wouldn't hurt a fly—could he kill someone?"

Dr. Herman bent forward, his bland, handsome features working themselves into a show of enthusiasm. "Not only could he, but the literature includes many documented cases of uncharacteristic behavior, frequently characterized by bursts of activity. It might take the form of acts of superhuman strength, or self-inflicted injury, or, as you say, violence. I mean, it doesn't happen every day, and it would have to be a situation of pretty heavy use, but yes, it's been known to happen."

Stella felt a chill start up along her spine. "And have no recollection of doing it?"

"Partial recall, in some cases, and in others, no recollection at all," Dr. Herman concurred.

"But—what about—" Stella thought about the mystery mummy woman, encased in her concrete resting place. It struck her as pretty unlikely that Neb had gotten himself loaded up, gone out to the site, cranked up the mixer, readied the frame, and all of a sudden got a hankering to commit a cold-blooded murder. No, if—and it was a mind-boggling if—he had killed the unknown woman, he would have had to come up with the plan to sink her in the foundations afterwards, not to mention get himself sober enough to carry out the plan without falling in himself.

"Here's the thing," she said, choosing her words carefully. There was no way she was about to give out details of the case; Goat would have her head on a platter. "What I'm wondering is, whether a person could commit this act of violence, this murder, and then figure out a complicated plan to, uh, cover it up and dispose of the body—a plan that would take a bit of complex scheming and some physical labor, maybe even some dead-of-night-type sneaking around—I mean we're talking a plan without a lot of margin of error—could a person all hopped up on Oxy do that and later not have any memory of it?"

Dr. Herman pursed his lips and looked even more earnest in his cogitations. He picked up a pair of half-moon glasses off the desk and slipped them on his nose, and peered at Stella over the top. The effect was a little bit condemning, and Stella had the uncomfortable memory of standing before the judge in his chambers the day he dismissed the case against her for killing Ollie.

"Well . . . ," the doctor finally said, drawing out the syllable. "In a high-use phase, which would be characterized by repeated dosage over several days with little if any periods of sobriety in between, it is possible for memory to be impaired, though usually it's episodic and short term. Which is to say, a person might forget bits and pieces here and there, but retain the general thread of events. Though there is something . . . what was it . . ."

He tapped a finger against his chin thoughtfully, and suddenly looked up at Stella in an *aha* expression.

"Kurtzoy syndrome," he said, "that's it. I saw a colleague deliver a paper on it a while back."

"Kurtzoy?"

"Yes—this is outside my area of expertise, but in the 1970s, Dr. Kurtzoy did groundbreaking work with, ah, episodic memory loss and opioids. He showed that a patient exposed to high doses over a prolonged period of time could suffer a more profound impairment . . . in lay terms, he could lose blocks of time as completely as if the memories were wiped clear of his brain, like erasing digital files from a hard drive."

Stella's heart sank. So it was possible that Neb truly was guilty—and didn't even know it himself.

She thanked Dr. Herman, receiving a second limp and soggy handshake, and left the office building with a head full of troubled thoughts.

She almost wished she hadn't come on this errand. She'd been so certain a quick check would clear up at least one avenue in the case, but instead it had only deepened her nagging worries that she had a guilty client on her hands.

Stella stopped by the Wal-Mart on the way home and picked up a collar, leash, giant bag of dog food, and—on a whim—a big soft dog bed with moose and rifles and hounds printed all over it. By the time she got home, it was nearly four o'clock and she was beat.

Stella felt a little swell of anticipation when she parked the Jeep in her garage. Part of it was dread at discovering what Roxy had managed to destroy in her absence, and part of it felt suspiciously like cheer, looking forward to an affectionate reception, even if it was from a creature whose IQ hovered around twelve on a good day.

Inside, a quick survey of the kitchen showed no dog, a torn Flaming Hot Cheetos bag, and a generous sprinkling of orange crumbs on the floor.

"Roxy?" Stella called.

In answer, there was a familiar thumping sound under the table. Stella knelt down: there was Roxy, lying flat on her side with her tongue lolling, her snout crusted orange. As if in greeting, she sneezed, looked surprised, and sneezed twice more in rapid succession.

"Oh, you big dummy," Stella said, extending a hand. Roxy got to her feet and licked Stella's hand, tail accelerating. "You didn't try to eat those nasty things, did you?"

There was one person who really loved the snacks, and Stella was not surprised to see that he'd come and gone, leaving another note as well as the evidence of his pantry-raiding.

I walked Roxy
She was hungry so I gave her that fryed chicken you
had in the frige
(DO NOT FORGET TO TAKE THE BONES OUT!!!
OR SHE COUD CHOKE ON THEM!!!!!!)
She did 4 number 1's and a big number 2

Stella rolled her eyes, figuring Todd had left Roxy's deposit for her to clean up—but she was pleased the boy had come by. He was a pain in the ass, but a sweet and generally dependable one.

As Stella hitched the new collar and leash on her dog for a tour of the backyard, the phone rang. Stella picked it up and let herself out the screen door, Roxy bolting ahead of her in a show of great enthusiasm.

"Hello?"

"Stella . . . this is Brandy. I need you to come over right now. Hurry, all right?"

"Brandy? What are you talking about?"

"I'm scared, Stella. I'm out at Goat's house alone and he's not going to be home until later and now he's not even picking up on his cell and—and—"

"Calm down. What exactly are you scared of?" Stella asked, allowing Roxy to pull her around the perimeter of the yard. When they were nearly at the hedge separating Stella's lawn from her backyard neighbors, Roxy caught a scent and tugged Stella so hard as she strained on her leash to follow it that they both crashed through the shrubbery, branches scratching at Stella's legs.

"I—well—there's . . ."

Stella waited, but Brandy sputtered into silence. "Damn you," she muttered at Roxy, who dragged her to the base of a big tree and took up baying into the branches. A squirrel, no doubt, who was relishing taunting the big dumb beast.

"What?"

"No, no, it's just my dog. What's got you so spooked, anyway?"

"There's—it's—I think I'm in danger." Her voice tapered off to a whisper, and Stella jammed the phone against her ear.

She pulled hard on Roxy's leash, and only by putting all her weight into it was she able to drag the dog back toward her own yard. She found a thin spot in the hedge and was able to get through without too much more flesh-scraping.

"What kind of danger?" she asked.

"Like . . . maybe . . . someone trying to hurt me."

"You think someone's in the house, like an intruder? A robber?"

There was a short pause, and Stella waited while Roxy found two or three patches of lawn that she hadn't yet urinated on.

"Could be," Brandy said in a very small voice.

Stella sighed. She wouldn't have figured Goat's brassy ex for the type, but plenty of people got spooked out in the country at night, and Goat's place was especially remote, set far back from the main road. There was no road noise once you drove down his long gravel drive. Only the sounds of night in the country: the owls and crickets, the jostling mooing commentary of cattle in close quarters for the night, the din that went up in henhouses and cattle pens and dog runs when the occasional coyote or fox came visiting. But most of all, it was the silence—long uninterrupted stretches of it that could be disconcerting for anyone who'd lived their whole life in town, even a small town.

"Have you locked all the doors?" she asked, finally getting Roxy's attention and starting back to the house. "Checked the windows?"

"Yes . . . but still, I was thinking, if you aren't busy . . . I mean I think Goat has some beer in the fridge, I could make us some grilled cheese sandwiches. . . ."

"Brandy," Stella said, "thanks so much for the invitation, but I don't know if it's such a good idea for you and me to get to drinking together every night of the week, you know? And besides, I'm beat. I really am."

"But if you—"

"Look, I'll be up for another hour. If you want, call me back before you go to bed. Goat'll probably be back by then anyway. And I'm sure everything's fine. Prosper's not exactly a hotbed of criminal activity."

"Yeah, 'less you count folks getting murdered," Brandy muttered, and hung up on her.

Stella stared at the receiver in her hand, irritated. She didn't care to be hung up on, especially not by spoiled high-maintenance interlopers from the past who showed up at exactly the wrong time.

"Pansy-ass," she murmured softly as she started up the back porch steps.

Then she stopped.

Over by the hydrangea bushes, underneath the windows, something caught her eye. In the porch light, she could just make out a trampled section, her coral impatiens crushed to a flattened mess, the storm-soaked earth bearing a pattern of shoe prints.

She went to check it out, bending down and tracing her finger around the outline of a footprint. It was a deep one, the impression of a lug sole distinct in the soft earth. She straightened and ran her fingers along the window sashing. There—there were loosened flakes of paint, and several gouges in the wood.

Someone had tried to force the window open.

They hadn't tried very hard, and they'd given up when it became clear that they wouldn't succeed—Stella locked all her windows from inside—but someone had been here with more than a friendly visit on his mind.

While Brandy conjured imaginary intruders a few miles away, a real one had visited Stella.

"Well, fuck," Stella mused, and let herself into the house, pushing Roxy ahead.

Suddenly, having a guard dog—even a tail-wagging, trash-digging, worthless specimen such as Roxy—seemed like a good idea. Stella made a circuit of the house, her hand on Roxy's collar, opening every closet door and looking behind the shower curtain. Roxy didn't seem to mind, but she didn't show any signs of excitement, either.

"If there *was* a bad guy," Stella asked when they'd been through the whole house, "you'd tell me, right?"

Roxy sat down and whapped at the kitchen floor with her tail.

"I mean, you'd know the difference, wouldn't you?"

More spirited whapping. Roxy cocked her head to one side and whined.

Surely a human being bent on evildoing would give off a different vibe than a regular good citizen. And dogs were supposed to pick up on that, weren't they?

Or maybe that was just vampires and robots and that sort of thing, like in the Terminator movies, when the dog went berserk whenever Arnold showed up.

"Look here," Stella said, getting a cereal bowl out of the cupboard and pouring some kibble from the bag she'd bought. "No more people food for you. But tell you what, you turn out to be a good watchdog, maybe I'll get you some of those Snausages they got over at Wal-Mart. You'd like those, wouldn't you?"

Roxy didn't answer—she stuck her snout right into the bowl and set to work—but the phone rang again. Stella jumped. Nothing like an unseen hostile presence to get the blood moving.

"Hello," she said.

"Stella, I need you to come over here and babysit. Immediately would be preferable."

"Chrissy, you better not be calling to tell me you got the heebie-jeebies," Stella said. "I've had about enough of that for tonight."

"The what? No, I'm—hang on a minute." There was a sound of shuffling and a door shutting and then Chrissy's voice came back on, slightly muffled. "I'm fixing to get me some tonight, is what's going on, so I need you to watch Tucker for me."

"You what? Girl, you ought to have thought of this a while ago. I love Tucker like my own and I'm happy to sit him anytime with just a little notice, but I can't go clearing off my schedule just because you get it in your head to go out and wet your whistle." Stella was crabby enough without having to muster up much in the way of encouragement for her partner's plan. "I'm too tired."

"Stella," Chrissy hissed. "I ain't doing this for *me*. I mean, not entirely, anyway. It's Larry Klipsinger who I'm seducing here."

"Larry who?"

"Aw, come on, Stella. He was in my high school class, star of the Mathlete team? Remember? Smartest kid to ever graduate Prosper? He had a free ride to MIT, but he stayed here to help his folks with the farm."

Stella had a vague memory of a newspaper article, a photo of a tall, skinny kid holding a plaque, shaking hands with a bunch of guys in suits over in Jefferson City. "He couldn't have been all that smart if he gave up a chance to go to MIT."

"Bite your tongue, Stella. He's plenty smart. All that higher learnin's not for everyone. Larry *likes* it here. And listen, he's already showed me how to hack into the DMV. I got Cory Layfield's license plate number. He drives a 2002 Ford Expedition. White."

Stella whistled. "No shit. Well, I stand corrected. Maybe you got yourself a hot one."

"Yeah. I guess so. But look, I had to show him my tits to get that far. I figure, if we want to get into the evidence files and what-all, I'm going to have to take him around the bases."

"Chrissy," Stella exclaimed, alarmed, "you can't go bartering sex for favors, honey. We don't run that kind of operation."

There was a short pause in which Stella could fairly well sense her partner rolling her eyes.

"It ain't like that," Chrissy whispered fiercely. "I was gonna go for it anyway. He's gone and filled out nice, you oughtta see him. Got him a little stubble makes him look like Keith Urban."

"Well, you didn't know that when you asked him over," Stella protested. She was delighted with the girl's ingenuity, but theirs was a pro-woman business, and trading sexual favors seemed somehow slightly antithetical to the whole corporate philosophy. "What did you tell him, anyway?"

"Just we had a new computer at the shop and would he mind taking a look. He works part-time at the library doing their computers, and it's not like I'm the first person around here asked him for help. I was just gonna try to sweet-talk him into a lesson, is all."

"And he agreed to come over? Just like that?"

"Stella," Chrissy scolded. "I was smokin' hot in high school. I b'lieve Larry would of cut off a arm just to slow dance with me back then."

"Well. Excuse *me*."

"Looka here," Chrissy said. "You think we can quit flapping jaws now and get this show on the road? He's upgrading the OS right now, but I think I got him all primed up and interested, and that's the kind of thing that don't keep."

Stella watched as Roxy inhaled the last of her dinner then belched contentedly. "I was gonna get to bed early," she sighed.

"Ain't no one stoppin' you. Fix Tucker some fish sticks and applesauce, and then you can both crash. I imagine we'll be pretty busy here at the shop for a good long while."

"Awww . . . the *shop*? You all aren't gonna do it on the counter, now, are you?" Stella had a sudden vision of the pair of them toppling the cash register on the floor in the heat of the moment.

Chrissy giggled. "I ain't promising anything like that, but we'll be sanitary. I'll put down some fusible web or something first."

"Ah—why'd you have to—that's just disgusting," Stella said.

"I was just messin' with you, we'll probably go back to his place. Besides, it ain't disgusting. It's just natural, and you're just jealous. Now git on over here 'fore Larry goes and fries all his circuits, waitin' on me."

Chrissy hung up in a fit of more giggling.

Geek humor, Stella thought darkly as she rounded up her purse and keys. An hour later, she was rinsing out a very messy bib in the little sink in Chrissy's microscopic kitchen, trying not to think about what was going on in the darkened shop across the parking lot. Tucker was fast asleep, curled up sweetly with his bottom in the air in the crib that shared the bedroom with Chrissy's twin bed and an old dresser.

Larry had been everything Chrissy promised and then some; it was hard to see a whole lot of computer geek left in the hard-muscled, tanned, compact young man who was somehow managing to type and mouse while staring at Chrissy's ample, softly rounded behind with his lips parted in anticipation while she got Tucker's diaper bag and toys ready for Stella.

Stella had been curious to see what the amorous pair had discovered in all their online sleuthing, but between her fatigue and Tucker's hungry whining, she figured she might as well leave them to their varied pursuits. She'd crash in Chrissy's bed, and the gal could explain it all in the morning.

She got the latest J. D. Robb paperback out of her purse—she couldn't wait to see what that badass lieutenant Eve Dallas was up to now—and poured a tumbler of purple grape juice, ready to settle in for a few minutes of reading before she nodded off, when her phone rang.

"Damn you!" she exclaimed, pulling the thing out of her purse. She hadn't gotten this many calls on a single day in ages.

Goat's number showed on the caller ID.

"Brandy—"

"It' ain't her, it's me," a deep and desperate-sounding male voice cut in. "Get over here, Stella. It's an emergency."

Unbelievable. By the end of the night, everyone Stella knew was going to have called with some made-up emergency that demanded her immediate attention. "Is it her imaginary burglar?" she demanded. "'Cause I'm not going anywh—"

"I'm telling you, Dusty, for the love of everything you hold dear, if you don't get here now, I'm liable to kill this woman with my bare hands."

"What's she done now?" Stella couldn't quite keep a smug

note out of her voice. It should have been obvious that Brandy was going to prove her own undoing, with her fragile little poor-me helpless act.

"Oh, not much," Goat grumbled, "unless you count hitting me on the head, knocking me out, and stealing my pants."

NINE

. . . .

didn't say I was knocked out for very *long,*" Goat protested when Stella arrived half an hour later with Tucker in tow.

"Yeah? Well, what about your pants?" Stella nodded at the faded old cargo pants that were slung nicely around Goat's athletic hips, held up by a burnished brown belt with a silver buckle. Nothing, that she could tell, was amiss *there.*

"She didn't get them *all* the way off, but she would have, if she hadn't been too drunk to deal with the buckle. You don't know how she gets when she's drinking."

Stella was not happy. She'd gotten Tucker out of the crib, bundled him into the car seat, listened to him wail all the way over to Goat's, only to fall asleep just as she arrived, and now he was twenty-eight pounds of back-breaking weight slumped against her chest.

Not to mention the fact that she'd flossed and brushed and swigged a bolt of Scope and redone her eye makeup. None of that was Goat's fault, of course, but it still made her irate that she'd gone to the trouble, only to arrive and find out that Goat was suffering only a knot on the side of his bald head, and he'd locked Brandy in the guest room.

"I thought for sure she'd pass out by now," he added conversationally. "She drank every one of my beers and made a dent in some schnapps that probably goes back a decade."

"Guess she can hold her liquor," Stella observed. There were regular thumps on the door of the guest room, accompanied by occasional bursts of singing alternating with muffled hollering.

"She always could put it away, but I wouldn't say she *holds* it all that well." Goat gingerly touched his head and scowled. "She gets a little excitable. It was one of the things that got between us—me having to talk her down all the time, well, *that* got plenty old."

Stella couldn't help it—her ears pricked up at Goat's criticism of his ex. That was an avenue she would have liked to explore further—she could probably listen to Goat trash the woman for hours without getting bored—but Tucker was getting terribly heavy.

"Is there somewhere I could—?"

"Oh, sure," Goat said, and grabbed Tucker from Stella before she could protest. To her surprise, though, he did it like a champ, smoothly easing the little boy into his own arms, settling him high on his shoulder so that Tucker's cheek tucked perfectly into the hollow of Goat's neck, and balancing him there like a sack of chicken feed. "I'll set him down on my bed here in a second. Just let me get you something. Uh, I'd offer you a beer, but I'm fresh out. I think I got a bottle of pinot noir in there somewhere—"

"Water," Stella said, "and I guess you best brew up some

coffee if this is going to take any kind of a while. Though it does look like you got things under control here, so maybe I can just turn around and head home."

As if on cue, Brandy sent up a high-pitched wail. "I got to peeeeee," she cried, and Goat gave Stella a deer-in-headlights look.

"You take care of her," he begged, "and I'll make you a damn good cup of coffee."

Stella rolled her eyes. Not much of a trade.

"The door's not really locked," Goat added, "it just gets stuck to where it's hard to open from inside. Put a little shoulder in it—that'll do the trick."

Stella did as he suggested, wondering at her own sanity the whole time. Helping Brandy was like encouraging a relentless suitor: it just guaranteed she'd keep coming back.

When she shoved, the door burst open, knocking Brandy over. She landed hard on her butt, hiccupped, looked up at Stella in surprise, and laughed.

"You *did* come!" she said. "I knew you would. I ain't scared no more, but Goat's being no fun. Maybe we can pop us some corn."

Stella put out a hand to help her up, noticing that Brandy had changed into a snug terry knit jog suit at some point in the evening, a little yellow set with athletic striping down the side. It was hard to imagine the sport it might have been designed for, seeing how it scooped astonishingly low over Brandy's energetically uplifted breasts, and the pants didn't cover even her hip bones, leaving a wide swath of midriff bare to the world. Stella spotted a fussy little gold-and-bead ring poked through Brandy's navel, and felt a twinge of envy; childbirth and a close personal relationship with the Frito-Lay product line had pretty much ensured her own navel would stay adornment-free and out of sight.

"Oooh—my—I'm just a little light-headed," Brandy observed as Stella tugged her upright.

Suddenly there was a huge flash, a thunderous crashing sound, and the room tilted sideways as Brandy came hurtling toward Stella, knocking them both out the door and into the hallway, where they fell in a heap.

An explosion of some sort. Stella, heart pounding, hastened to untangle Brandy's floppy arms and legs from hers. Out the window she could see an orange fireball shoot flames toward the sky.

Goat rounded the corner at a gallop, Tucker wide-eyed in his arms. "Are you—? Is she—? *Stella*—"

He grabbed her in a not-unpleasant fierce embrace and then released her, eyes roving up and down her body, before he handed her Tucker and bent down to check out Brandy.

"I think I peed myself," Brandy said, and yawned.

Goat scowled and let her slump against the wall. He grabbed Stella's hand and pulled her with him at a jog, through the house to the front door, but as he reached for the knob, he hesitated. "You stay inside," he ordered.

Stella got Tucker hitched up a little more comfortably in her arms. He pointed a chubby finger outside and said, his voice full of awe, "Hot."

After Stella put out a hand to test the air, she followed Goat onto the porch. Out in the gravel drive, the slightly tarnished red Camaro in which Brandy had delivered herself to Goat's house just two nights earlier had been reduced to a burning pile of rubble. Smoke poured from the chassis, and flames licked out from the rear of the frame. Bits of glass winked on the ground, and pieces of metal thrown by the blast lay smoldering on the drive.

"Holy cow," Stella breathed. "I don't believe she'll be driving that thing anywhere any time soon."

"What—? How—?" Goat sputtered and stepped in front of her, throwing a forearm out protectively. "Stay right here, Dusty," he finally said.

Stella was torn between the urge to push him aside and the lovely sensation of that hard-muscled arm brushing against her clavicles . . . that, and a taste for personal safety. Heading into all that molten metal and leaking fuel and fiery devastation just didn't strike her as all that smart.

Her pocket gave a little start and began to shriek, and Stella fished out her phone and answered it, coughing from the smoke fumes. "Hello . . ."

"Stella? It's me," a voice said in a scratchy whisper.

Stella jammed the phone harder against her ear and stepped back into the house in an effort to hear better. She kept an eye on Goat, who stepped off the porch toward the blaze. Damn fool man, more guts than smarts. Though there was something kind of appealing about his broad-shouldered frame silhouetted against the flames.

"Me who?"

"Todd!" the voice barked indignantly.

Stella checked her watch. "It's almost ten," she said. "Aren't you supposed to be in bed or something by now? Besides, I'm involved in a—a little drama unfolding here."

"No, it's Friday. I can stay up as late as I want. Besides,

Stella, reason I'm calling—you got an *intruder*. I got rid a him for you."

"I got a what?"

"An intruder. I put the hose on him and he ran away."

Stella took a last look at Goat, who was edging into the yard toward the wrecked metal, despite the fact that flames licked around the ruined carcass of the car. She retreated farther into the house where the reception was better, and settled down on a couch with Tucker, who yawned and snuggled down into the cushions. "At my house? You saw someone at my house?"

"Well yeah, where'd you think? I saw him come sneakin' down the street acting like he was just out walkin' or whatever, and when he got to your place he looked all around and then kind of ducked down and ran over to your front porch. He knocked a bunch of times and then he put his head right on the door, trying to hear were you inside, I figure, and I guess he decided you weren't and that he was going to wait for you to get back, 'cause he went back of that big old bush you got next to your porch, kind of wiggled in behind it, and then he just stood there hiding."

"What? When was this?" Stella thought of the broken glass at the back of the house, the gouged sill, the footprint in the soft earth. Looked like her peeper had come back.

"Like around . . . I don't know, half an hour ago."

"What were you doing, that you saw him?" Stella demanded.

"I was . . . uh . . . playing Pokémon on my PSP?"

"Wrong," Stella said automatically. There was only one good reason for Todd to be outside alone after dark, and that was to come visit her. If this intruder had spotted him coming down the street . . .

126

"This is important," Stella added. "Code of Silence rules apply."

She could hear Todd breathing in the phone and knew he was thinking that over. Code of Silence was their agreement, made at Stella's suggestion, that in some instances she would hear Todd out with the understanding that Sherilee would not be notified as long as Stella was satisfied that the boy had told the entire truth and, if it concerned something ill advised or even stupid, he would not repeat the infraction. So far, it had been invoked only once, when Todd had left a Tupperware full of live bait on the front seat of the brand-new Lincoln belonging to mean retired neighbor Rolf Bayer on a sweltering morning last May, and had second thoughts and called Stella from his first class at school.

Stella had removed the bait before it could disintegrate in the heat and add a permanent olfactory taint to the car, and it was not spoken of again. She figured Todd's belated guilty conscience made up for the stray mischief. Besides, Bayer truly was an asshole.

"Okay," he said. "Chanelle Tanaka gave me some clove cigarettes. I was, uh, smoking them on Mrs. Granick's porch—she's in Florida."

"Todd!" Stella said, horrified. "*Smoking?* That's the nastiest—"

"Calm down, Stella. There ain't any tobacco in them. They're like all natural and—"

—and Chanelle was the hottest girl in eighth grade, Stella thought darkly. "Todd," she interrupted him sternly, "we'll talk about your slow and painful lung cancer death later, but for now, just tell me this guy didn't see you."

"Okay. He didn't see me."

"Well, did he?" The notion of a Peeping Tom at her window had taken a turn for the more sinister since the car bombing a couple of minutes earlier. Some unusually violent force was at work in Prosper, and the thought of Todd wandering, innocent and unsuspecting, into its midst was terrifying. "Or didn't he?"

"Uh, well, I don't think so. When I snuck over to get the Knowleses' hose, I—"

"When you did *what*?"

"Stella," Todd said patiently, "you gonna let me tell you or you gonna keep interrupting me?"

"Continue," Stella said through gritted teeth. "Please."

"I went down three houses before I crossed over to your side of the street, then I came back the other way in the backyards, and when I got to the Knowleses' I came around the side real slow, and the hose was all coiled up on that hook thing Mr. Knowles got on the wall there and I got it unwound enough without making any noise. Then the faucet handle creaked just a little—"

"What the hell were you doing with the hose?" Stella could feel her heart pounding in her throat. The Knowleses lived next door to Stella to the right; Todd would have been a mere fifteen feet from the intruder in the bushes—an intruder who could have been armed or even wielding bombs or grenades or something. "And what kind of fool idea—"

"I was *saving* your ass," Todd said, raising his voice to a powerful whisper-bellow. "I didn't have a phone with me and what was I supposed to do, let him murder you when you got home?"

"What makes you think he was going to *murder* me?" Stella

demanded. "He could of, I don't know, wanted to borrow something or—"

"Stella," Todd said in a withering tone, "men don't come around your place askin' to borrow shit. They come around fixin' to maim you and kill you."

Naturally, the boy knew all about her recent brush with death—he'd visited half a dozen times in the hospital and asked a hundred questions. Stella had tried to soft-pedal her answers, but she figured the boy was entitled to a good helping of truth, seeing as smart kids generally know a lie when they hear one. So he was well aware of the nearly half dozen assorted crooks and ne'er-do-wells who'd attempted to kill her.

"Okay," she sighed. "The hose?"

"It had one a them attachments on it? You know, with all the settings? Well, good thing it was set to jet, 'cause I just pointed it at the guy and blasted the shit out of him. Man, you shoulda seen him come flyin' outta that bush! Soaked him good 'fore he took off running, too!"

Todd chortled at the memory as Stella's pulse skyrocketed. If the man had come *at* Todd, rather than fleeing . . . if he'd turned and looked and noticed that his attacker wielded only a garden hose . . . if he'd decided to come back and finish the job—

"Please tell me you didn't stick around to watch," she said.

"Naw, I went home the back way, he wouldn't a known how to find me. Turned the water off, too," he added. "I guess you're gonna say to go wind that hose back up, huh?"

"I'm—I'll—" Words eluded Stella as she tried and failed to come up with a way to convey to her teenage bodyguard the recklessness of his actions. "I'll talk to you tomorrow. Now get your ass in bed. Lock all your doors first—then straight to bed."

"Don't you mean, *Thank you, Todd*? For getting rid of your armed and dangerous killer?"

"Thank you, Todd," Stella repeated, trying to keep the agitation out of her voice. "Gotta go. Get your butt in *bed*."

She hung up and slipped the phone back in her pocket, and covered Tucker with an afghan that was folded over the couch, touching his cheek to make sure he was sleeping soundly. Then she returned to the porch, where she watched Goat jabbing at a smoking pile of rubble with a garden rake. A sound behind her in the hall caught her attention, and she turned to see Brandy, vertical at last, leaning against a wall with a tumbler in her hand.

"Isn't *that* a sight," she said, sighing happily. "I do love a bonfire. Whyn't cha fix you a drink and we can go cook us some wieners."

TEN

. . . .

Stella was short on misgivings when she left Goat to deal with both Brandy and the firebomb in the front yard. She had Tucker to consider, after all, and she figured he'd seen about enough mayhem for one evening. They were back at Chrissy's apartment and in bed by eleven, and Stella even resisted the urge to see if the lights were still on over at the shop.

Around seven the next morning, she was lying in a sleep-stupor, Chrissy's fluffy pink comforter pulled around her like a cotton candy cocoon, enjoying the last of a dream that was slipping away. A few feet from the bed, Tucker was doing his own early-morning ruminating in the crib, humming to himself, making the occasional comment in unintelligible toddler speak, playing with his green fuzzy horse.

Stella was trying to hold on to the image of Goat in those low-slung pants—the very ones Brandy had been trying to take off him—and no shirt, when she heard the key in the door.

"It's me and I got doughnuts," Chrissy called. She came clomping into the bedroom in her high-heeled mules and went straight for the crib, scooping Tucker up for a volley of kisses and giggling. Then she lay down next to Stella, the baby between them, the bed pleasantly jammed.

"Well, you don't look much worse for wear," Stella said as graciously as she could. "What kind of doughnuts you got?"

"Three cream-filled, three chocolate sprinkles, but you cain't eat 'em in here."

Stella rolled her eyes. "Considering what-all you probably been doing for the last dozen hours, I don't know if I'd be acting all prim and proper over a few crumbs."

"Oh, envy ain't pretty on you," Chrissy said.

She yawned extravagantly and crawled out of bed. Tucker snuggled in closer to Stella, his well-chewed green horse butting her in the chin. "Whore," he said. No. *Horse.* Had to be horse.

Chrissy opened her tiny closet and started rummaging through hangers.

"Well, while you and your fancy man were making whoopee over in the shop—"

"We went back to his place," Chrissy interrupted. "He's got him a nice apartment with a Jacuzzi tub over by the Applebee's."

"Well, la-di-da," Stella said. "I guess it's nice for some folks to be floating around in bubbles while other folks were being blown up."

Chrissy turned around, startled. "What have you gone and got yourself into now, Stella?"

Stella laid out the events of the last evening while Chrissy changed into a fresh pair of shorts and a tank top with complicated crisscrossed peekaboo strands of ribbon highlighting her cleavage. There were no obvious hickeys or bite marks or rug burns on her that Stella could make out.

"Hoo-ee," Chrissy said when Stella finished. "Well, I guess you're gonna want to know what-all I dug up on that ex-wife of the sheriff for you."

"You mean Larry looked her up online?"

Chrissy turned around mid-tug on her lacy pink bra. "What do you mean *Larry*—I'm the one tracked her down while he was makin' us some grilled cheese and tomatoes."

"Oh—sorry." Stella held up her hands in apology. It was never a good idea to underestimate Chrissy. She had a chip on her shoulder big enough to flatten a less robust person, left over from several decades of being told she wasn't smart. "What did you find, then?"

"Well," Chrissy said smugly, unmistakable pride in her molasses drawl, "Larry showed me how to get past these encryption thingies they got, and then I checked where her mail was going. Turns out she's been shacking up with this guy name a Wilbur Vines. He owns him a trilevel house and did you know, he bought it in 1992 for sixty-five thousand bucks? Don't that just beat all?"

"That's real estate for you, I guess."

"Yeah, well, anyway he's got him a couple of arrests on his record. One for burglary and one for fraud, acquitted both times, but you gotta figure he did it or why would they arrest him. Wouldn't surprise me a bit if that Brandy, after being married to Mr. Squeaky Clean for a couple years, went lookin' for something a little more downtown."

Stella ignored the amateur psychologizing for the moment. "They were married only a couple of years? Her and Goat?"

"Not even, just twenty-two months. Got married at the Morgan County courthouse, almost five years back."

"Well, then they've been split up longer than they were together."

"Hey, you don't have to convince me—ain't no reason you got to stand back from that man on account of any holy union or that shit," Chrissy said. She had been married twice before; besides her dead ex, she had a first husband who still carried a torch for her, plus a spate of admirers in between, one of whom had fathered Tucker, though Chrissy wasn't sure which one that was.

"Anything else you dug up on her? Like something that would explain why a person would want to incinerate her, for instance?"

"Nah . . . she's been working at a place called Dinette Superstore, but she musta got laid off a couple months back 'cause she's been drawing unemployment."

"No kidding. Usually it's laid-off folks that do the workplace violence to their old bosses and such, not the other way around."

"What, you think it was someone she worked for that blew up her car?"

Stella pondered that. "She is awfully annoying, but that seems kind of extreme. I guess maybe I'll check out that fella she was shacking up with. Like you said, he was acquitted, he probably isn't such a bad guy. Maybe I can get him to come and get her and take her back to Versailles."

"Now, Stella, are you trying to help this gal, or are you just trying to get rid a her?" Chrissy demanded. "I mean, you're always flappin' your jaw about helpin' out women don't got anywhere else to turn, blah blah blah, and seems to me this Brandy don't really have nowhere else to go if she had to come bunk with her ex. Plus she's got someone trying to kill her."

"What's your point?" Stella demanded.

"Only if—well, if you want me to work for you, we got to have this one thing clear: I ain't doin' your dirty work just so you can clear out the competition for a man. That ain't what these skills is for." She held out her hands in front of her and made a typing gesture with her fingers.

"Point taken," Stella said dryly. "Whyn't you type us up a corporate ethics policy while you're at it."

"Maybe you oughtta git that smart mouth a yours out of bed," Chrissy retorted. "Come on, you two lazybones, have a doughnut."

Stella complied, setting Tucker down on the floor; he hit the ground running in his rumble-seat jammies, barreling straight for the white paper sack on the kitchen table.

"I found out some other stuff," Chrissy said after she'd made them coffee and polished off a sprinkle doughnut plus the abandoned crumbs of Tucker's. "I looked up all the missing girls from when Neb and them were building that snack shack, in all seven counties around Sawyer. There's only a couple cases that ain't got solved yet. I printed out the details for you."

"Wow—that's great," Stella said. "Looks like you might have to keep makin' that Larry happy—I mean, until he's taught you all his tricks and you can do everything yourself," she added hastily as Chrissy opened her mouth to protest.

"Shouldn't take long. I figure I already know about a million times more about computers and shit than *you* do."

"Okay, okay, you can be like the tech support department. Or CIO. Chief Information Officer. Would you like that?"

"I don't know. Is that a high-paying job?"

"Sure thing. Second highest in the company, in fact."

"Oh, great," Chrissy said sarcastically. "All that means is I'm one step away from the poorhouse. Maybe I'll stick to selling elastic and whatnot."

"Suit yourself," Stella said, shrugging indifferently; it wasn't lost on her that Chrissy had been more excited about the online sleuthing than most of the tasks she'd undertaken since starting to work for Stella. It seemed clear that she had a gift. "But don't you figure you ought to jump in the shower, girl, and wash off all that sinnin' before you go open up the shop?"

Chrissy gave her a dazzling smile, the fetching little gap between her front teeth making her look as innocent as a baby lamb. "Considering all the places Larry used a bar of soap on me in the Jacuzzi this morning, I believe I'm clean enough I won't need to shower for a month."

Stella's own shower, while a solo effort, was just what the doctor ordered. She turned the heat up high and stood under the stinging spray with her face upturned for as long as she could stand it. The night, with all its interruptions and sur-prises, hadn't been the most restful she'd ever passed.

Toweled, moisturized, deodorized, glossed, shadowed, and blown dry—feeling like an entirely new and spiffier woman—Stella added a spritz of White Diamonds and had a brainstorm.

She went to the laundry room, stepping over Roxy, who after a brisk walk and a generous bowl of kibble was snoozing on her new bed. Stella fetched the soap flakes and the liquid laundry starch and mixed up a gruely paste in a mixing bowl.

"Coming, mutt?" she asked, and Roxy bounded to her feet and skittered across the kitchen floor to where her leash was hanging on a hook. In the yard Stella let Roxy wander free while she took care of her little task, a variation on a Girl Scout project she had done years ago with Noelle's troop, helping the girls make casts of fossil imprints out by the quarry.

She carefully poured the gucky stuff into the footprint her peeper had left the day before. She had to use her fingers to smooth out the top. It felt unpleasantly slimy, but Stella pushed the mixture into all the nooks and crannies.

She straightened and called Roxy, who'd made it as far as the neighbors and was peeing on a patch of tuberous begonias. Roxy finished and pawed daintily at the tender flowers before loping back, ears flopping.

"Now, you stay out of that, hear?" Stella said, pointing at her makeshift cast.

She picked up the leash, and the two of them strolled around the house and down the street to the Groffes' house. Seeing as it was Saturday, Sherilee would undoubtedly be home, trying to cram a week's worth of housecleaning and bill paying and laundry into one day. Saturday nights she got a sitter for her twin daughters, who were nearly seven, and took Todd out for a little quality time—a slice of pizza or a movie.

Tomorrow was Sunday, which meant Todd would come to Stella's house while Sherilee took the twins out for their weekly girls' night—a trip to Chuck E. Cheese or a spin around the mall. It was a sacred and unshakable commitment, and Stella mentally readjusted her schedule so she'd be ready in time for Todd tomorrow—any crime-solving that remained unfinished at that point would just have to wait.

Stella knocked on the Groffes' door, straightening a faded wreath of plastic leaves and silk flowers. She heard the girls scrambling for the door, giggling and shouting, and then it opened, and one of the girls fell backwards with a thud while the other one grinned up at Stella with a couple fewer teeth than the last time she saw her.

"Nice look, Glory," Stella said, taking a chance and tapping her own teeth.

"I'm Melly," the girl replied with a dramatic sigh, "but it's okay, I forgive you."

Glory picked herself up off the floor and poked her sister in the side. "*I'm* the one with the extra *freckles*," she said with exaggerated patience. In truth, Stella didn't think there was a single difference between the girls. Even their mother got them confused. Sherilee rounded the corner holding half a plate and trailing Todd, who was scowling at the ground.

"All's I said was, if Melly hadn't left it there, it wouldn't have got broke," he muttered.

"And if you hadn't been skateboarding inside the house, you never would of broke it," Sherilee shot back. "Hi, Stella.

You come to take this boy a day early? 'Cause you can sure enough have him."

"I'll pass," Stella said. "I got to rest up before he comes over. I just really wanted to tell you that I got a new dog."

Sherilee fanned herself with the broken plate and gave Todd a shove back toward the kitchen; the girls followed him, tripping over each other's words. "A dog. Huh. Wouldn't be a black-and-white one, about yea high?"

"Hmm," Stella said. "Sounds about right."

"Oh . . . that *boy* of mine, I'm gonna have to tan his hide."

"I just thought I ought to ask if you knew where it came from."

Sherilee rolled her eyes to the heavens and shrugged. "Come in with the storm, is what Todd told me. Found 'im in the culvert, half drowned, and cleaned him off with my guest towels. The *nice* ones, with the lace."

"Bet that fried your bacon. Well . . . I guess I'll keep her, anyway."

"It's a girl dog?"

"Yes. Name of Roxy."

"Roxy? Did Todd give her that name? 'Cause this girl from school left her backpack over here the other day. Said 'Roxy' on it 'bout fifty times, and then she's got it wrote on her T-shirt and on the butt of her shorts." Sherilee sighed. "My girls don't *wear* words on their butts."

Stella clucked sympathetically. "The other thing . . . ," she said, not sure quite where to start. "Well, I guess there's been a peeper in the neighborhood. Looking . . . into windows and whatnot. Just thought I should tell you, maybe you could convince Todd not to go out after dark, least till we get this cleared up."

"Oh, he doesn't. I don't *let* him."

"Oh." Stella considered enlightening Sherilee on her son's peripatetic evening ways, but a scream from the kitchen distracted her.

"Mom! Glory's got her hair stuck in the toaster!"

As Stella let herself out the front door, she figured she'd just convince Todd herself. Tomorrow, when he was a captive audience.

ELEVEN

. . . .

t wasn't really a surprise that Jelloman Nunn wasn't picking up his cell. He routinely slept until noon. Which wasn't a sign of sloth; most of his business was conducted in the evening, so he was generally awake until the wee hours of the morning.

Stella pulled into the weedy side yard where Jelloman's customers parked. His house had been a bungalow of the three-room sort that sprang up a hundred-odd years ago when early Prosper dwellers were still pulling rocks out of the fields, but enterprising homeowners in the intervening years had built additions and nooks and sheds and a sun porch roofed with corrugated plastic and hung with a half dozen Missouri Tiger flags, giving the whole thing a festival air.

During football season, Jelloman cut back on his motorcycle repair business—though his weed-dealing sideline remained brisk—and on Saturdays, he and his buddies dragged a big-screen television into the shop and set up folding chairs and a couple of kegs. Mizzou was playing Kansas at two o'clock today, so Stella figured she was doing Jelloman a service by pounding on the door and waking him up so he'd have plenty of time to prepare for his guests.

He came to the door after about five minutes of knocking and hollering, rubbing his eyes and pushing his long gray ponytail out of his face. He wasn't wearing his black leather vest, but otherwise it looked like he'd slept in his clothes—a Metallica T-shirt from the Summer Sanitarium Tour with a flannel shirt over it, and jeans slung low to give his impressive gut the breathing room it needed.

Jelloman's cross expression evaporated the minute he opened the screen door. "Stella! You come to watch the game?"

Before she could reply, he folded her into a hug, and Stella leaned into it and hugged back, breathing in the not-unpleasant odors of home-rolled cigarettes and Mitchum and sleep. It was good to be hugged. It didn't happen often enough—though Stella certainly enjoyed the baby-powder drooly embraces of Tucker, not to mention the squeezes from Noelle and Chrissy and ex-clients she bumped into here and there.

But this was a man-hug. Jelloman didn't light any fires for Stella, but he had big forearms and his chin landed squarely on top of her head and his sloping gut made just the right angle for leaning in to, and Stella gave in to the whole thing and hung on tight.

And then it was on into the reception area of the house for Jelloman-style hospitality, which included offers of pot, beer, and finally sun tea, the last of which Stella accepted.

"Listen, I need a favor," Stella said once they were settled in a pair of old recliners with a view out the picture window onto a dirt-bike track Jelloman had built for the neighborhood kids.

"Hell, Stella, anything, you just ask—you know that."

A couple years back, Jelloman's mom—a surprisingly sweet and dainty woman in her early eighties—was wooed and conned by a dapper septuagenarian lothario. He'd nabbed nearly half the old lady's life savings by the time Jelloman got Stella involved.

Now the funds were restored and there was one wiser and older old coot who was using a cane that might not otherwise have been strictly necessary.

Stella had done that one pro bono, and now Jelloman was her go-to guy for all sorts of sticky problems.

"It's Todd, that kid who lives down the street from me. I'm worried about him."

Jelloman exhaled a thin stream of smoke and set down his spliff. "What's he gone and got into?" he demanded in a tone of outrage. He was old-school when it came to raising kids; he believed in strict rules. His own daughter, a polite, soft-spoken brunette gal, was in the pre-med program at Mizzou.

"Nothing much, other than the usual teenage buttheadedness. But I think there's someone hanging around my house. Could be nothing, could be something."

"Something having to do with a case a yours."

"Yeah, like that. And you know kids—I tell Todd to stay clear of my place for a while, why that's practically a guarantee he's going to camp out in the front yard. And I got a few things on my agenda where I can't be home all day for a while, anyway, so I was wondering if you'd mind coming over and staying for a few days."

"*After* the game, you mean," Jelloman clarified.

"Yeah, of course, I don't expect any problems during the day. But maybe if you could come over, say by dark . . . ?"

"I'd be honored," Jelloman said formally. "Can I bring Sabine?"

"Absolutely. In fact, tomorrow night's Todd's regular visit, why don't we have us a little party—I'll ask Noelle to stay, and maybe we can get Chrissy and Tucker over, maybe Chrissy's new boyfriend."

"I'll get Sabine to fix them wieners she does in the garlic and red wine sauce."

Sabine was Jelloman's French girlfriend. His main girlfriend, anyway. They had a complicated open relationship with rules governing who could step out on whom and when—this must be one of their "on" weekends. Stella figured Sabine for forty or so, but an accumulation of hard miles had rendered her ageless in a wrinkly, nicotine-stained, raspy-voiced way.

Stella liked her plenty.

"Well, I gotta go," she said.

"You're doing the Lord's work," Jelloman said, standing chivalrously and tracing a quick sign of the cross on himself.

As Stella made the drive back across town, she queued up Miranda Lambert and did her own quick prayer. She tried to check in with the Big Guy every day, and she always led off with gratitude.

Back in the days when Ollie was still around to curse every minute of her existence, Stella forgot the gratitude part for a while. She dutifully found her place in the pew every Sunday, but her mind tended to wander or, more often, just shut down, a one-hour respite when even Ollie wouldn't dare raise a hand or his voice to her.

Now, she didn't get over to church much. Mostly, it was a factor of her ever-expanding business, which made her Sundays and Tuesdays—her days off—too busy for much more than chores and delivering brutal justice to woman abusers.

Ironically, her talks with the Big Guy had become more frequent and far more important to Stella. They left her feeling . . . calmer. More sure of her priorities. Almost, some days, within spitting distance of some peculiar brand of contentment.

So as Miranda sang her way through "Mama I'm Alright," Stella murmured her gratitude, for Chrissy and Tucker and Noelle and friends like Jelloman and clients like the Donovans, and as she pulled into the Popeyes parking lot, she sneaked in one tiny little request, which she didn't put exactly into words but which had the general outline of a certain law enforcement officer who had been taking up extra room in her dreams for a while now.

Popeyes, at eleven thirty on a Saturday, was jam-packed, but the Green Hat Ladies had staked out their usual claim and dragged over a spare chair so Stella could join them with her tray of chicken and biscuits.

"You're looking well," Shirlette Castro observed.

Linda Becker pushed her John Deere cap up above her tight-permed curls so she could peer closely at Stella's face. "Mmm-mmm," she said, shaking her head. "I swan but them doctors can do wonders nowadays. Git you a little makeup on, Stella, and won't nobody need to know how bad off you was looking there for a spell."

Since no-nonsense directness was one of the things Stella treasured about the elderly ladies, she let the comment pass. The half dozen old gals met nearly every day to trade gossip—which made them valuable allies—and show off their matching ball caps, which made them a startling sight to any out-of-towners who happened to have a hankering for fried chicken. The ladies, however, liked how their caps set them apart from the red-hatted, purple-wearing gals who had formed a rival club over in Quail Valley.

"You needin' our help again, Stella?" Novella Glazer asked, picking a bit of corn out of her teeth with a frill-ended toothpick.

"'Fraid so," Stella said. The gals loved to help, especially when it meant an entrée into a juicy bit of speculation. "I got this list of women who went missing a few years back, thought I'd see if you all remembered anything."

She pulled the piece of paper from her purse and unfolded it, slipped on her reading glasses, and read out loud.

"Okay . . . so this first one's Ashley de Boer, twenty-two when she went missing, student at Southern Missouri State . . . she came home to her folks' house up in Independence in August three years back, just for the weekend. She was working at the university library for the summer and hadn't seen her folks for a while. Saturday night about nine she went out to meet a friend for a drink and never showed up."

"Ashley, huh," Lola Brennan said. "I don't recall any Ashley."

"I remember that one from the paper," Shirlette said, clucking sorrowfully. "Pretty girl. I bet she's in a ditch somewhere picked clean over by the buzzards. That's how those college girls generally end up."

"Not all of them," Gracie Lewis chided.

"All the missing ones, anyway," Shirlette said defensively.

"Then there's June Dunovich," Stella said. "She was local. Well, over in Fairfax, anyway."

"Well, sure, I remember that," Lola said. She leaned forward conspiratorially. "I'd bet you a hunnert bucks she ain't missing, though. She had those gambling problems—"

"Riverboats," Linda confirmed, bobbing her head. "It was up in the thousands. She tried to clear out her and Rex's accounts, he only found out when the bank called him."

"Suze Orman says you should have all the accounts in your own name. Not your husband's," Novella said.

"Oh, she says no such thing," Gracie said. "What she said was—"

Stella interrupted to read the final name, but there was general head-shaking and mystification all around.

"Wait," Gracie said. "That last one—Laura Cassel? That rings some kind of bell."

"She was thirty-five, says here. Lived alone, up in Picot, worked for a company called Glecko-Goldin."

"Drug company!" Shirlette exclaimed. "They make my blood pressure medicine. Greedy bastards."

Drugs. The connection loomed obvious and unwelcome in Stella's mind—what with OxyContin being prescription, was it possible that Laura Cassel could have been some sort of supplier for Neb? It seemed like drug companies would have all kinds of procedures in place to make sure their products didn't wander off the premises on the persons of their employees, to make their way through shady channels and end up in the hands of addicts, but it wasn't the sort of news that had Stella feeling extra-optimistic.

"Says she didn't show up for work, her boss got worried, had them check out her town house. Didn't ever find anything out of place or anything."

"I think it was on the news," Gracie said. "Good-lookin' gal, kind of that pinup girl look. With the bosoms and the rouge. And blond hair cut in a pageboy."

"A *bob*," Gracie said, touching her own steel-gray hair, which was cut in an unflattering line that bisected her jaw. "That's called a bob now."

Stella remembered the pale hair around the freakishly shrunken face of the mummy. "White blond?" she asked. "Platinum?"

"Yes, that's right," Gracie said. "They interviewed all these gals in the singles club up there. I guess that woman ran around some with them. If it's the same one I'm thinking of."

"Was there an ex-husband, do you remember?" Stella asked.

"Well, if there was one, I don't recall him coming on TV or anything. You know like they do sometimes—all crying and saying all we want is our loved one back? I never believe that, anyway—it was me, I'd want my loved one *and* to gut the kidnapper like a fish."

"It's never just a kidnapping," Lola said ominously. "There's generally crimes of a sick and twisted nature gets done on these gals 'fore they get dismembered and all."

Stella started to correct her, to point out that the mystery mummy was, as far as she could tell, not dismembered a bit—but then remembered that she was here to *gather* information, not feed it into the grapevine. The Green Hat Ladies needed more grist for their gossip mill like their blood pressure needed a heaping serving of sodium.

She thanked them, finished up her spicy chicken deluxe sandwich, and refilled her Diet Coke for the road. It was starting to look like an extra-caffeine kind of day.

TWELVE

· · · · · · · · · ·

On the forty-minute drive to Versailles, Stella rolled the windows down and enjoyed the Indian summer warmth of the breeze that blew through the car. She came to a flashing red at an intersection and waited her turn behind a little parade of traffic. No one seemed to be in a hurry today.

Off past the fields beside the road, she saw an old barn that had been flattened in the storm, silver-gray boards scattered like pick-up sticks. An old man in a straw hat moved among the debris with slow, deliberate movements like he had arthritis in his joints. Two young men helped, lifting and hauling shattered wood as though their burden were weightless. One had stripped off his shirt in the autumn sunshine, and Stella could see he was a young man, barely out of his teens, his muscles defined against his pale skin and hairless chest. He called something out and the others stopped their work to laugh, the old man wiping at his eyes with his sleeve, the other—his brother?—tossing a clump of earth that hit the boy squarely on the shoulder.

The cars in front took their turns through the intersection, and Stella put her foot on the gas and cruised forward. A strange sadness hit her in the gut, a memory of what her father had said that day as he and Horace left to help the folks caught in the storm. *Why do you have to go, Daddy?* she'd asked, and she'd never forget the gentle smile on his face when he answered: *'Cause helpin' folks is what men do when they grow up.*

Someone had taught those two boys right. They were out helping their neighbor or uncle or whoever it was, it didn't matter, he was someone who needed help and they did it without a second thought. If Stella'd had sons, they would have missed out on that lesson. Her father died from a heart attack right after Stella got married.

How was it that she'd forgotten that simple message when she went out to pick a man to settle down with? Ollie hadn't just been a cruel and worthless husband; he hadn't been much of a friend or neighbor either. Ollie looked at his fellow man and wondered what they could do for him. He found humor in other folks' misfortune and had a keen eye out for the extra share, to which he helped himself without qualms.

Well, Stella was making up for all of that. Who said it always had to be the men who went out and set the world straight? Sometimes there were no men around to do the job, and sometimes, it seemed to her, a woman was the better candidate anyway. A woman might not have brute strength, but she had cunning and determination and creative problem-solving skills. Women were used to juggling six things at once and working inside a system that didn't always cater to their needs.

So Stella's work didn't always mean coloring in the lines; so what—she was helping out those who needed help. Doing the right thing had taken the place of just getting by—it was who she *was* now, and Stella realized she had her father to thank for that. Buster Collier never turned away from someone in need because he didn't feel particularly helpful that day. And Stella had taken that lesson and tucked it away, deep inside, and now that her life had taken all these strange turns and put her on a new path, she brought out her father's gift and put it to work.

Chrissy had been right—there was no way she could send Brandy packing when by all indications, she was in exactly the kind of straits Stella specialized in.

Stella glanced at the clock and remembered she needed to call Noelle. All this thinking about fathers and sons reminded her how grateful she was to have her daughter back in her life. So she'd never had a son—she figured if her father could see Noelle, he'd be mighty proud anyway. Not long ago, Noelle had got herself hooked up with a bunch of her beauty shop pals who went up to Kansas City a couple times a month and set up a free clinic in a neighborhood where there wasn't a whole lot of money to go around for milk and medicine, much less extras like manicures and haircuts. Their clinic was proof—there were a million different ways to do the right thing.

Stella called Noelle and left her a message about dinner the next night. Noelle usually came over on Sunday afternoons anyway, to do her wash and catch up on things, and she figured the girl might like a home-cooked meal, even if it was likely to be Jelloman and Sabine doing the cooking.

Stella cruised into town, glanced at her notes, and found Wil Vines's house with no trouble. It was in a shabby little cul-de-sac of '70s-era tri-levels. The driveways were cracked, the bushes overgrown, and the garage doors peeling paint. The good times had apparently rolled on past this part of Versailles.

She parked around the corner and dialed the number Chrissy had turned up in her online trolling. It rang and rang, never going into voice mail or a machine, though Stella tried twice. After thinking a moment, Stella got out of the car and made her way back through the backyards toward Vines's place. They were sizable yards, and Stella had no trouble skirting the wooded edges, staying out of the sight line of the houses. She cut across the back of Vines's place and let herself into the screen porch, which smelled of mildew, and knocked on the back door.

She knocked softly at first, then louder, and finally she gave the door a couple of good hard kicks. There was no sound from within the house.

She inspected the door. Luckily, the rock that was holding down a yellowing newspaper on a plastic table worked just fine to break the glass in the door. Stella pulled a couple of quart Ziplocs she'd stuffed in her pockets earlier and slipped them over her hands and managed to let herself into the house without cutting herself on the glass shards.

Inside the dim kitchen, it smelled like stale coffee grounds and moldering rags. All the drapes were pulled shut, giving the place a funereal air. Stella commenced to give herself a thorough tour of the Vines residence.

Make that the Vines-Truax residence. Brandy's presence was everywhere: she may have split up with Wil months earlier, but there were snapshots of her on the fridge and a framed glamour-shots-style portrait on the side table beside his bed.

In the closet, near the back, were a couple of women's blouses, carefully buttoned to the neck and hung by themselves so they weren't jammed up against other garments.

The real bounty was in the drawers of the vanity in the bathroom. The top one held a few men's grooming items, but the other two held a carefully arranged trove of what Stella had to assume was Brandy memorabilia. In one, half a dozen makeup containers were arranged in a neat row, eye shadows and blushes in various stages of use, some nearly empty, some practically new. A fluffy powder brush lay on a nest of tissue, and there were two folded scarves—one hot pink, one gray paisley—rolled and tucked in next to a wadded plastic shower cap. In the other drawer was a hair dryer with the diffuser still attached—not an instrument any man Stella knew would have use for. There was also—in case there was any doubt these were Brandy's things and not some subsequent girlfriend's—a fall of platinum-blond teased hair that could be clipped in place to add a little extra vavoom to a fancy hairdo.

So Wil wasn't entirely over his ex. Could this be some sort of stalker thing, the jilted boyfriend gone nuts, his actions escalating as his girlfriend not only ignored him but also left town to go back to an old lover? One thing was obvious: Brandy was holding out on her. Stella needed to have a heart-to-heart with her, and find out what else the former Mrs. Goat Jones wasn't telling her.

Stella searched the rest of the rooms and the basement, didn't find anything else interesting in the house. Wil Vines was a pretty good housekeeper, for a guy, and the carpet was vacuumed and the floors swept. Magazines were stacked in a neat pile on the coffee table. Running a plastic-covered finger along the top of the dining room table produced only a tiny bit of dust.

She went back outside and tried the door of the detached garage. It was open, and Stella slipped inside and turned on the light.

The garage was as neat as the house, with rakes and snow-blowers and so forth hanging from pegs on the bare studs. But what caught Stella's eye immediately was the large panel van taking up half the garage.

Chrissy's explorations had turned up only one car registered to Wil, a late-model Ford Taurus. Certainly there hadn't been any record of him owning a windowless white van—or the pile of magnetic signage Stella found piled neatly on a work-bench:

MORTIMER & SONS PLUMBING

CENTRAL MISSOURI HEATING AND AIR CONDITIONING

CHEERY MAIDS—LET US CLEAN SO YOU DON'T HAVE TO!

LISA DEE'S FLORIST BALLOONS GIFTS

Stella rifled through the stack, then set it back, neatening up the edges. Well, now this was interesting. She found it hard to believe that Wil ran all these businesses out of his home, and it wasn't that difficult to imagine that the quick-change nature of the anonymous van and the signs lent itself to the kind of mischief that the law generally frowned on. Like dealing drugs out of the back, for instance. Or snatching college girls from parking lots and dismembering them—Stella remembered

Shirlette Castro's words with a shudder. Or, at the very least, making the kind of house calls that left homeowners scratching their heads and wondering how they could have misplaced the jewelry and silver.

It was always possible that the van and the signs were a new hobby, something Wil Vines had taken up to get his mind off his breakup, but Stella figured this added to the list of questions she'd have to ask Brandy.

Stella was letting herself out of the garage when her phone went off, making her jump. She still wasn't used to her new ringtone, a trill of instrumental flute music that she thought would be a nice change from the head-banging crap Todd put on every time he got his hands on her phone, but which was turning out to be surprisingly annoying.

"Hello?"

"Stella, this is Irene. I just thought you might want to know that that Detective Simmons just took off outta here, headed back to Fayette."

A warm little goody-goody sensation ticked in Stella's stomach, but she kept her voice neutral. "Ain't that a shame. Guess she didn't care much for our local color, huh."

"That ain't quite it, hon. She took Neb Donovan with her. And he's headed for jail."

Donna Donovan's hysterical call followed not twenty seconds after Stella hung up with Irene.

"Stella, they cain't take him off to jail like this!" she wailed. "He didn't do anything wrong!"

Stella kept her thoughts on the matter to herself. The unsettling visit with Dr. Herman had changed her perspective on her favorite parolee, and not in a good way. "Calm on down, honey," she said soothingly nonetheless. "Just 'cause he's arrested, doesn't mean he's guilty."

"But they don't have any, any evidence!"

As a matter of fact, Irene had let slip that they did, but she wouldn't say what it was.

"Listen, Donna," Stella said. "There's a couple of names I'd like to run by you. All's I want to know is whether these names mean anything to you. Even if you just think you might have heard them somewhere, and you don't know where, I want you to tell me."

"Why? What's that about?"

"It's about . . . just maybe ways of helping me prove Neb didn't do anything wrong."

"Like alibis or something?"

"Uh, yeah, kind of like that. So one of them is Ashley de Boer."

There was a brief pause, during which Stella could hear Donna breathing on the phone. She sounded winded, like she'd jogged up a flight of stairs, but Stella knew it was her nerves. It was a wonder the woman didn't fly into pieces, she was so upset.

"No," she finally said. "I've never heard of her."

"All right. How about June Dunovich?"

"Well, sure, Stella, everyone knows about her—she gambled away her and Rex's savings and ran off with a fellow that worked on the riverboats. Don't tell me they think she's the one dead out at the track?"

"It's been suggested," Stella admitted. "But just as a, you know, remote possibility."

157

"Well, I don't think it's June. Everyone says she and her new man went out to New Mexico. I knew her from when the boys were in Little League, and she was a hot one even then. Sticky fingers, too, we always figured she was stealing the money she collected for the team parties. I mean, I doubt anyone got mad enough over *that* to kill her."

"Okay." It had been a distant possibility anyway. "There's just one more—Laura Cassel."

This time Donna didn't even hesitate. "No. I have *never* heard of her. Is she another one that's missing?"

"Yes, she was from up in Picot, never showed up to work one day. Thirtyish gal, single. The timing's about right. There wouldn't be . . . uh, any reason that Neb might have met someone? You know, away from work?"

Stella chose her words as carefully as she could, but there just wasn't any pretty way to say it. She was thinking drug dealer, maybe someone who hooked Neb up with the black market OxyContin he'd been hoovering up back then, but given the fact that all these names were women, she feared she knew exactly where Donna would go.

And she was right. "Are you saying there was a woman?" Donna demanded, voice rising in pitch. "That he was having an affair?"

"No, I am not saying that, Donna. There could be a thousand reasons he might have met some woman, and I mean just *met* her, all innocent, like maybe waiting in a doctor's office or I don't know, ordering supplies for work or, or maybe shopping to buy you a birthday present—"

She was reaching, and they both knew it. "Neb isn't like that," Donna said, voice hoarse. "He doesn't—he's *shy,* Stella, when he ain't with me. That's why we always go everywhere together. He's not one to go and introduce himself to any strangers or like that. He prefers it if I make the small talk. He just, you know, he likes to listen and—and—"

"What about . . . maybe who he was getting his Oxy from? Could that have been a woman?"

"Oh, no, Stella," Donna said. "I don't think so, Neb would of told me."

She ended up, as Stella had feared from the start of the conversation, in sniffles. At least she wasn't sobbing, but Stella still felt like a real heel when she begged off the phone, promising to check in again later and extracting a promise from Donna that she would call her niece, the fresh-minted law school graduate, and get her started on some sort of defense strategy.

"You just *find* the person who *did* this," Donna wailed. "You find 'em, Stella, so I can get Neb home where he belongs."

Stella stood indecisively on the walk between Wil Vines's house and garage for a moment and then shrugged—Neb wasn't going anywhere, and it would be a shame to cut this snooping expedition short.

Stella slipped around the side of the house and, after looking both ways, out to the street. In the time that she'd been inside, the sky had darkened; there were traces of blue here and there, but an accumulation of white clouds rolled into a ridge of gray and purple. It looked like rain again. Stella remembered her little footprint project and considered calling Todd to go get it into the house, as it should have been hardened by now, but she didn't want to risk having him come over until Jelloman was in place.

Which he wouldn't be for quite a while, as the football

game was in full swing. She could hear it wafting from the house to the left of Vines's, where a woman in a fuzzy pink sweatsuit swung lazily on a glider, sipping on a glass bottle.

When Stella got a little closer, she saw that it was a bottle of Mike's Hard Lemonade. Stella knew from experience that there was a kick in that bottle. "What's the score?" she called, producing her friendliest smile.

"Hell if I know," the woman said. "I come out here to get away from it."

"Oh. Ah . . . I was looking for Wil Vines. Have you seen him around lately?"

The woman glanced up from her magazine and regarded Stella suspiciously. "You trying to sell him something?"

"Oh—no, ma'am. I'm his . . . second cousin. I thought he ought to know that my, uh, dad's on life support. His great-uncle?"

"That wouldn't be his great uncle," the woman said doubtfully. "If you're Wil's second cousin, then your dad's his second cousin once removed."

"Oh. Yes. We just say great uncle to make it all simpler. But they were close, those two."

"He into the model trains, too?"

"The . . . trains?"

"You know, the model trains Wil's got in the basement? Them train guys are always over here lookin' at that setup he's got. Wil's just awful proud of them. He keeps sayin' how he's gonna have the whole neighborhood over to see them, time he gets it all set up just so."

Stella hadn't seen so much as a single length of miniature track, despite a thorough scouring of the house and basement.

Visitors to Wil's place might have been enthusiastic, indeed, but it wasn't itty-bitty trains that were getting them all hopped up. "Is that right. No, um, we're just a close-knit family. Why, we do *love* that Brandy he took up with . . . such a shame those two split."

The woman raised her plucked and penciled eyebrows. "Is that right? I didn't find her to be all that friendly, myself."

"Well, maybe if she'd managed to get settled in," Stella gambled. "After all, how long were they together, just . . ."

"Near upon two years," the woman said. "I believe that's plenty long enough to make a civilized call on a person's next-door neighbor. I tell you, I don't know what Wil saw in her."

Oops. "Seeing as he's such a gentleman," Stella guessed, crossing her fingers behind her back.

The woman nodded. "Uh-huh, that's right. And working two jobs, no less, when *she* couldn't hang on to a job to save her life. Why I think she was out of work more than she was in it, layin' around that backyard in her bathing suit while decent folk are out trying to earn a living."

"Oh? I forgot Wil got that other job. The uh, uh, what was it . . ."

"Cozy Closets," the woman said. "He does the measuring for them, on top of all that construction work. Course there won't be so much of that now that winter's coming."

Well, that was interesting. If Vines was measuring for closets, that was taking him into lots of folks' houses, where he could get a real good look around at their valuables, figure out their coming-and-going schedule, and then make another call a few weeks down the road when the hapless homeowners didn't even know they needed the services of a plumber or a furnace repairman. And meanwhile, Vines would be relieving them of whatever goodies he could sneak out to the van.

"He always was the industrious one," she said.

"Isn't that the truth." The woman sighed, giving the glider a good solid shove with a pink-sneakered toe. "I tell you, I wish my mama would of sat me down before I got married and explained that pretty don't count for near as much in a man as decency and hard work."

"You're telling me," Stella said. On the way to the car, it occurred to her that she ought to have business cards made just for occasions like this.

Of course, then she'd have so much business that she wouldn't have time to sleep, Stella realized as she headed up the interstate toward Fayette. She was practically halfway there already, and figured Neb might appreciate the visit.

She queued up her *Driving & Thinking* playlist, one she saved special for times like this. The iPod and the interface kit for the Jeep had been a get-well present from Noelle, and Stella had to admit it sure did beat carrying all those old CDs around. Eliza Gilkyson started up "Coast," her sittin'-on-the-porch-with-you voice dancing in and out of the gentle guitar picking.

Did you ever think that it would be like this?
Ah, the price you pay for lo-ove . . .

Stella's thoughts wandered ahead to her visit with Neb. She wasn't exactly keen on visiting the jail, a place she half figured she'd be calling home someday, what with all the varieties of lawbreaking she found herself having to commit.

Why was she bothering with Neb, anyway? At this point, it seemed pretty certain that the man was guilty. It was a shame if it was the demon Oxy that made him do it, but Stella figured that taking a life was serious enough business that she ought not get in the way of the law on this one.

On the other hand . . . he wasn't proven guilty yet. And Stella wasn't confident that Priscilla, Donna's attorney niece, would be much help.

A thought nagged distressingly close to the surface of Stella's mind, tickling her guilt buttons. If this was one of her regular clients, which was to say one of her *woman* clients, nothing would get in the way of Stella making sure she got exactly as much defending and protecting and avenging as Stella could possibly provide, long hours and personal danger be damned. If the waters were muddy, if the gal appeared a bit guilty of this, a little responsible for that, Stella would disregard those factors in her quest for the overriding balance of good stomping the crap out of evil.

Of course, her clients generally had a fair amount of beatdown victimhood stored up that made them significantly more sympathetic in the harsh light of Stella's consideration. What about Neb? Fond of the man as Stella was, much as she'd thought of the Donovans as practically an extension of family, you couldn't exactly make the case that anyone had beaten or threatened him onto the troubled paths that led to addiction and cult involvement. He'd more or less made his own bed and climbed on in.

The outskirts of Fayette came into view, alfalfa fields giving way to saggy-porched bungalows with wash hanging on clotheslines. A tall sign announced WELCOME TO FAYETTE PRIDE OF SAWYER COUNTY! COURTESY OF YOUR ELKS LIONS KIWANIS OPTIMISTS FAYETTE WOMENS CLUB.

The thing was, Stella had always wished for a brother. A big brother, preferably, a tough and scrappy boy who would have beat the tar out of anyone who picked on her. Neb, for all his faults, was the grown-up version of the boy Stella longed for. Generally a man of few words, get him on one of the topics for which he carried a burning passion—his wife, say, or the Cardinals' chances for the play-offs, or the fact that Hinomoto and Sitoh were building circles around American tractors— and he'd hold forth with a fervent light in his eye.

In a way, that was what led to his entanglement with the Eternal Realm of the Savior cult. Neb was attracted to beauty and righteousness and fiery rhetoric. The fact that he'd gone overboard and thrown his lot in with a bunch of zealots—well, there'd likely been more than a few belts of corn whiskey, not to mention all those confusing warm feelings that drinking with distant relatives can bring on, where the folks you can't stand the rest of the year suddenly strike you as kind of charming in their I SURVIVED THE DONOVAN FAMILY REUNION T-shirts— Stella could see that. Not smart, but understandable.

What she could *not* see was the kind of brutality that led a man to kill. Stella sighed as she took the exit toward the center of town. Maybe she ought to call up Dr. Herman again. She'd asked him about what Neb might have forgotten—but what she really should have asked was if the drugs could so scramble a person's brain that they'd mix up their fundamental principles and values to the point that a decent family man suddenly figured it was a good idea to bash or strangle or shoot some blond-bobbed gal and shove her into a pool of concrete, watching the gloppy gunk burble over her like so much Duncan Hines frosting and smoothing it over with nary a niggling bit of guilt.

THIRTEEN

. . . .

I t was a damn good thing Stella was a woman of the cloth.

She'd almost forgotten that little fact about herself. It was only after the Fayette County Jail corrections officer manning the desk had patiently explained that visiting hours were over for the day—and then explained it a second time with considerably less patience when Stella pressed the point—that she noticed a small hand-lettered sign tacked to the wall behind the officer's desk.

CLERGY PRESENT IDENTIFICATION FOR ADMITTANCE DURING NON-VISITING HOURS

"Well, I declare," Stella said softly.

"You still here?" Officer Halpern—identified by the little plastic tag askew on a uniform that needed a good pressing— managed to glare and sneer at the same time. Stella couldn't blame him too much, as he probably had to deal with unhappy folks all the time, folks who'd made the trip to see their incarcerated loved ones outside the appointed hours and didn't care to be turned away.

"I believe I forgot to mention that I am an ordained minister," Stella said in as reverent a tone as she could muster. She folded her hands piously in front of her and added a benevolent smile.

Halpern snorted. Stella wondered how you had to screw up at prison guard school to land not just the weekend, but second shift, a time when all the other guards presumably had dates or family obligations or even just a cold brew and some Saturday-night television lined up. Well, she'd drawn the short end of the stick enough times herself to have some sympathy for the guy.

"Let me just get my ID," she said, and rummaged through her purse for the worn case in which she kept all the cards that wouldn't fit in her wallet: the buy-eleven-bagels-get-one free cards with only a punch or two, the worn Serenity Prayer card, an OfficeMax Rewards card. Near the back she found it— *Universal Life Everlasting Church* was emblazoned in fancy gold lettering across the top, and her name—REVEREND STELLA JEAN HARDESTY—printed below. It was even signed by a Mortimer Blaise Cunningham, Vice President and Coordinating Minister.

And—best of all—it featured a photo of Stella that had been snapped after Thanksgiving dinner at Jelloman's a year ago, late in the day after everyone had got into the eggnog. Stella thought her slack expression and rosy glow—courtesy of the Bacardi folks—could easily be mistaken for devout piety. Jelloman had taken pictures of his guests and then lined up mail-order ordination for all his best friends for Christmas, and Stella had been a card-carrying member of the clergy ever since.

Apparently Halpern thought she looked plenty holy, too, because after squinting at the ID for a few moments, he scrambled to his feet and picked up the phone's handset. "I'm sorry, Reverend," he said as he dialed a few numbers. "You just wouldn't believe all the folks trying to get in here after hours. Next time you just show that card right off and we'll get you in quick."

"Thank you, son," Stella said gravely, and assumed her most beatific expression.

"Kinhara?" Halpern barked into the phone. "Need an escort to Nebah. . . . Nebah . . ."

"Nebuchadnezzar Donovan," Stella stage-whispered. "It's a *biblical* name."

Halpern nodded smartly. "To Mr. Donovan. A member of the clergy is here to see him."

Kinhara seemed less impressed with Stella's credentials. In fact, Kinhara, a gangly gal with an abbreviated nose and bangs in her eyes, didn't seem too impressed with much of anything, including the contents of Stella's purse and the results of the wanding she delivered with a lackluster "stand on that line there."

"I got to take you to the cell," she said over her shoulder as she led Stella down a hall with painted cinder block walls and waxed linoleum floors. It was clean enough, but a fly buzzed by Stella's ear and the air was stale and overwarm. "Phones in the visitor booths ain't workin' right."

"How long have they been broken?" Stella asked, curious. Given the slightly run-down state of the place, she figured maybe the old Hardee's wasn't such a bad deal for the Prosper team after all.

Kinhara snorted. "Oh, they work fine—when they want to. Maintenance'll come around and wouldn't you know that's the day there ain't a thing wrong with them. Then the next day nothin'. Put the phone to your ear and all's you hear is like a buzz or some such. And getting those maintenance guys to come—mmm-mmm."

She shook her head sorrowfully as they came to a heavy metal door with a small glass window. She unlocked it with a keypad and they entered a vestibule with an identical door on the other side. Once the first door clanged shut, she tapped in the code for the second one and they went through.

But in the brief moment they were in the small space between the doors, Stella experienced a little heart-quickening note of panic. The closeness of the walls, the silence of the room, the view down the halls in either direction, not a window in sight—this, Stella figured, was what it must feel like to be locked up.

She didn't like it.

Not one bit.

In all the times Stella had imagined the day when the law caught up with her, when the string of bashed and intimidated husbands she left in her wake somehow engineered her ruin, she'd never allowed herself to think about the reality of prison.

She didn't like to be closed in. All those years ago, shut into the little basement storm cellar, the thundering and howling of the twister audible even as her mama sang and clapped her hands to distract her—the memory of that day came back with a ferocity that pounded at her temples and left her hands clammy and her stomach churning. She'd waited along with her mother and her sister, eyes on the bolted door, thinking about Daddy and Uncle Horace as Patches whined and pawed helplessly at the floor.

Mama kept saying everything would be fine. But Mama had been wrong.

"Getting the maintenance guys to come," she mumbled, repeating the last thing Kinhara had said, stumbling after her and touching the wall for support as they approached the long row of cells, white metal grids forming the wall between them and the prisoners.

"Yeah, you know state budgets. Governor couldn't fund the paper to wipe his own ass, you ask me. We ain't had a raise in two years. And them maintenance guys, they got them covering all the admin buildings and impound and the garage, cut their staff in half, they can't hardly keep up. . . . Here we go."

They stopped in front of the white grid, and Stella peered through. There, in a narrow rectangular cell, sat Neb, looking much diminished on his plastic-covered cot. The small space was crammed with a tiny sink and steel toilet and shelf and abbreviated desk, but somehow Neb still managed to look lost, his hands clasped in front of him, his head bowed.

"Hello, Mr. Donovan," Stella said, clearing her throat. "I'm here for my *clergy* visit."

Neb leapt to his feet, appearing both startled and relieved. He approached the bars and wrapped his rough, callused hands around them. "Stella! What clergy? Who all'd you bring with you?"

"Nobody," Stella said, winking and furtively giving him a cut-throat gesture. "Seein' as I'm an ordained reverend and all. I'm here to pray with you. In *private*."

She turned to Kinhara. "I'll let you know when I'm through," she said. "Thanks for the escort."

Kinhara hooked a thumb over her shoulder. "I'll fetch us a couple a chairs, but won't hardly be private, 'cause I got to stay here with you. I got a magazine, though, and I won't pay you no mind."

She dragged a couple of metal chairs from the end of the cells. They made a screeching sound on the floor. Stella accepted one, and Neb fetched his own matching chair from under the little desk. They sat down, their knees inches apart but separated by the bars. Stella reached through for a squeeze and Neb squeezed back with surprising strength. Stella tried not to wince.

"I'll be right in here," Kinhara said, dragging her own chair down the row a ways. Voices from the other cells greeted her, but she ignored them and pulled out her magazine. "You got fifteen minutes, just like if you was at the booth."

"What was that clergy thing about?" Neb asked quietly once Kinhara turned her attention to her *True Romance,* scratching at a spot below his left ear. Stella took it for a nervous gesture, one he'd apparently been employing all afternoon, as the skin was rubbed raw. He was not going to make a very sturdy prisoner, Stella decided.

"I just had to say I was a reverend to get in here."

"Oh. I guess that's okay."

"You doing all right?"

"I suppose." More scratching. "The food sucks. You know how they always say that, in prison movies? That the food sucks? Well, it really does. This thing they brought in here, I don't know if it was supposed to be some sorta tofu or somethin'—

man, you do *not* want to know what it did to my digestive system."

Stella darted a glance at the dull-finished steel toilet in the corner and figured he was probably right—she didn't much want to know.

"Course, one good thing was, I guess they'll finally believe I'm off the OxyContin, seein' as I had to pee in a cup. Twice."

"Gave you a medical exam, huh?"

"Medical, mental, searched—well, pretty much everywhere they could think of, I guess. Hey, Stella, *you* know I didn't do it, right? That I didn't kill nobody?"

Stella couldn't quite meet Neb's eyes. She wanted to tell him she believed him—but after her visit to Dr. Herman, she couldn't be sure. Oh, she believed he *thought* he was innocent, all right.

"They told you who that gal was?" she asked, avoiding his question.

"Yeah, some woman named Laura."

"Laura Cassel."

"If you say so."

"Neb . . . I got to know. You swear you never had anything to do with this gal? Never met her, even just in passing, nothing like that?"

Neb's lips quivered as he spoke, his voice hollow with exhaustion. "Stella, on my life. On *Donna's* life. I never even heard that name 'fore today."

Stella, watching closely, figured there was no way he was lying. If he *had* killed her, it was without even knowing who she was.

"What do they got on you, anyway?" Stella asked, darting a glance over at Kinhara, who held her magazine a few inches from her nose and appeared to be absorbed in the small print, evidently uninterested in their conversation.

"That's the craziest thing," Neb said, shaking his head. "They got a letter I wrote, sayin' to come and meet me at the track. It was on that dead gal they dug up, in her pocket or something. It's got my signature and everything."

"You sure it's your signature?"

"Well, I don't know," Neb said. "I only got a quick look. It sure looked like mine. The rest of it was typed. Or printed on a computer or something. They got some handwriting expert going over it now—I guess after he gets done looking at it, I'll know if I wrote it or not."

"Well . . . that letter could have been faked."

"It gets kind of worse, though," Neb went on. "There was, uh, blood on the body? They're doing all that DNA testing on it, and they took swabs from me. I guess they'll know before long if it's a match or not. But already they're sayin' it's type B negative and how only two percent of folks got that type. And Stella . . . I'm B negative."

Dang. That *was* bad.

"Look, Neb, you haven't been talking, have you? I mean, not without Priscilla here . . . right?"

Neb toed the tiled floor dejectedly. "Aw, maybe one or two things," he mumbled. "Priscilla couldn't get away early. You know, she's low man on the totem pole at that law firm and all. But she's gonna come up first thing tomorrow if her boss lets her."

Stella's heart sank. "What have you told them, Neb?"

He shrugged, but try as Stella might, she couldn't get anything further out of him. She could only hope that the questioning hadn't gone too far—she could just imagine Simmons with her pinched face, staring Neb down in an interrogation room, looking for angles to make him incriminate himself.

"Look," he finally said, "I'm kinda tired. I'm thinkin' I ought to hit the hay. It was really nice of you to come, Stella, but I reckon I ought to be fresh for tomorrow. Donna's gonna . . ." He paused as a little hitch stuttered through his voice, cleared his throat, and tried again. "Donna's gonna be here soon's visiting hours start, plus Priscilla and all. But I sure do appreciate it. . . ."

If ever there was a man who needed a hug, Neb was that fellow, but as Stella stuck her hands through the bars to try to grasp his hands, he shrank away from her and retreated back to his cot.

Stella could tell that he was ashamed. And not just because he wasn't sure if he was a cold-blooded murderer or not, but because Stella had to see him here, stripped of his dignity, his pride—even his shoelaces. Stella read his misery and nodded briskly.

"All right, then," she said. "I'll be back soon's I can. Meantime you just—just—hang in there, and keep the faith, hear?"

The fact that she was pretty sure he hadn't heard, not through his layers of misery and humiliation, did not quite make up for her embarrassment at having uttered a platitude so inadequate that even a minister of the Universal Life Everlasting Church ought to have been able to do better.

. . .

Kinhara walked Stella back through the echoing halls and the suffocating little double-doored chamber to the visitor desk.

Officer Halpern practically jumped out of his chair and nodded smartly. "Reverend," he said. "Sheriff Jones was just here asking after you."

"Reverend Hardesty," boomed a familiar voice before Stella could react. Goat strolled into the room from a hallway leading in the other direction and held out his hand. A hint of mischief showed in his navy blue eyes as he took her hand in his and pressed it delicately. "I'm so sorry I've missed services lately. Duty . . . you know. It *calls*."

Stella blushed furiously, staring at a button halfway down his uniform shirt. "Sheriff," she muttered hoarsely. "Good to see you."

"Yeah, I was just meeting with my colleague, Detective Simmons. . . . Hey—" He snapped his fingers. "—you know, I wonder if she might like to attend services sometime. As my guest. You got a copy of the schedule on you? We could . . ."

He tilted his head back down the hall the way he'd come, where, presumably, Simmons was gnashing her pointy teeth in her lair while she worked on her plans to string Neb up and get her claws in Goat.

"Actually, I'm kind of busy," Stella said. "I'm just on my way to, uh, do my hospital ministry. Got a . . . scarlet fever victim. Probably be dead by morning, I gotta do the last rites and all."

"Ah. No rest for the soldiers of God's army. Well, at least let me walk you out."

175

"It's really not necessary. . . ."

Goat took her arm and guided her firmly toward the door.

"Good night, Reverend," Halpern called.

Stella scowled, but she had no choice but to go along with Goat down the hall to the exit.

Out in the parking lot, Goat chuckled. "I guess we're even."

"How do you figure?"

"Well, I dragged you out to my place last night for nothing . . . made you deal with Brandy and all."

That was true. Stella brightened at the idea of evening a score with Goat while pulling off her little jail-cell ruse.

"Does Simmons know?" she asked. "About my . . . um, visit?"

"Naw, I just saw your name on the register when I was saying good night to Halpern. You get anything out of Neb?"

"Nope."

"He tell you what we found on the body?"

"Nope."

Goat regarded her for a long moment. Clearly, he didn't believe her, but he wasn't going to make an issue of it, for which Stella was tremendously grateful.

"You seen Brandy today?" Goat asked as they started walking across the lot toward the visitor parking, where Stella had left the Jeep.

Stella glanced at Goat to see if he was yanking her chain. "No, but I've been gone since this morning."

"Oh . . . she didn't call you, maybe? Leave a message on your cell or something?"

"No. What's the matter, did you go and misplace her somewhere? 'Cause I got to tell you, last night it seemed like you wouldn't mind being shut of her."

That was putting it mildly—as Stella beat a hasty exit, Goat had been trying to fend off Brandy, who was following him around the smoldering mass of metal that had once been her car, making suggestive comments and sloshing her drink. It was a miracle the alcohol on her breath didn't catch a wayward spark and set her on fire.

Goat didn't say anything, just scowled and lengthened his stride so Stella had to practically jog to keep up.

"Look," he said, stopping abruptly when they got near her Jeep, "how about a beer? Or a cup of coffee? I mean, if you don't have plans or something."

Stella did her best to hide her surprise. "Well . . . I guess. I can maybe move some things around. I just—let me make a quick call, okay?"

Goat jammed his hands into his pockets and waited, gazing out to the street, where one of the older residential areas of town sloped gently away from the municipal buildings.

"Oh," said Stella. "I mean, you don't have to wait for me or anything."

"Uh." Goat's face, a little stubbly after all the hours of crime-solving that had intervened since his morning shave, screwed up into an embarrassed expression. "You mean you want to make a *private* call."

"Eh, uh, yeah." Stella felt her own face reddening. It wasn't so much that she needed privacy; she was planning only to check in with Sherilee to make sure she knew where Todd was, and Jelloman to make sure he found the key under the rock— and Chrissy, to make sure things had gone all right at the shop. But somehow these homey conversations, with people she cared about, were too intimate to have in front of Goat.

Which, Stella realized, was ridiculous. Except . . . it almost, maybe, felt *too* good, *too* tempting to open the door on everything she held dear, to let Goat in where she'd promised herself she'd never let another man tread. Her personal stuff. Her private world. The things she cared about enough not to risk anyone hurting her with them.

Thirty-some years ago, she'd married Ollie Hardesty and let him drive his huge smoke-belching bulldozer of an evil-ass presence right into her life. She hadn't known how to set boundaries. She never thought to demand her share. For decades, she just let Ollie ride roughshod over her feelings, her memories, her dreams.

And while Stella was well aware that she needed some manly attention, while she hoped and intended to indulge in all manner of sins of the flesh and other varieties of rollicking good times, her *heart* remained off-limits.

That's how the promise went, anyway. It had seemed obvious and even necessary at the time, when Ollie was still fresh in the ground and the prospect of building a future was terrifying. Which made it so darn peculiar that every time she got around Goat, that damn heart she'd worked so hard to protect started banging a spoon on the bars of its cell and demanding to get out.

FOURTEEN

. . . .

'll just be a minute," she said, her voice wobbly. .

"Okay. There's a bar . . . can't remember the name of it, nothin' fancy—I mean, we could drive somewhere if you rather—"

"No, I'm sure it's fine."

"Block or two that way." Goat jerked a thumb to the right, down the darkening street, and ambled off without looking back, hands still stuffed in his pockets.

Stella watched him go, until he disappeared under an overhanging dogwood branch, ducking his lanky frame to avoid being scratched. She stood rooted to the spot a little longer before she remembered that she was supposed to be making calls.

No one was home at the Groffes; seeing as it was Saturday, the girls were probably already at the sitter's and Todd and Sherilee would be digging into their Taco Bell Fiesta Gorditas right about now.

A call home got her a very cheerful Jelloman. "Tigers,

twenty-three to twenty-one!" he shouted into the phone, nearly bursting her eardrum. He sounded like he'd already got into the postgame celebratory substances, but Stella didn't mind. A tipsy Jelloman would be just as effective against a prowler as a sober one, perhaps even more aggressive, and it would take so much to actually knock him out that Stella figured he'd run out of things to drink and inhale first.

"This is one fine dog you got here," Jelloman said after he assured her that nothing was amiss. "I'm teachin' her to fetch me a beer from off the table. She's only bit a hole in one can so far. Gotta see if I can teach her to open the fridge."

"My, that sounds useful."

In the background, she heard Sabine holler something.

"Sabine says Roxy got a package of wieners off the counter. She's threatening to make hamburgers out of her. Hey, listen, I had her out in the backyard doin' her business, and I come across some sort a plaster mess on the ground outside the back windows. Picked it up and it looked to me like you got you a footprint there. This have something to do with that guy who was hanging around here?"

"Uh—yeah, maybe. Yes. Did you take it in?"

"Yup, got it sitting here in the kitchen. It's about the only thing your dog ain't tried to eat yet. Gotta tell you, that's a dainty foot your fella's got. Probably only a size nine or so."

Stella smiled. "Well, then I guess he's probably no match for you, so I guess you can quit worrying."

Jelloman laughed, a hearty, welcome sound. "Worry? Stella, the only thing I'm worried about is if Sabine gets to him first, there won't be nothing left for me to take a swing at. She's all worked up 'bout this."

"Be careful!" This time Stella could make out Sabine's voice loud and clear—she must have snatched the phone away. "There are *keelers* out there!"

Stella promised not to get killed and made her final call.

"You're goin' drinkin' with him?" Chrissy demanded. "With the *sheriff*? He gonna let you drive home? He shouldn't, you know. 'Less you plan on stickin' to Fresca."

"What's got into you?"

"Nothing . . . I just put in a long day at the shop an all . . . Nadine Schleusner was in tryin' out the Husqvarna again."

"Oh. You have my sympathies." Nadine came in at least once a month with a basket of mending and sat herself down in front of the most expensive Swedish sewing machine, loaded it up with her linty cheap-ass thread, and sewed crooked patches on her husband's dungarees. Which wasn't really a problem, since the demo machines were there to be used, except that the old woman's real reason for coming was to talk. Loudly. Incessantly. Mr. Schleusner had long ago learned to turn down his hearing aid, and so Nadine sought out her conversational fill from Stella and Chrissy, bobbing her snowy bouffant-coiffed head along with her running commentary and keeping the volume full blast. There was no stopping her until she ran out of things to sew and say, which could take hours.

"And . . . well," Chrissy continued. "Larry was wondering could I come over and barbecue, and he's all like go ahead and bring the baby, but I know where he'n me would end up and it's no place to have Tucker around, you know what I'm sayin', and I was hopin' you—Oh, sorry, Stella, that totally makes it sound like I take you for granted, and I don't, I would have tried to get someone else to watch Tucker but—"

"You know I'd ordinarily love to," Stella interrupted. It was true—she'd love to watch Tucker, but not quite so much as she'd love to head down to that bar and rub knees with Goat in a booth back in a dark corner. "Maybe later . . ."

"Aw, to tell the truth, I'm a little beat from last night. Maybe I'll just get Tucker to bed and take a hot bath or something."

"Thought you said that after getting in the hot tub, you were clean enough to last a few months, remember?"

"Yeah . . ." Chrissy yawned audibly. "Only, I been having these dirty thoughts all day—I figure I might just need a good scrub."

Stella almost walked right past the bar. It was set back from the street in between a couple of shabby brick apartment buildings, the old-fashioned kind with concrete stoops and windows open to the breeze and abandoned balls and scooters on the lawn. The bar was a humble affair, little more than a converted shed, with no sign to identify it. A single neon COORS light burned in a grimy window.

Inside, it took a minute for Stella's eyes to adjust to the gloom. An Alan Jackson tune played in the background while a few older gents studied the lay of the break on a pool table. Two or three solo drinkers looked like they were settling in for a long night at the bar, and a bartender was stacking glasses on a shelf. Goat was sitting by himself in a booth, a couple of tall frosty beers sweating on the table, a basket of pretzels untouched in front of him.

Stella slid into the booth and picked up her beer straight

off, raising the chilly glass to her lips and getting down a good, soothing swallow. She had too much on her mind, and as pleased as she was with this unexpected opportunity for a little time with Goat, she appreciated the nerve-steadying powers of that first icy delicious sip.

"It's Bud," Goat said. "I seem to recall you being a Bud gal."

When he wasn't plying her with red wine, Stella thought wistfully. The ruined evening seemed much longer than two days ago. She decided not to mention that she usually liked her beer to follow a nice neat slug of Johnnie Walker Black.

"Thanks . . . I'll get the next one."

"Your calls go okay?"

Stella nodded. "Just had to check in with Chrissy. Make sure the shop didn't fall down while I was gone."

"How's that young lady faring?"

If it hadn't been for Goat and the Ogden County emergency services' quick response to the bloodbath down at the Lake of the Ozarks a few months back, Chrissy wouldn't have lived to raise her baby and draw men like flies and act as Stella's partner in crime. Goat had taken a shine to the girl, and visited often while she was hospitalized.

"Fit as a fiddle," Stella said. "Well, maybe fit as an old guitar with busted strings, but she's getting better every day. She ought to be good as new by the holidays."

"And the boy?"

Stella grinned; couldn't help it. Sometimes she felt like Tucker was her own grandbaby. "Couldn't be sweeter. You'll have to—"

She had been about to say, *You'll have to come over and visit him when I'm babysitting*, but the old familiar awkwardness stopped her midsentence. Casual visiting . . . that implied a level of ease, of intimacy even, that Stella could only imagine, since every sighting of the man brought on stammering and blushing.

There was a silence as they pushed around their little cardboard coasters and sipped at their beers. Goat couldn't maintain his smile; it slipped by degrees, his broad mouth turning down at the corners and his eyes reflecting trouble.

Stella figured it was up to her to jump in. "So what's this about Brandy going missing?"

"I called her a few times today," Goat said. "She wasn't picking up. I mean I imagine she's got her a hell of a hangover, and maybe she decided to sleep it off all afternoon—or hell, maybe she's still pissed at me for, uh, for . . ."

Not giving up the goodies, Stella thought. For which she had to give the man credit. She'd seen for herself how determined Goat's former spouse could be when she wanted something. Lots of men would have just given up the fight when the first few attempts to peel off a horny woman failed.

Stella didn't figure Brandy for giving a man the silent treatment, though—not when spite wouldn't get her anywhere she wanted to go. The gal had to be working some new angle.

"You tried the cell and the house phone?"

"Yeah, and I was about to go by the house and check, when . . . well, you know, Daphne called about hauling Neb in. Things moved kind of fast after that."

Stella could only imagine. With that note they'd taken off the body, and the blood evidence to boot, it was no wonder they'd grabbed him up so quick. Putting Brandy out of her mind for the moment, she decided to see if she could get anything more out of Goat, any details about the body that she could use. At the very least, maybe she could confirm its identity.

"I know you can't tell me who the dead woman is," she said. "But it seems to me that if I guess right, you could maybe tell me that I wasn't wrong, or something."

"Stella . . ."

"It's Laura Cassel, isn't it?"

Goat didn't look so much surprised as resigned. He sighed heavily and picked a pretzel out of the basket, broke it in half, and tossed the pieces into his mouth. He stared at her thoughtfully as he chewed, then followed up with the rest of his beer. Stella signaled to the bartender to bring him a new one.

"I ain't even gonna ask you where you got that from. I mean, unless you feel like telling me."

No chance. "Um, just . . . around. Lucky guess."

"I *know* it's not Irene. . . ."

"No, Goat, I swear on—on my folks' graves, it's not Irene."

"Good. 'Cause I do *not* want to fire that woman. Whole damn place would fall apart, I'd never find anything again. And if I ever find out you've been trying to dig something out of her . . ."

"I won't," Stella said, though she had to cross her fingers under the table on that one. Though digging Goat's whereabouts out of Irene hardly seemed like it should count, seeing as he was a public servant and all, who had to answer to the public, of which Stella figured she was a bona fide member.

"Good. Now, look here, Stella. You and me, we got to come to some sort of understanding. You got to realize that my job is on the line each and every time there is even a possibility of, even the *implication* of a possibility of, me sharing information with you."

"Well, first of all, I'm the most discreet person I know. And it ain't like I'm asking for something for nothing," Stella said hotly. "It's, you know, a two-way flow here. Plus we both want the same thing, which is to figure out who the hell killed Laura. Plus can't you just call me an anonymous source or something? I mean what are you worried about, your girlfriend Daphne—"

"This ain't about Daphne," Goat snapped. "Or anybody else. It's about what's *right*. Bottom line, I can't do my job the way it's got to be done if I'm compromising the integrity of the investigation, the evidence, all of that."

"All's I'm asking," Stella said, and then stopped when the bartender—an indifferent-looking fireplug of a squat ruddy-faced man—plunked a new beer in front of Goat and took away the empty. She waited until he was out of earshot. "What I'm asking is, and we can make this about an *unidentified* victim, is if y'all are thinking this is a random thing or a lovers'-type quarrel or, I don't know, a hate crime or a robbery or what. I mean, you got to see why I'm asking—so I can figure out if there's any way Neb might be responsible or not."

There was another long pause while Goat took the foam off his beer and dropped the level some. He watched her the whole time, and Stella forced herself not to blink first, even though his gaze on her felt disconcertingly electric.

"Look here," he said finally. "Neb's a *man*. And, well, I do know a little something about your, you know, leisure-time hobbies, let's call 'em. And what I don't get is how you got hooked up with, uh, Neb's welfare here, him being a man like I said. I guess I might feel a little better about this conversation we're having if I understood your interest in the case."

With the tables flipped over on her, Stella felt her skin flush. She'd long wondered how much Goat knew, or suspected, about her little justice business.

There was a level, deep below the surface, where women in need connected with each other, where they found out about solutions of last resort, where Stella's number was passed along in whispers and secrecy was guaranteed by all those terrible layers of fear and desperation.

Stella was unshakably certain that Goat hadn't infiltrated that secret system. No man, not even—maybe especially not—a lawman would ever be allowed in that place.

And that, on second thought, was the reason Stella could never tell him any more about what she did. No matter how much she believed in his decency, or trusted his intentions. She had to keep him as far as she could from the secret core of her business, where women had very little trust left to call upon.

"Neb's a friend," she said. "Like a brother to me, really. I'd— I'd just do anything to prove he didn't do it. Besides, you know me, I've just got a real curious mind. Plus—I just might have something to trade. Something to help you folks out with your, you know, investigation."

"Trade?" Goat said sharply.

"Yeah. I'm going to give you a suspect. A good one, that you all don't know about yet. Only before I do, here's what I want: You got to tell me what you know about Laura. And I ain't asking for anything I couldn't find out on my own, if I had more time, I'm just asking for you to—what do you call it, expedite the process some."

"Stella, you know I can't tell you who—"

"And you don't even have to identify the victim, the way I figure it. Let's just say that you knew a thing or two about that Laura Cassel woman, like maybe she was a friend or an acquaintance or something, it doesn't really matter, you're just someone who happens to know a few little facts about her, facts I could ask any of her friends or family about, if I had more time, which we both know I don't, not if I'm going to be my most helpful with this mess."

Stella had spoken in a rush to get it all out without Goat interrupting, and now she sipped at her beer and peered at him over the top of her glass to see how it went over. Goat's scowl stayed fixed for a moment while he regarded her straight-on, and then he seemed to relax just a fraction of a bit. He leaned back against the booth and folded his arms across his chest.

"So . . . I guess I might know her," he allowed. "She was thirty-five years old, single, never been married. Had her a nice little town house over in Picot and a late-model Toyota. Worked as a drug rep for one of the big companies. Which, as I guess I don't need to tell you, don't look too good for your addict buddy."

Stella kept a poker face. *Ex*-addict, she was thinking, but she couldn't blame Goat for his suspicions. "What kind of family does she have?"

"Just her parents," Goat said. "No siblings. Aunts, uncles, cousins all over in Kansas. Folks there in Picot, the dad runs a printing business, mom teaches grade school."

"Did you talk to them?"

"Yeah . . . I did."

Stella could tell that Goat was torn about giving her details of the conversation. She waited with lips parted, not daring to prod him any further.

After another long draw on his beer and some more inscrutable thinking, he continued. "They got a nice little place up there, a couple acres. Pictures of that gal all over the house, like to break a person's heart, they still got her baby pictures on the breakfront. Softball team, graduation, pictures from family vacations. Said she still kept up with her best friends from high school, most of them were married now and Laura was like an auntie to their kids, and they were always trying to set her up and get her married off, but her mother said she just hadn't met the right guy."

"She wasn't seeing anyone back then?"

"Well, her parents thought she was, but she said she didn't want to talk about it. They said they figured it was an old boyfriend, one she'd got back with a couple of times. You know, the kind of situation where they never quite break up, neither one really moves on? All that drama."

If Goat caught the similarities to his own marital status, he didn't let on. And Stella certainly wasn't about to point it out. "Did they, uh, like the boyfriend?"

"No . . . no, I would say it was pretty clear they didn't think much of him. The dad said he didn't have any initiative, you know, how he wouldn't ever amount to anything."

"Dads talk that way, I guess. Nobody good enough for their little girl, and all."

"Yeah. But the mom didn't like him either. She didn't exactly come out and say it, but I could tell. Like she didn't much trust him."

Well, now, that was interesting. "Don't suppose you'd want to share his particulars?"

"No, I'm pretty sure I don't. Hell, Stella, I got Mike on that. Can't you trust the department to do anything without your interfering? I promise, if it turns out this guy was anywhere near Laura back when she was killed, he'll get looked at better than any civilian can do, okay?"

"Okay."

"I mean it, Stella. Stay out of that one. Now, what have you got for me?"

"There's this guy," she said carefully. Stella's experience with the vagaries of human nature had taught her to play her hole card with caution. "Now, you know that I would never dream of telling you how to run an investigation. But it seems to me if there's someone who had access to the crime scene, someone with an itinerant-type past"—that was stretching it a bit—"with a mean streak and a reputation for knocking heads"—and that was pure fabrication—"that you folks might want to know about it."

Goat lowered his eyebrows, fine expressive dark brows that communicated oceans of sentiment. "Stella, if you know something you haven't been telling me, and this an active investigation, you know way better than to—"

"Calm down, calm down," Stella said hastily. "It's something I only just found out." Lie number three.

"Yeah? So?"

"His name is Cory Layfield. Did some work for Neb on the

side, some of the heavy lifting out at the fairgrounds. Young kid, twenty or so. And you got to admit, if Neb was all hopped up and still recovering from a recent surgery, and what's concrete weigh, got to be all kinds of cubic tons or metric tons or something—"

"Quit sellin'," Goat said, his voice low and gravelly and threatening, irritation sparking glints in his eyes, which had dialed down from indigo to a shade closer to ebony in the poor bar lighting. "I *do* know my ass from my elbow. I think I can judge if this guy's worth lookin' into."

"Well, there's one more thing. I, uh, I mean, just in case it's connected, like if it's maybe the same guy. Like if he figured out I was looking into things. Well, it's just that there was someone maybe trying to break into my house the other night, and I got his footprint—well, like a *cast* of his footprint, I guess you would say—which I thought you might want to use to compare or whatever if you find him—"

"Someone tried to break into your *house*?"

"Well, I mean, I assume that's what he was doing, there was like gouges on the windowsill and whatnot plus him tromping around in the mud—"

"Stella, goddamn it, why didn't you call me *then*? Shit, you have got to be the most stubborn, impossible, reckless female I have ever in my days—oh, for fuck's sake—if you could just—I mean, just, just one *speck* of common sense—"

There it was, that little shiver-me-timbers thrill Goat unleashed on her whenever he was angry. Stella figured there must be something very wrong about the way she enjoyed provoking him, about the liquidy yum sensations in her gut when his voice went all deep and growly.

It was crazy. After all, she'd spent several decades letting an angry man take out all his meanness on her. You'd think any sane woman who'd been through what she had would turn and run at the first sign of a man's bad mood.

Only . . . when Goat got mad, despite the glowering, despite the snarling, it was very clear to Stella that he was all bark and no bite. That he'd sooner saw off a leg than let fly on a woman. That he'd been brought up with the old-fashioned kind of ideas that made a man stop in his tracks and remove his cap, offer an arm, light a cigarette. Pound the shit out of a guy who sneaked into his woman's yard.

The thrill, Stella admitted to herself, was pushing Goat right to the edge and knowing he couldn't do a damn thing about it. He was like a beetle on his back, waving his legs in the air, and though he might make noise and throw lightning bolts, Stella knew that nothing in the world would ever make Goat hurt her on purpose.

And that was so thrilling, so new, so delightful, that Stella wanted to keep him there, to incite him a little, get him all riled up, just for the thrill of it. Just because . . . she *could*.

Was that what they meant by feminine wiles? Was this the trick that other women, women smart enough not to marry the first man who asked or stick around once the beating started, kept ready in their arsenals? For a delicious slow second, Stella considered meeting Goat's irritation with lowered eyelids, with a slow swipe of her tongue along her lower lip, with a few more sassy words guaranteed to get his ire even further up.

And then her stupid cell phone rang, the annoying trilling flutey tones instantly evaporating the thin layer of bad girl that Stella had worked so hard to conjure.

"'Scuse me," she muttered, and got the cursed thing out of her purse, flipping it open without bothering to check the ID screen. "Yeah, what."

"Stella, don't you hang up!" It was Brandy's unmistakably breathy voice. "You're the only one can help now. I've been kidnapped and left to die."

FIFTEEN

. . . .

What the—?" Stella started, and was instantly interrupted.

"Now, listen good, Stella," Brandy said. Her voice
had a strangled, terrified quality to it that went a long way to
convincing Stella to do as she said. "I'm sorry I didn't tell y'all
sooner, but I know who killed that gal in the track."

"You *what?*"

"I said, I know who did it. The whole reason I came to
Prosper was for protection. I thought I'd be safe with Goat,
only now he's gone and kidnapped me 'cause I know too much.
I can *identify* him. Which is what I'm about to do, but you got
to promise me you'll take care of this yourself."

"*Me?* What—?"

"And *not* Goat. Hear? He's a good man, and now I think
about it, I guess you can have him, seein' as I'm probably gonna
be dead here in a bit, but he can't do what needs done to this
guy. Only you can do it."

"For criminy's sakes, who the—?"

"It's Wil Vines. My old boyfriend. That's who killed her. And blew up my car. It was like a warning or whatever, but now he thinks I was fixin' to tell Goat, which is why he's going to kill me, only I didn't tell Goat, I only—"

"Your *boyfriend* killed the woman at the track?" Stella's mind practically ran over itself trying to absorb the new information.

"That's what I'm trying to tell you—"

"But why don't you want Goat to know? He's—"

"Is he there?" Despite her predicament, Brandy managed to get a fair amount of outrage and suspicion into her voice. "'Cause he *can not* know about this."

"But he's the—"

"*Promise* me," Brandy hissed with such force that Stella drew back from the phone a little.

Stella had no idea what was going on, and she had half a mind to suspect that Brandy was up to another of her tricks, except what if she was telling the truth and—

As if reading her mind, Brandy yelped, "My battery is about to *die,* Stella. Now, do you want to hear the rest or *not?*"

"All right . . . Noelle," Stella said haltingly. She glanced at Goat to see if he bought the ruse; he picked up his beer and drained a good stretch of it. There was enough noise in the bar that she figured he couldn't hear Brandy, screeching or not.

"Now, listen good. Wil, he's up to all kinds of shit. That's why I finally left him, he's never let go a chance to make a dirty buck. Drugs, stealing, all kinds of—"

"But why'd he . . . you know, what did he have to do with that gal?"

"Well, that I don't quite have a handle on. But I know he

195

did it. He come home that night, the night they laid in that foundation, all covered with concrete dust and tells me this story how it was *guns* he buried in there. All this song and dance about how he was just holding 'em for a guy but they were hot and he didn't want 'em traced back to him, he just tossed 'em into the foundation and wouldn't you know I fell for that like I fell for every other line of bullshit he ever fed me. *Men*." She spat the last of her impassioned speech, and Stella figured they had that little bit in common, anyway; both of them let down by poor representatives of the other gender.

But she wasn't sure that was enough to convince her to go after a killer without the backup of the law, even if it did mean clearing Neb. After all, Wil sounded like a worse brand of trouble than she had him figured for.

But it was a heck of a lot of coincidence to swallow for the two cases to be connected. What were the odds of Goat's saucy ex appearing at the very same time that *her* ex's murder victim got unearthed?

"Why don't you just tell . . . our friend?" she demanded. "Let him deal with it?"

"Stella, don't forget that I *know* what you do," Brandy said, her voice dropping conspiratorially. "To men. The ones as have it coming, anyway. So you can quit pretending. Now, look, you got to *kill* Wil. If Goat gets him, there's gonna be all kinds of red tape and he'll probably end up getting off on some dumb-ass technicality and then he would have killed me for nothing. You got to find him first and, and, you know, drop him like a rabid dog."

Stella didn't bother to point out that Brandy was operating on bad information—that she wasn't available to hire for murder, even for a good cause. "You ain't, uh, gone yet," she said instead. Trying to speak in euphemisms to keep Goat in the dark was difficult. "Don't you want me to find him and get him to tell me the, ah, location, and come get you?"

"Oh," Brandy said dubiously. "I guess you *could,* if you wanted. Except I'm ninety-nine percent sure I'll be dead here in a bit. No sense holding you up."

"Where the hell *are* you, anyway?"

"Well, if I *knew* that, don't you think I'd *tell* you?" Brandy demanded crossly. "Wil got me in the car and put a blindfold on me, then we drove around in circles for like three hours or something. I couldn't even tell you if it was night or day. I might be in—in Arkansas, for all I know. Then we went on this bumpy road, you know, like in the wilderness or whatever, and after a while—a few miles, I guess—we stopped and Wil made me get out and he wouldn't take off my blindfold or nothing, so I was just kind of stumbling along. And I could feel weeds and shit on my legs, so I'm thinking it was the middle of nowhere. And then Wil told me to sit my ass down and I did and my legs went in this, like, hole and he gives me a shove and bam I'm falling into this hole he dug, it's probably twelve, fifteen feet deep—and I think I busted a leg or something falling in here. Then there was all this thumping around, he dragged some kind of boards or something over the top, and then I could hear the dirt start to hit the boards, and that went on like forever until I couldn't hear nothing. And there's barely room for me to lay down in here. Plus it's cold."

"What—you mean, he buried you *alive*?"

"Yeah, that's what I'm tryin to *tell* you. All's I know is I'm sealed in here and it's dark as pitch, and it took me forever to get the rope off my wrists and the whole time my phone's beeping 'cause it's almost out of power and I knew I only had enough battery left for one call so you better make it good, Stella, 'cause I think I've breathed up just about all the air in this here hole and my phone's about to go and you're my only hope." Her voice trailed off in a thin waver and she coughed delicately a few times, and then the phone went dead.

"Holy shit," Stella exclaimed.

"What the hell was *that* about?" Goat demanded, his eyes wide and startled.

"It was . . . uh . . ." For a moment, Stella thought she ought to just tell him everything. Stella plus Goat plus that detective from Fayette and all her little helpers seemed like a far better bet when it came to tracking down a raging criminal than just plain Stella.

But if what Brandy said was true, and Wil had killed once—and depending on whether Stella could find her dirt grave in time or not, possibly twice—then she made an excellent point: The man needed a bullet in the brain way more than he needed to be a guest of the federal justice system at the taxpayers' expense, only to be unleashed on an unsuspecting public down the road to get right back into the mayhem business.

Stella wavered, thoughts skittering back and forth across the deep divide between her longing for justice and her nagging worries for her own personal safety—and distracted only a little by Goat's lips parted expectantly and the look of alarm that had his eyebrows doing that bent-down thing—and then she came down exactly where she knew she would, her mettle having been formed once and for all the day she dropped her husband to the ground with a wrench.

It wouldn't be such a stretch to suppose that—having discovered how easily a living, breathing, cruel bastard can be turned into a mush-skulled, harmless, dead one—a woman might decide to turn killing into a regular habit. In for a penny, in for a pound, as her mother always said; once you dip a toe in that water, what was going to stop you from jumping on in? Especially when there were so damn many jerks littering the planet, running around hurting and humiliating innocent women with impunity, practically begging to be sent packing to Hell?

There was just one problem: Stella was not a killer.

Yes, she'd taken her husband down, and she'd had to drop a couple of crazed mobsters who had tried to kill her first, but those had all been self-defense. That was different, and no court of law or philosopher or Bible thumper would ever convince her otherwise.

But when those deeds were done, Stella sought out the Big Guy and prayed for His guidance, and when she came to the end of her reflection, she knew in her heart that self-defense was the only excuse for the taking of a life. She knew with divine certainty that unless she was saving herself or her loved ones from imminent peril, justice of the capital punishment variety was off the table. Because that was getting into the Big Guy's territory. It wasn't, to be blunt, Stella's place to decide who should live and who should die. Her job was only to set His more wayward lambs back on the path of righteousness, and if that occasionally took the crack of a whip or delivery of a few thousand volts or the slow and painful removal of a few fingernails, well, she figured the Big Guy would understand.

What He probably would not be very pleased about was

Stella taking on the Wil-hunt without every resource available, not when one of His children—even if she was an annoying, overblown, man-stealing, hussy type of child—was in jeopardy.

She allowed herself one short sigh. "You're not going to believe this," she said, and then she told Goat all about the call, even as his face went from alarmed to chalk white to a ruddy shade of pissed-off red. He was practically out of the booth before she was finished, pulling his phone out of his pocket and throwing some bills on the table.

"Guess we got to go find Brandy now, huh," Stella said, scrambling to follow.

"There ain't no 'we' about it, Stella." Goat stopped in his tracks and laid one large and heavy hand on her shoulder. "You hear? Go on home and mind your own business. This don't have anything to do with you."

He was out the door before she could come up with any kind of response, leaving her in the middle of the shabby bar with a few curious patrons giving her the once-over.

Stella picked up her purse and made her way slowly back down the street toward the municipal center, which was lit up bright in the autumn evening, energy conservation be damned. Ahead she could make out Goat sprinting across the parking lot, yanking open the door to his cruiser. A moment later, he peeled out onto the street, his flasher strobing blue light into the darkness.

As Stella trudged back to her Jeep, she reflected that Goat was moving awfully fast for a man who wasn't still stuck on the stupid woman who'd managed to unhinge Stella's life in the process of fucking up her own.

SIXTEEN

. . . .

When she pulled onto her darkened street half an hour later, dispirited and tired from the drive back from Fayette, Stella was so relieved to see Jelloman's restored El Camino in her driveway that little prickly tears formed in her eyes.

She blinked them away fast as she went into the house and found Jelloman taking loaves of fresh-baked bread out of the oven. One look at the man—not even a fraction of his bulk covered by her favorite red apron, flour dusting his cheeks, a wide and welcoming smile on his face—caused Stella to burst into delayed-reaction tears and tell him, if not the whole story, at least the part about hankering for a man who was still hung up on his ex. The whole saving-her-from-death angle seemed, at that point, superfluous.

Jelloman gave Stella the extra-long version of his trademark bear hug and then between the two of them, they polished off nearly an entire loaf of seeded challah with a generous melty layer of butter. Then Stella allowed him to shoo her off to bed while he went about the business of cleaning up the kitchen, whistling and whipping a dish towel around the kitchen's surfaces like an oversized, bearded Betty Crocker.

Before going to sleep, though, Stella made one more call. Even though she was certain she wouldn't have any more luck trying to find Brandy's burial site than a whole county's worth of trained professionals, it didn't feel right to her not to try. She was more than a little skeptical about Brandy's claim that she was running out of air already, in a hole of the size she described, so to reassure herself, she'd called Chrissy and had her get Larry on the line for a three-way chat.

If she'd had any doubts about Larry's geekiness before the call, they were put to rest when the boy didn't bother to ask her *why* she needed to know how long the air in a hole ten to fifteen feet tall and five feet around could sustain a person. He immediately started mumbling numbers and equations to himself and then wandered away from the phone, though they could occasionally hear him talking to himself as he typed furiously, the clack of the keyboard as loud as if he were typing with hammers.

"He's got a lot a finger strength," Chrissy explained while they waited, "and whaddaya call it, manual dexterity."

Stella took advantage of the lull to fill her partner in on everything that had happened since the morning. Chrissy felt like they ought to set out right that minute to add their womanpower to the search efforts—"Just 'cause she's got her hooks in your man don't make her less deservin' to live," she pointed out—but when Larry came back on the line and told them that in a hole that size, Brandy probably had at least a couple days' worth of air, Stella convinced Chrissy that they'd be a lot more helpful with a good night's sleep behind them.

Then she'd gone to bed and slept like a rock, and if she'd dreamed, the dreams were forgotten by morning.

Stella woke to the smell of bacon and coffee and the feel of warm breath on her face. She slowly opened one eye and then the other and found herself staring into Roxy's freckled snout, and she wondered for a moment if she was imagining the delicious smells, until she remembered that Jelloman had taken over her kitchen.

Stella lingered under the covers for a while, penned in by fifty pounds of affectionate dog, trying to convince herself she should be happier. If Brandy was right about Wil, Neb should be in the clear. There was the little matter of the evidence to consider, but whatever they had on him ought to seem a lot less significant when viewed in the light of them having produced an entirely separate killer and kidnapper.

And since Brandy had a couple of days' worth of air left, surely they'd find Wil and get the information out of him in time to find and free her. That is, if Brandy didn't claw her way out first—those long scarlet fake nails, combined with her relentless need for attention, ought to make easy work of all that digging.

Which was all good . . . real good. Crime solved, bad guy put away, Neb out of jail, Brandy rescued, the town recovered from the spate of twisters, and Stella free to get back to her regular life.

As Stella pushed hard against Roxy's plump and spotted rib cage, and Roxy rolled onto her back and waved her paws in the air, letting her tongue loll out, Stella tried hard not to admit to herself that getting back to her life was a lot less appealing without the prospect of Goat being in it.

But if there was one thing harder to compete with than a sexpot ex-wife, it was a sexpot ex-wife who'd just been rescued from the jaws of death. If the man of your dreams was the valiant, come-to-the-rescue variety, that is, and Goat fit the bill to a T.

Stella wasn't a victim. Not anymore, anyway, and never again, if she could help it. She was a badass in her own right, which meant she wasn't exactly catnip for would-be heroes.

"Move it, you worthless beast," Stella muttered, and gave Roxy an extra-hard shove that rolled her right out of the bed and onto the floor, where she stood wagging her tail and grinning a big doggy grin. Stella sat up and scratched her mutt behind the ears for a while. At least one creature on the planet seemed pleased to have her around.

Make that two. After Stella took a quick shower and picked out a pair of stretchy pants and a loose top suited for a day of victim-hunting, Jelloman squeezed her in a hug, sat her down at the kitchen table, and slid a big plate of challah French toast and bacon in front of her. She nibbled at it and endured Jelloman's admonishments to slow down and appreciate life and not be in such a fuckin' hurry all the damn time.

He fussed like a mother hen until she made it through nearly a whole slice of French toast and most of her bacon, and then he handed her a steaming cup of coffee in a travel mug and demanded one last hug before he let her out of the house.

Stella told Jelloman that she was headed over to do inventory at the shop, which was closed, seeing as it was Sunday.

She saw no need to worry him with the petty little details of buried rivals and riled murderers on the loose. But as she got in the Jeep and headed over to pick up Chrissy, her glum mood threatened to evaporate the little bit of enthusiasm she'd managed to stir up for the job that needed doing.

When the man of your dreams was a justice-hungry knight in khaki polyester armor, there just wasn't any way to compete with a woman whose ass needed saving—especially if that ass was sporting skimpy thong underwear.

Tucker came to the door and mashed his face against the screen, yelling "Sow, Sow!" Stella let herself in and found Chrissy sitting at the kitchen table, looking extremely smug.

"What're you so dang cheerful about?" Stella demanded.

Chrissy fluffed her tumble of damp blond curls and sent them springing around her pale china-smooth cheeks.

"'Cause I'm a genius, is why," she said. "Listen up, once you hear what I figured out, you can go home and change outta them nasty-lookin' rags and into something decent, 'cause we ain't gonna have to go hunting today after all. Not in any dirty old holes, anyway."

"What do you mean?" Stella reached down for Tucker, but he darted away and ran through the apartment, hollering unintelligibly. In seconds he was back, carrying a glittery platform sandal with pink and yellow fake gems all along the straps.

"Soo!" he yelled, and held it up to Stella.

"That's right, it's a *shoe*," she said. "Very good."

Tucker, barely able to contain his excitement, jumped up

and down a few times and pointed at her shoes. Today Stella had on her yellow rubber clogs. She had four or five pairs in a variety of colors; they were comfy, could be hosed off if her work took her into unsavory or dirty conditions, and on most surfaces they were silent, which made them good for sneaking up on people.

Tucker loved Stella's colorful clogs. She kept meaning to get him a pair of his own, except she was pretty sure he didn't exactly want to wear them. No, he liked putting his little action figures and cars in them, and putting them on his bears, and most of all, he loved running around the house carrying them and using them as bumpers when he smashed into things.

"I got a couple of things I think you'll be interested in," Chrissy said. "You know that whole story Brandy told you? About the hole and all?"

"Yeah . . ."

"Well, you remember that movie Jennifer Garner and Matthew McConaughey done a couple years back, where Jennifer's a model with three months to live and Matthew plays her boyfriend and then she gets kidnapped—it was what's-his-name played the bad guy, the one who used to be hot like a hundred years ago and now he looks—Alec Baldwin, that's it—well, anyway, turns out she's just one in a whole mess of girls? Like, there's a serial killer?"

"I must've missed that one." In truth, Stella made it a policy to avoid movies that featured violence, since she figured she got enough of that at work. Which certainly cut down on the pop culture offerings she could stand to watch, but she was too busy to see very many anyway.

"Well, when we were talking yesterday, it hit me that there

was something awful familiar about that whole cockamamie story Brandy was feedin' you. In the movie, Alec Baldwin hits Jennifer over the head in a bar parking lot and then he takes her out into the woods up in Montana, and he's got a whole bunch of big old holes dug out there. I guess there ain't very many folks living up in that entire state, so you can do shit like that and no one pays any mind."

"That so. Huh."

"Well, least in the movie that's how it was. So anyway, he puts her in the hole and then he drags a piece a wood over the top and—is this startin' to sound just a little familiar, Stella?"

"Either you're sayin' Brandy's been picked off by a serial killer who's been poking holes all over Sawyer County, or—"

"Or Brandy made the whole thing up and she couldn't be bothered to come up with an original *plot,* even." Chrissy seemed more outraged at the lack of originality than by the lie itself. "Only I can't figure why she'd go and kidnap herself."

Stella snorted. "Well, girl, I gotta hand it to you. I think you might be on to something. The whole thing sounded pretty stupid to me when she was telling me about it—like Wil would let her keep her cell phone, I mean, come on—and it would just *happen* to have enough juice for the one call. Course, she's got more tits than brains, I guess."

"Hey—watch it," Chrissy snapped. "Just 'cause someone's got a nice set—"

"Yeah, yeah, I'm sorry. You know, you gals that got the looks *and* the brains just make it tough for the rest of us. Have a little sympathy."

"Oh, now," Chrissy said, mollified. "You got your own look. We just got to dress it up a bit."

Stella chose to ignore the comment, but Tucker was getting more and more agitated as he tried to pry the yellow clogs off her feet.

"Soo! *Soo!*"

"Oh, all right, you can borrow them," Stella said, slipping off the clogs. Tucker immediately bundled them up in his arms and ran off, hollering "Da-doo!"

"Was that—?"

"Yup, 'thank you,'" Chrissy said, beaming. "His first sentence!"

"Oh, my," Stella said, and she took a break for a few minutes to chase the little towheaded toddler around long enough to tackle him and blow a congratulatory raspberry on his plump tummy.

"The reason she did it," she said when she caught her breath, "is this way she thinks I'll go after Wil and kill him. If she just told Goat, she was afraid they wouldn't be able to make any charges stick and Wil'd just go after her again, and maybe shut her up for real."

"Huh," Chrissy sniffed. "Me, I'd face my problems head-on. I personally wouldn't go tellin' no tales tryin' to get someone to do my dirty work for me."

"Yeah, but Brandy ain't got half your starch," Stella said. Not a quarter. Not one little *tenth,* truth be told.

"She ain't got my brains, neither." Chrissy lifted a couple of sheets of paper off the kitchen table with a flourish. "Looka here!"

"I don't have my reading glasses on me, doll. Whyn't you tell me what you got there."

"Only the last four transactions on Brandy's Visa card,"

Chrissy said. "Larry showed me how to hack in and see it on-line. Why, I had half a mind to go charge a few things on her account."

"Like maybe a few nice long books to read for when you get put away for fraud?" Stella said, but the truth was she was impressed. Seriously impressed.

"I ain't done a fraction of all the shit you done," Chrissy said, "and you're just jealous 'cause you cain't hardly turn that Mac *on* and plus I'm gettin' laid in the process and you ain't."

Stella didn't need reminding of the latter truth. But she had to grudgingly admit that the former might take a little acknowledging.

"See here," she said, "I suppose these might be some handy skills you're picking up. If you can figure out how to do all this without Larry—'cause I can't hardly afford to put *him* on the payroll, too—then I guess there might be some sort of bonus in this for you, assuming Donna's willing to pay us for clearing Neb."

"Hey, I'm getting the hang of that whole hacking thing. I b'lieve I might have a *calling* for it. I don't really need anyone holding my hand and telling me what to do. And besides, Larry's just after my sugar," Chrissy added. "He'll do whatever I want for free."

Must be nice to have that kind of effect on a man, Stella thought wistfully. "So what-all did our girl charge on that Visa?"

Chrissy tapped the sheet of paper with a sparkle-polished fingernail. "The Bluebird Motel in Casey. Plus sixty bucks at Beau-T Nails. Got her a new set of tips and a lip wax."

"You could tell that online?"

"Nah, I called, acted like I had a question about my bill. Details, Stella, remember?"

Stella did remember: She'd once told Chrissy that the secret to running a successful business, whether you were maiming wife-beaters or selling sewing machines, was in the details. The preparation. The meticulous records. The follow-up to ensure customer satisfaction.

The fact that her young protégée had taken her advice to heart gave Stella a little swell of pride. "So . . . partner," she said, her voice a little husky, "what do you say our next step is?"

"I say we go bust into that Bluebird Motel and call out the bitch. It ain't right that she's got the sheriff'n them running around lookin' for her while she's layin' out by the pool sipping margaritas."

"All right, then, sounds like a plan."

"You know what, Stella," Chrissy added as she slipped a couple of juice boxes into a diaper bag, "I sure don't care to be lied to, you know what I mean?"

"Mmm-hmm, I surely do."

The proud little swell lodged in her chest expanded into something like a tidal wave of good feelings. Because there was a *we* in there—Chrissy was thinking like half of a team. Brandy lying to Stella was as good as her lying to the both of them; that's what the girl was saying. And that felt just about right to Stella.

Partners. Two of them, watching each other's backs. Stella figured there wasn't a whole lot that could stop them.

"To the Bluebird, then," she said, and grabbed hold of Tucker's arm as he dashed by. "Now, honey, Auntie Stella's going to need her shoes back."

But ten minutes later, Tucker was holding the clogs tightly in his little fists, sitting in his car seat in the back of Stella's Jeep, while Stella drove down Broadway with a pair of sparkly jeweled flip-flops on her feet.

Sometimes you just had to go with the flow.

SEVENTEEN

. . . .

Casey was a dusty little town fifteen minutes up the interstate and then another ten miles out Route 72, smack in the middle of nothing. It had been built up in the 1930s and enjoyed a nice tourist business when Harry S. Truman himself declared that the bubbling sulfuric waters had done all number of nice things for his various ailments. A handsome old hotel was set into a wooded hill above the springs, with wide green lawns and lovely gardens and beautifully tended paths and fountains.

The Bluebird Motel wasn't it.

The Bluebird was a tacky yellow-sided affair wedged between a 7-Eleven and a Cigarettes Cheaper on the edge of town. It had plastic geraniums planted at rigid intervals in fake-stone urns lining the stretch of pavement that served as a walkway along the rooms. It looked fairly clean, Stella gave it that much, but it was hard to tell from the parking lot.

"How we gonna do this?" Chrissy asked as they pulled into a spot near the double doors leading to registration. Inside they could see a bored-looking middle-aged fella watching the little television that sat on the counter, his lips parted slightly and moving, as though he was singing along with the program.

"Well, I guess we either bribe him or scare him," Stella says. "All's we need's Brandy's room number, way I see it."

Chrissy turned her wide lavender eyes on Stella indignantly. "I don't b'lieve I care for either of those options. Why don't you just let me handle this one."

Stella shrugged and got Tucker out of the car seat. He was in a sleepy baby-haze, his eyes fluttering closed and his chin drooly, and he was happy to snuggle in against her neck and hang on. He was sure getting heavy lately, with his second birthday looming in a few months, but Stella figured hauling him around might be a nice segue back to the Bowflex now that she had the doctors' go-ahead to return to her regular exercise routine.

Chrissy led the way toward the office, but she paused outside the door and adjusted her top, a sweet blue eyelet affair with a drawstring under the bust and little cap sleeves with just enough puff in them to suggest a bit of naughty schoolgirl.

She turned to show Stella. "Good?"

Whatever yanking and tugging Chrissy had effected had caused her breasts to swell up and over the soft cotton fabric of the top, and her blond curls looped and rested against her pale bare shoulders. "Well, now, I guess it's fine if you're aimin' to get your own show on the Playboy Channel."

Chrissy stuck her tongue out at Stella and pushed the door open.

The man behind the desk, who Stella could now see hadn't managed an even shave this morning—he'd missed a patch along his red-pocked jaw—was playing with a plastic top. He spun it with his thumb and finger and watched it spin down, as the television blared some talk show that featured angry guests lunging at each other and cussing. He turned down the volume as the top spun itself out and lay on its side; Stella could see that it read SOOKY'S PIZZA IS TOPS.

"Melp you," he mumbled, glancing their way. Then an interesting thing happened. His eyes opened wide and he jerked his head up and his palms smacked flat on the counter and he raised himself up into an approximation of good posture that might have been convincing if his narrow caved chest hadn't sloped down to such an impressive beer gut. His gaze took a quick circuit of Chrissy's face before landing with finality on her bosoms.

"Uh, melp you," he said again, just a touch louder, but with considerably more enthusiasm.

He didn't look at Stella and Tucker at all.

Chrissy sidled up to the counter and leaned into it so that her breasts had a nice stretch of Formica to rest on.

"We're here for Brandy Truax's bachelorette party," she said. "Oh, are these free?"

There was a basket of Starlite Mints on the counter, and Chrissy plucked out a candy and stuck one cellophane end between her teeth.

"Uh, yeah," the clerk said. Stella rolled her eyes and squinted at his name tag, which bore the unwieldy moniker HAL USTOR HOW CAN I PROVIDE EXCELLENT SERVICE TODAY?

Chrissy held the other end of the wrapper between her fingers and pulled gently. The mint spun lazily out of its wrapper and dropped into her waiting palm. Chrissy licked her lips and popped the candy in.

"Oh dear," she said, "do you have a trash can for the wrapper?"

"Sure, just—"

Hal held out a hand but Chrissy ignored it and came around the counter and bent over, peeping under Hal's desk and coincidentally practically unleashing her breasts right into Hal's trembling hands. He dropped the pen he was holding and swallowed hard.

"There it is!" Chrissy exclaimed, and tossed her trash in. She patted Hal's arm before returning to the other side of the counter. "Thanks, hon."

"The bachelorette party," Stella prompted. This was all very entertaining, but she figured it was about 500 percent overkill; Hal looked like he'd hand over the deed to the joint if Chrissy let him cop a feel. "You want to ask Hal here where they're having it?"

"Oh my yes," Chrissy said. "Now is it in one of your special event rooms or are we meeting at Brandy's?"

"Uh, I don't really know what—"

"He just works here," Stella said. "He's not going to know what-all they've got planned."

Chrissy turned a dismissive gaze her way. "Whatever, Mom."

"I can check. . . ." Hal tapped a keyboard in front of him a couple of times and frowned in concentration. "There's nothing in the conference room today."

"So we must be meeting in her room. Oh. You know what would be really cool? Is if we could surprise her. Have it all

ready by the time she and her sister get back from the salon."
Chrissy leaned across the counter and stage-whispered a few
inches from Hal's chapped lips. "I got this, like, naughty cake?
With the frosting like coming out the one end like . . . well, I
can't really say with *her* here. She's gonna watch the kid so
Brandy and me and the others can party."

"Oh," Hal managed. "That sounds fun."

"So I was thinking if you could let me in her room we
could, like, decorate it? I got all these streamers and shit and—
oh, don't worry, we're not gonna trash the room or nothing,
we're just having champagne first before we head over to my
friend Jill's. Hey, would you want to come? We need more *guys*."

A purplish flush crept out of the burgundy polyester collar
of Hal's shirt and across his face. He gulped air a couple of
times and Stella thought he might pass out. "Well, I'm not off
until three—"

"But that's perfect," Chrissy said. "We're gonna head out
to Jill's pool around then. Don't worry if you don't have a
swimsuit—it's gonna be suits *optional*."

"What . . . what did you say your friend's name was?" Hal
asked faintly, his fingers tapping spasmodically at the keys.

Three minutes later they were standing outside room 138,
Chrissy waving the card key smugly at Stella. "No bribing,"
she whispered. "No threatenin'."

"You're the master," Stella said sarcastically. "I'm just your
long-suffering mother who doesn't know anything. Though
before you go busting on in there, how about telling me what
you got planned next?"

"How about you beat the shit out of her? Ain't that what
you usually do?"

"I don't hit *women,*" Stella protested. Tucker was snoozing on her shoulder, snoring gently in her ear, and her arm was falling asleep under the weight. She was desperate to set him down.

"Well, that's just plain *sexist,* Stella."

"I also don't resort to violence when diplomacy will do," she said primly.

"Well, okay, Madam Diplomat, since you got it all figured out why don't you just go ahead and show me how it's done."

"Well, get on out of the way and I will."

"Okay, fine."

"Fine."

When the door swung open, they were both so started that they backed up and Stella almost dropped Tucker—but Brandy looked most surprised of all, with a towel wrapped around her head and a thick green paste spread all over her face.

"My, my, that's quite a look," Stella said as she gave Brandy a good shove that sent her toppling back into the room onto the bed. "Look at you, all dressed up and nowhere to go."

EIGHTEEN

. . . .

N ow we only got a couple hours 'fore this pool party we're s'posed to be at," Chrissy said as she followed Stella into the room and stood with her hands on her hips, glaring down at Brandy. "So you better git to talkin'."

"Who's she?" Brandy demanded as she glanced nervously over toward the TV stand. Stella tracked her gaze to where a pert white purse sat on top of the giant flat-panel television. "And what the hell are you doing with a *kid*?"

"This is my associate, Chrissy Shaw," Stella said, crossing the room and snatching the purse, "and her little boy, not that it's any of your business."

She upended the purse on the other bed. Along with a host of combs and lipsticks and a travel-size hair spray and a packet of condoms and a handful of loose change, a little steel .38 fell out.

"My, my, my," Stella said. "Change of plans."

Chrissy was at her side reaching for Tucker in a split second. They managed the hand-off without Tucker even batting a sleepy eye, and Stella grabbed one of the pillows and yanked the case off and slipped her hand into it before picking up the revolver, while Chrissy retreated watchfully to the other side of the room, where she sat in the upholstered chair and cradled Tucker close.

"Know what the secret of my success is, Brandy?" Stella asked. "I mean, one of 'em, anyway—well, it's improvisation. That means making do with what's around. This here pillowcase'll take care of prints, but I gotta admit I don't feel like I have so much control on the trigger, you know what I'm sayin'?"

"Stella, put that down," Brandy said. "No need to get all dramatic."

"You think *I'm* bein' dramatic? Let me tell you about dramatic. I thought we were *friends*. I thought we had a *deal*. I kept up my end. And then there you go, lying to me, taking advantage of my good nature, hiding out here in all this luxury while you send us on some wild goose chase through the boonies looking for a hole in the dirt that doesn't even exist. Why—it's enough to hurt my feelings."

"Well, I *told* you not to look for me," Brandy said. "So you can't blame me for that. If you would've just nailed Wil like I asked, then none a this would be a problem, now would it?"

Stella let loose an exaggerated sigh. She considered explaining that she didn't do contract killing. But she was also pleased that her reputation for violence, which was, after all, the cornerstone of her little side business, had spread so far and wide. No sense poking any holes in the illusion. What was it Warren Buffett said? *It takes twenty years to build a reputation and five minutes to ruin it.*

"You figure I was just gonna kill him for free?" she demanded instead. "Out of the goodness of my heart, or something? Look here, chicky, I don't do pro bono work."

Brandy had recovered most of her composure and stretched her legs out in front of her on the bed. She was wearing the hotel's white terry robe, and it fell open to reveal a length of smooth, creamy, cellulite-free thigh, which somehow irked Stella just about as much as being lied to. Though, given the rest of Brandy's cosmetic alterations, it was probably the result of lipo, not incredibly good genes.

"How old are you, anyway?" she demanded, dragging over the desk chair with her free hand and settling in next to the bed, gun trained on Brandy the whole time. With Chrissy sitting on the other side of the bed, it almost felt like they were visiting someone in the hospital. The slutty cousin no one liked, maybe.

"A lady doesn't tell," Brandy said primly. "How old are *you*?"

"None of your fucking business." Though there was more Stella would have liked to know—like how much work Brandy had done, how much it cost, if it hurt—she certainly hoped it had—and whether Goat had encouraged the whole thing.

If it took this kind of gussying up to snag a man, then Stella was pretty sure she wasn't the woman for the job. And not because she wasn't willing to exert her fair share of effort either.

Even good relationships took hard work, she knew that—all those *Redbook* articles made that clear. But if she made herself over into a dish like Brandy, she wouldn't be herself anymore. And while not so long ago that might have struck her as a not-terrible trade, back when being Stella Hardesty felt like a ticket to the Victim Olympics and her self-esteem had been stretched to its breaking point, in the last couple of years she had grown comfortable with the person she'd come to be, warts and all.

"You didn't ask *me*—I'm twenty-nine," Chrissy said. "But I'm kind of a genius, see, so I doubt you're going to be able to put anything over on me, Brandy Truax, even if you do got twenty-five years on me."

"Twenty-*five*?" Brandy sat up, features suddenly rigid. "You better get you some glasses, girl, 'cause I'm closer to bein' your *sister* than your mama's age."

"Dang, Stella," Chrissy said, "I know you were sayin' you thought she was rehabilitatable and all, but I gotta say I think you were mistaken this time. I say we go ahead and let Wil know where she's stayin' and let them work it out."

"You found him?" Brandy, cool as a tarted-up cucumber who'd been dipped in green goddess dressing, suddenly went shrill. A gob of facial mask dripped down off her cheek onto the white robe, but she didn't seem to notice. "You talked to Wil?"

Stella exchanged a glance with Chrissy. "Look here, cupcake, why do you think we bothered to hunt down your skanky ass in the first place? First off, I want you to tell me all about this ex of yours and why you're so dang sure he's tryin' to kill you. And if you can convince me of that, then I'll want everything else you got on this guy. Cell numbers, car, where he's likely to be hiding, all that."

"Listen, Stella—I told you what happened. He was *there* that night, at the track. He was the one put that woman in the ground and poured concrete over her."

"Maybe. Maybe not. Maybe there was two of them. Like he was working with a partner or something. Maybe he accidentally stumbled on someone else doing the job, and—"

"It was him, Stella—I know, 'cause of the *shoes*."

"Huh?"

"The shoes. Wil called me just as soon as the tornado went through, 'cause he heard on the radio that the snack shack got pulled right out of the ground. He figured it was just a matter of time until they found the body. He told me I had to get the shoes off of it. Said she had on black patent shoes—skimmers, you know, like them little ballerina flats everybody was wearin' a few years back?—and his prints was all over them."

"What—how the hell was he thinkin' you'd get the shoes? I mean, that's like *evidence*," Stella said.

Brandy sighed theatrically. "Stella," she said, enunciating slowly and clearly, "you got to remember I got a little extra that most females don't. And Wil knows that, he knows exactly what kind of effect I have on men. I mean, I can't even help it."

Stella caught Chrissy rolling her eyes heavenward, but the girl kept her mouth shut.

"Do tell," Stella said dryly.

"So Wil says to me, go on back to that ex-husband of yours—he never could stand it that I used to be married to the law—why, I think that's half the reason he got so dang intent on breakin' it all the time—anyway he says go and do whatever it takes to get them shoes."

"You're saying this man of yours was willing to let you get in another man's pants?" Stella said dubiously.

"Of course not, Stella—Wil knows I got all kinds a different techniques and whatnot. Why, I could have a man turned to putty in my hands without even lifting my skirt. I got *ethics,* you know."

Stella snorted. "Right. This hardened criminal boyfriend of yours figured the sheriff would hand over evidence if you just batted them fake eyelashes at him a few times—"

"It don't matter what he *thought,* anyway, Stella, 'cause he said if I *didn't* get the shoes and keep my mouth shut about it, he was going to kill me."

"He said he'd kill you. In those exact words."

"Yes, Stella, that's what he said. Well, he said he'd make me very, very sorry. What do you think that means? I mean, how much sorrier could I get than dead?"

"Mmm." Stella wasn't convinced. "Why would Wil of left the shoes on that body in the first place, if he knew his fingerprints were on them?"

"Well, 'cause he didn't think the body would ever get dug up. I mean, who could of foresaw a act of God like that twister?"

Chrissy sniffed. "Sloppy, if you ask me."

"And this whole time he's ordering you around, telling you to dig through the evidence locker for him, did he ever bother to explain why he killed that woman in the first place?"

At this, Brandy's composure threatened to give way for the first time. She bit her lip and glanced away. "He just said he didn't do it."

"Huh. Did he say, maybe, who *did* do it? Seein' as he didn't and all?"

"Well, now, Stella,—I didn't ask a whole bunch of questions. I was scared out of my mind. But what Wil said was he hadn't ever met her before and he was just burying her for a friend."

Stella snorted. "I've heard of watering plants for a friend when they go on vacation," she said. "I've heard of picking friends up at the airport and driving them to the doctor and loaning them yard tools. I ain't much heard of burying bodies they accidentally killed, though. That seems to go above and beyond, you ask me."

"Well, fuck you, Stella," Brandy said. "I'd like to seen you do any better, with some crazy man threatening to kill you. I don't guess you would have got him to confess much either!"

"She ain't afraid of crazy men," Chrissy offered. "I mean, look at her face. She got herself all cut to pieces by a crazy man and didn't never back down."

Stella touched her face automatically, fingertips going to the fading ridges and lines of scars. Nice as it was for Chrissy to defend her, it was a painful reminder of her ongoing beauty challenges.

"Look, no matter what Wil was telling you, letting him order you around was about the dumbest thing you could have done," she said crossly. "Seems like if you'd had any sense, you would of just told Goat what was going on and asked to be put in protective custody or whatever."

Or witness protection—that might not have been a bad idea; Stella didn't imagine Sawyer County would be much worse off if Brandy had been shipped off to, say, Wyoming to start a new life.

Brandy blinked as some green slime dripped into her eye. "Well, that was my plan B."

"Plan B? So when you showed up that night, when Goat and I were having a perfectly good dinner—"

"I saw he made you his mama's chicken," Brandy said. "He

made that for me, too—first time he cooked for me. Guess I better let you know, he ain't got much of a repertoire."

"Maybe for *you* he didn't. Could be he's learned a few new tricks," Stella shot back, and then regretted it—she'd been bluffing, and Brandy arched her thin brows skeptically.

"Mmm-hmm. Yeah, I guess, seein' as what you two got is so *special* and all. Anyway, I knew if I could just, ah . . . look, I don't want to hurt your feelings here, Stella, but if I could just get Goat where I wanted him, why, he'd just be ready to do anything for me, like always. He never could refuse me anything once he quit thinkin' with his head and got to thinkin' with—"

"I get the picture," Stella snapped. Though it wasn't a picture she much fancied lingering over. "But if you're so damn irresistible in the sack, how is it that I had to come spring you from a bedroom he locked you into?"

Brandy's scowl was evident even under all that goo. "All's I needed was a little time. I was wearin' Goat down, but then Wil got tired of waiting and blew up my car and that's when I knew the jig was up."

"The *jig*?" Chrissy interrupted. "What the hell kind of talk is that? You been watching too many old movies. Like the one you based your whole stupid come-get-me act on. Anyway, way I hear it, you were so trashed, you didn't even know it was your car got blown up. I heard you was tryin' to roast weenies out there."

Brandy glared hard first at Chrissy and then at Stella.

"Hey, don't look at me, sister," Stella said. "I only told it like it was. And you ain't exactly done a whole lot to get on my good side."

"I told you you can have Goat, okay? All I want now is for you to get rid of Wil."

"You still haven't explained exactly how you're gonna convince me you're telling the truth."

"What? I laid it all out for you. I ain't got no reason to lie—"

"You mean, other than all the lies you've already told, that's got the entire sheriff's department out searchin' for you? What if there was some kind of *real* emergency and you got Goat and all them off beatin' the bushes all over the county?"

"What, this ain't a real emergency? You want to wait until I truly am dead?" Brandy's voice had gone shrill. "You want a big old knife poking out of my chest? Maybe a couple of bullets in my forehead?"

At the moment, Stella thought those options didn't sound too bad. But the truth was that she really couldn't come up with much of a reason for Brandy to be lying. "Okay," she said, sighing heavily. "Give me what you got, and Chrissy and I'll go find him."

"And then you'll kill him."

"And then we'll turn him in. Let me explain how this works. I got a client who's gonna pay me to make sure her husband, who just happens to be innocent, doesn't fry for sticking a gal into a concrete grave. All I got to do is get the proof that somebody else did it, and then I collect my nice big fat paycheck and let the law take it from there."

"When you say 'the law,' what you really mean is Goat, right? Goat's gonna hunt him down like the mongrel dog he is?"

Stella drew a breath, giving herself a second to steady her nerves. "There's a team," she said. "A law enforcement team with support from up in Fayette. They'll book Wil in there, but I bet we're talking all kinds of federal laws here, so I imagine he'll end up doing time in Springfield. Though I don't know why it matters to you. Gone is gone. I know you want him dead and all, but he won't be getting out of prison any time soon, not after he makes a full confession."

"Well, he ain't gonna do *that,* Stella. What do you take him for, some kind a idiot?"

Stella was getting a little tired of arguing with this woman. Her sassy mouth was bad enough, but the fact that she looked better covered with green mud than Stella did after a full-tilt beauty assault—and she'd shared carnal knowledge, and plenty of it, with the man Stella had in her sights—was just about too much.

"What do you take *me* for, Brandy, some kind of *amateur*? Believe me, I've made plenty of men do things they didn't plan on doing. The ones come in with the most confidence—why, after we go a few rounds, they're generally the ones that end up whimpering like kicked puppies. Trust me, when I'm done with your boyfriend, he'll be begging to confess to selling swampland and rigging elections on top of doing that gal at the track."

"I gotta tell you, Brandy, it's just *painful* to look at you," Chrissy cut in, rubbing circles on Tucker's back as she held him. "With all that nasty shit on your face. How about you go wash it off and put on something decent? 'Fore I lose my breakfast."

Brandy gave Chrissy a withering glance as she slid her way off the bed. She walked carefully past Stella, clutching the robe tight around her, and pulled a small, slinky pink garment out of a drawer, along with a few matching silky underpinnings. She minced to the bathroom with her chin in the air and slammed the door behind her.

"Man, she just don't give up anything, huh?" Chrissy asked. "Acts like her farts don't stink."

"Just a cover-up. She's nervous. And she oughtta be. I'm not leaving until I get everything she knows about Wil Vines, right down to the birthmarks on his hairy ass."

"You know, Stella," Chrissy said thoughtfully. "I'm not sure she's really all that *afraid* of him. I mean she's kinda nervous right now, yeah, seein' as he blew up her car and all, but I think what she really is is *mad* at him. And hurt."

"Huh? Chrissy, they been broke up for six months. And she's trying to get back with Goat."

"No, see, you ain't thinkin' it through. She came here to Prosper 'cause she *wanted* something from the sheriff. That's different from hopin' to get down his drawers. I mean, I guess a gal can go after both, kinda like with me and Larry, but just think how quick she was to give him up. What was it she said to you on the phone?"

I guess you can have him now. The words came back with a delicious little thrill. "Well, but that's 'cause she thought she'd be dead."

"She wasn't in no hole. She was in the Holiday Fucking Inn here, eatin' bonbons."

"Only 'cause she was afraid Wil would find her."

"Maybe, a little."

The door to the bathroom opened and Brandy came out. With the towel unturbaned from the woman's head, Stella was startled to see that her hair, unsprayed and unteased and un-pouffed, was as flat and dull as a mutt's fur after a dip in the lake, plastered over her ears in a style that didn't do a whole lot for her face, which on careful examination was a trifle too round with a bit too much room between her small eyes and her hairline.

There were purple smudges under her eyes, and her lips were nearly colorless. Even her hoochie little body looked a bit forlorn stuffed hurriedly into the pink top and shorts, unaccessorized, as it was, without the benefit of bangles and platform shoes to draw the eye away from a poochy midsection and a set of round hips that had seen just about as much middle age as Stella's own.

"Well, go ahead, take a good look," Brandy grumbled. "'Cause you ain't never gonna see *this* again. I don't *ever* go out without my face on."

Stella did, enjoying the sight plenty. As a matter of fact, it just might be that Brandy's hips were lumpier than her own. And that butt—*flat*. Decidedly flat. Like, you could iron on it.

And, really, what man likes a flat butt?

"So how about we get going on the information sharing, Truax?" Stella said with considerably more cheer than she was feeling just a few minutes ago.

"Now, look here," Brandy said, perching on the edge of the other bed. "I don't know that you have to go messing the man up, all right? I mean, no need to go overboard."

"What's your problem, Brandy?" Chrissy demanded. "Here we are, ready to take this problem permanently off your hands, so you can go back to whatever pathetic little life you were leadin' in Versailles, and all of a sudden you want us to play nice with the guy who's been trying to kill you?"

"I didn't say be *nice,* exactly, I just don't know if it's necessary—"

"You still love him!" All of a sudden Chrissy snapped her fingers. "Stella, that's it—Brandy here still loves that no-good man of hers. Don't you?"

"I never said—"

"You didn't have to. I mean, look at you. You're all twitchy like, worried we're gonna mark up his pretty face. What did that neighbor lady tell you, Stella?"

"She said he was charming," Stella said doubtfully. "And easy on the eyes, though that's the kind of thing that has a fair bit to do with the beholder—"

"Aw, come on, Stella. I been married to a no-good man, and you have, too. We don't neither of us need to go pretending we don't know what it's like to fall for a fella that'd just as soon bust your lip as kiss you."

"Wil ain't *never* hit me," Brandy said hotly. "He was always gentle."

"Holy Christ, Brandy, he tried to blow you up, and he killed some poor woman—hell, he was probably screwin' her, too. Just how much punishment do you need to take from a man, anyway?"

"He ain't never messed around on me, neither." Brandy set her lips in a thin line and crossed her arms and fumed at the two of them. "And if he did kill that gal, there had to be some good reason."

"There's never a good reason to kill a woman!" Call it a hot button—Stella felt her blood surge in her veins.

"Trust me, I've messed around on a lot a guys and a whole bunch of them probably think the same thing, sister," Chrissy said. "Just 'cause you don't want to know it, don't mean it didn't happen."

"Shut up. You don't know him. Not like I do."

"And yet you're willing to let me kill him," Stella said. "You're one confusing, crazy, mixed-up kind of sister."

"Well, yeah—if you kill him *quick*. Hell, that'd be better than locking him up. He's a—a wild spirit. You can't fence that in." A little hiccupping sob followed this declaration and Brandy dotted her eyes with a tissue.

"Oh Lord, as I live and breathe, now I think I've heard it all," Chrissy said. She picked up a TV channel guide from the nightstand and fanned herself and Tucker with it. "I think you may be just about the dumbest person I ever met. And trust me, I know all about dumb—I've dated it, married it, and had its baby. Difference between you and me is, I *learn* from my mistakes."

"Well, maybe I just won't tell you anything, you think you're so smart. You go ahead and figure it out yourself," Brandy said petulantly. "I don't have to tell you his cell phone number or nothing else besides either. Why, go ahead and shoot me, Stella, if you want to. Only I don't think you got it in you."

It wasn't the smartest thing to say, but at least Brandy got one thing right: Stella couldn't shoot a woman, at least one as pathetic and self-destructive as Brandy.

But after Stella handed the gun over to Chrissy and ex-
cused herself and went and got her portable intimidation kit
from the Jeep, and got Brandy strapped down with a couple of
custom-made, chamois-lined restraints, and explained just
how she planned to shave her head bald with a wicked-sharp
razor, Brandy turned out to be a lot more cooperative than
any of them expected.

NINETEEN

. . . .

The new plan was simple enough: First, call off the search so the law enforcement staff could get back to looking out for the welfare of the citizens, in addition to locking up innocent civic employees like Neb Donovan. Next, find Wil Vines and ask him why he killed poor Laura Cassel. Then suggest he turn himself in . . . and pound his ass into a pulp if he wasn't feeling cooperative. And then have a nice celebration dinner with the Donovans, and work out a payment plan that would help keep Stella afloat for the next few months.

Only . . . Stella and Chrissy hit a snag right about step two.

The visit to the sheriff's department went as well as it could, considering the sheriff himself wasn't there. Since he'd led a search team around the county's backwaters all through the night and into the morning, Detective Simmons had finally sent Goat home to get some sleep. Simmons, on the other hand, had caught a few hours of shut-eye back at the motel, and when Stella and Chrissy dragged a much-subdued Brandy through the doors with them, she was sitting in Goat's office, looking rested—if no more friendly than on Stella's prior visits. Tucker, bright-eyed after the nap that started in the motel room and continued on the ride over, wiggled to be put down and then scampered over to Irene's desk and helped himself to the bowl of Tootsie Rolls she kept there, holding just one of Stella's clogs pressed to his chest.

"Well, hi, girls. That Tucker's getting more precious every day," Irene said. Then she lowered her voice and leaned over her counter. Apparently Simmons still hadn't learned to play nice with the help, because Irene shot a significant look in the direction of the detective. "Now they got me babysitting the Wicked Witch of the North. Who you got there?"

"This here's the murder victim," Stella said. "Brandy Truax. Only she never really was in any old hole. Ain't that right, girlfriend."

"I guess," Brandy mumbled.

"You're talking to a lady member of the sheriff's department," Chrissy said, slugging Brandy on the shoulder. "Show some respect, and speak up."

"I said, I guess, *ma'am*."

"Well, my heavens. Nice to meet you. I suppose I best get Simmons in here," Irene said, and tapped the intercom, causing Simmons to start and then practically leap out of her chair. Irene might not like the woman, but she was passionate about justice. She bent and spoke into the speaker. "Detective Simmons, we got a situation."

Stella was secretly pleased that Goat wouldn't be taking Brandy's confession—no sense accidentally setting off any confused misdirected chivalrous feelings in the man. But as Daphne Simmons strode out of Goat's office, sharp nose jutting for-

234

ward like she was scenting blood, Stella managed to feel just a bit sorry for the gal.

"Brandy, may I introduce Detective Simmons, who's been kind enough to come down from Fayette to help put a stop to all the murdering that's been taking place around here," she said politely. "Detective, this is Miz Brandy Truax."

"I suppose you know that fakin' a kidnapping's a serious offense," Simmons said, not even sporting Stella a thank-you or a nod. "You've had my team running all over the place in unfavorable and dangerous conditions for hours."

All that running and digging, Stella reflected, and yet, Simmons looked surprisingly fresh. No creases in her uniform pants—no dirt caked on her shoes. She'd had the rest of them on the run while, for all Stella knew, she'd been playing solitaire on Goat's computer. Stella didn't think much of that kind of comportment—it wasn't any kind of teamwork that she knew about.

And—was that lipstick on the gal? And wasn't there some kind of fancy smell emanating off her—a floral kind of spicy perfumey smell? Now that was low—gussying up for a man in the middle of a murder investigation.

Stella tried very hard to ignore the fact that she'd done the same thing. Still, encountering yet another rival added more confusion to the situation—she found her allegiances slipping around like greased pigs. Suddenly Brandy didn't seem quite so bad.

"I'm sure you'll cut Miz Truax some slack, seein' as she has valuable information for you on the crime," she said.

Simmons pressed her lips together. "There's *protocols* that we got to follow."

"Guess our work here is done," Chrissy said, and gave Stella's sleeve an ungentle tug. She turned a winning smile on Irene. "Sure was nice seein' you again, Miz Dorsey."

"I believe you and I are going for a drive up to Fayette, Ms. Truax," Simmons said, glowering like if it was up to her, she'd throw the whole bunch of them into the paddy wagon. "Y'all watch her for a minute while I get my things."

When she was back out of earshot, rooting around in Goat's office, Irene leaned over the desk and said to Stella: "He ain't at home, you know."

"Uh . . . who?" Stella felt the color flooding her cheeks.

"Goat, that's who. Simmons sent him home, but he called me not twenty minutes later, sayin' he was going out on the lake and to call him if anything happened. So if you need to talk to him . . . or something . . ."

Irene waggled her eyebrows suggestively, and Stella realized something kind of funny.

She owed Daphne Simmons, ball-busting second-in-charge up in Fayette, heir apparent to the job of Sawyer County Sheriff, a debt of thanks. Much as she hated to admit it, before the woman had come to town and cast her line for Goat, Irene had only ever been polite and generally friendly to Stella—and if she'd noticed any sparks between her and Goat, she'd never done much to fan the romantic flame.

Now, though, presumably because she'd seen the alternative—and didn't fancy the thought of a romance between her boss and the interloper from Fayette—Irene was tossing cookies at Stella quick as she could catch them.

"He usually puts in at Calvin Wallach's place down near Barton Beach. You know where that is?"

Stella knew. In fact, she made good time, after she sent Chrissy and Tucker home with instructions to see if she could dig up anything further on Wil Vines's possible whereabouts.

It was only about twenty miles down to the silty, brackish branch of the lake where the Wallachs had built a low-floating dock just perfect for Goat to put his kayak in. On the way, Stella called Jelloman, who reported that Noelle had arrived and got her laundry started, and Todd had wandered over. Sabine had gotten off her shift at the Freshway, and the four of them were playing poker.

"Boy's catching on quick," Jelloman said. "Gonna teach 'em acey-deucy next. We're betting that jar of change I found in your pantry."

Stella had been tossing her spare change in an empty peanut butter jar for a couple of years. It was the start of a savings plan for a much-dreamed-about trip to New York. "I want it all back," she said. "Plus a cut for the house."

Jelloman laughed. "I b'lieve you're forgettin' who's cookin' your dinner tonight."

Goat's battered truck was parked in a choke of weeds. Down by the water was a rowboat, turned upside down and tethered to a stake pounded into the dirt shore. Stella managed to flip it over and, after a moment's hesitation, slipped off Chrissy's bejeweled sandals and tossed them into the boat, in an effort to keep them mud-free. Then she clambered in and pushed off and rowed until her shoulders started to ache, especially the one that had been shot, which still throbbed now and then. The effort got her a couple hundred yards out into the lake.

Only then did she call him.

"Stella," he said. "What a surprise. If you're calling to

gloat, don't bother. Simmons called, so I know about Brandy. Guess I should thank you for hauling her in."

There was a reason Stella had waited until she was in the middle of a lake to call. The way she figured it, Goat would tell her not to worry, to go on home and let him and his department hunt down Wil. And that would never do. For one thing, if Goat brought him in, she couldn't in good conscience ask for full payment from the Donovans. And for another, the minute he kicked her out of the investigation, she'd be off his radar as he focused all that steely-blue-eyed concentration on the case. And she wasn't quite ready to go gently out of the picture.

"Yeah," she said, "only I got a problem."

Stella didn't have much room for helpless in her life anymore. It hadn't worked out too well as a strategy in the past, and now she had to be strong and capable for all her clients. So it was with a big heap of misgivings that she picked up the oar and threw it as far as she could away from the boat.

"What kind of problem?"

"I'm stuck." Stella sighed, shut her eyes, and pictured Goat's long sun-browned arms, all bulked up from paddling. "I need you to come and get me."

TWENTY

. . . .

W hat did you think you were doing, coming after me like that?" Goat demanded. It had been a delicate operation, getting himself out of the kayak and into the front of the rowboat. He'd nearly fallen in, which probably wouldn't have done much for his mood; as it was, he had Stella holding on to the kayak, which trailed along behind as Goat stroked powerfully toward the Wallachs' dock.

"It's that dang cell service," Stella said. "I couldn't get through. I called and called, and then I figured I might as well come on out here."

"And yet Irene got me just fine. Go figure."

Stella shrugged and focused her attention on a dragonfly that was flitting around beside the boat. It was a warm afternoon for September, banks of cattails along the shore nodding gently in lazy breezes, and fish occasionally glinted rainbows near the surface, competing with the sunlit flashes Chrissy's shoes sent kaleidoscoping around the boat.

"Look," Goat finally said as they approached the shore. "I guess I know what this is about."

That was a surprise, since Stella herself didn't really understand.

"We got your boy in the lockup, and now it looks like we got another strong suspect—" He held up a hand to stop Stella from speaking. "—and I ain't gonna confirm or deny what we got on this Wil Vines, either, so don't ask."

Shoes—had to be the shoes, unless Brandy didn't know what she was talking about.

"That Cory Layfield of yours didn't pan out," Goat continued. "Mike's following up, but Layfield's a nurse's aid over at a hospice in Rolla these days. He told Mike that while he was taking care of his sick uncle he realized he was called to work with the sick. He offered to drive right on down and help out however he could, just as soon as he got off his shift. I mean, I could have Mike go measure his foot if it makes you feel better, I guess, but . . ."

Stella felt her face flame with embarrassment. "No, I don't guess that's necessary right now."

"Yeah. So the way I see it, you're here to make your case for your boy Neb. But I got to tell you, Stella, you know that it's gonna come down the way it always does, and that's just purely on the facts, and no amount of you spinning it up one way and down the other is going to make a damn bit of difference if—"

"I *know* all that—"

Stella couldn't stand to hear any more. She usually loved seeing Goat all worked up into one of his justice frenzies, seeing as it made the veins in his strong arms stand out in a most becoming way, and set his hard jaw in an even firmer line than usual, but the idea that he would think, even for one minute, that she would try to influence the outcome of a case—

—well, if that's what the man thought, then he clearly didn't get her. That was the thought that arrived in a mini-huff, an indignant self-righteous little push-back against the assault on her principles, her *honor,* for heaven's sake, and she wasn't about to stand for it.

Except . . . he was sort of a little bit right. She *did* make a habit of flouting the policing and judicial and corrective systems and doing everything her own damn way. She did it all the time, in fact. And she wasn't sorry.

The law had procedures in place for when one human being, generally of the male variety, decided to start taking out his frustrations on a weaker and less powerful person, generally his wife or girlfriend. Stella had read that an astonishing third of all women get abused at some point in their adult lives, a fact that helped explain why she never had a shortage of clients.

The law made it clear that the abusers should be prevented and punished. The procedures laid out exactly *how* they should be prevented and punished. There were training programs and guidelines and protocols and hotlines and websites and shelters. But even with all those resources, the abusers kept on doing their thing.

There were just too many things that could go wrong. Responding officers couldn't convince terrified women to press charges. Husbands learned how to hurt without leaving marks. Men got locked up and came out angrier than when they went in. Paperwork got misfiled, court dates got delayed, wealthy

defendants hired attorneys and poor ones honed their fury waiting for their court-appointed defenders to look at their cases.
Men skipped their court-ordered counseling; or they went
and the lessons didn't stick; or they cleaned up their act for a
while, until the day when the woman in front of them was once
again just too tempting a target for all their frustration.

And they kept on hurting. They kept on and on until someone even craftier and angrier and more determined came along
and made them stop. Someone who worked outside the law,
who was unfettered by red tape, who judged for herself just how
far to go to make sure that this time was the last time. Someone
whose toolbox included pain and terror and intimidation and
who answered to no one but herself.

This was a conversation Stella had never really had, in de-
tail, with Goat. And she wasn't exactly sure she wanted to. Even
if she was sure that he would never interfere with her work.
Even if he gave her his blessing.

Because despite the warts and flaws and setbacks in the system, and all its members who did a terrible or mediocre or
not-quite-good-enough job, there were those like Goat who
got up every morning and put on the uniform and went out
into the world with every intention of cleaning up messes and
straightening out jams and reeling in the misguided and locking
up the really bad ones. And Stella didn't figure she wanted to
put a dent in any of that. All of it was good. All of it was worthy.

Not all of it was Goat, of course. There were plenty of
deputies and sheriffs and police officers and lawmen out there,
perfectly hardworking nice gents—probably thousands of
them—who *didn't* get her all fluttery on the insides.

"I know all that," she repeated with a little less conviction.

Goat gave her a funny look and dipped his oar into the water a couple of times, moving the boat far more effortlessly than Stella had managed, and eased it up in through the water weeds and bumped it gently against the dock.

But there was still something else that had to be said. Something completely unrelated to the law enforcement situation. One more thing, if Stella was going to ever get the lid on the hurting envious corner of her heart. A sense of urgency stirred up Stella's breath as Goat reached out a strong hand for the edge of the dock and set a variety of words tumbling to her lips, though none of them seemed like the right ones.

"Wait up a sec," she said. "Just—Brandy—was she—is she—?"

It wasn't enough that Brandy had finally given Stella the blessing to go after Goat, that her interest in the man turned out to be entirely hatched from self-serving instincts.

Stella needed to know if Goat still wanted her.

"Who left who?" she finally blurted out.

Not exactly the question she'd meant to ask, but it would get the job done, seeing as it got straight to the heart of what had gone wrong between the two of them.

Goat slowly tucked the oar back along the bottom of the boat. He reached past Stella to take hold of the kayak, his arm brushing her thigh and sending little hot sensations along her skin. The kayak floated atop the surface of the water as if it were no more substantial than a paper boat, and Goat lifted it, dripping sparkly water droplets into the boat, and set it securely up onto the dock.

Then he sat and regarded her with his elbows on his denim-clad knees, long forearms crossed casually, looking like an aging Ralph Lauren model with a taste for trouble. The boat rocked against the silt for a moment, then floated out away from the dock, drifting with the breeze down the shoreline away from the Wallachs' place.

"Strange times, those were," Goat finally said, so softly that Stella had to lean a little closer to hear. "She left me. And ain't I a dang fool for letting it drag on so long . . . Stella, that was one show that was over before it even got started. Brandy, well, she has a knack for getting herself into jams."

"So I noticed."

"Yeah. See, a few years back—hell, must be about five years now . . . I got called out to a domestic disturbance over on the far side of town. I get there and there's this skinny little gal's pulled a knife on her husband, who had to weigh about three times what she did, but she had him backed into a corner shaking like a leaf, and she was screamin' her head off how she was goin' to cut off his balls and serve 'em for dinner."

"Brandy did *that*?"

"No, not Brandy—her sister. Her estranged sister now. But back then, Brandy was coming off a patch of bad luck, and she needed a place to stay, and she was sleeping on their sofa—until the day her sister kicked her out for calling the cops on her."

"And you . . ." *Rescued her.* Stella didn't even need a road map—she could see that one coming.

Goat sighed and looked out across the lake, where a bunch of kids were splashing around in inner tubes. "All I did, that night, was to buy her a cup of coffee. Out of the machine, at the station. We were trying to line up temporary housing for her, and I got her this crappy cup of coffee, and she's sitting there in a folding chair looking around the station over in Versailles, and if you've never been in that building, let me tell you it's nothing much to look at, smells like a locker room and looks like—well, a prison, I guess. Anyway, Brandy looks around and she gets this little smile on her face and she says, 'Is it always this quiet?'—and it's like midnight by then, so of course it's quiet, it's just the night guys, and she goes on to tell me how much she misses having a little peace and quiet 'cause she's been bouncing from one friend's couch to another, trying to get her life straightened out."

"So . . . you married her."

Goat flashed a rueful little smile. "Not *right* away. It took me about six weeks."

"Holy fuck, Goat," Stella said. "I mean . . . have there been others? A whole string of women who were down on their luck, maybe you dragged 'em out of homeless shelters and halfway houses and turned 'em into brides?"

"Hey, I never said I had any smarts when it came to women." His smile this time was genuine, if a little embarrassed. "But no, Brandy was the only one who—who took me for the long ride. Not that I'm blaming her."

"Seems like she might of earned a little of the credit for the mess—don't you think? I mean, is she tryin' to bleed you dry, what with the lawyers and what-all?"

"That? Nah." Goat managed a dry chuckle. "I ain't exactly got a whole lot to fight over, in case you haven't noticed. Brandy, she just needs the drama, plain and simple. Sometimes I think she stirs things up when she's lonely—she's always got to have something going on. That's what she left me over, if you want to know—not six months after we were married—there just wasn't a whole lot of excitement to be had waiting for me to get home at night."

"But you didn't get separated for twenty-two months—" Stella realized her mistake and shut her mouth, fast.

Goat regarded her with amusement. "I wonder how you figured that out, anyway," he said. "Guess there's a whole lot of things I don't know about you, Stella Hardesty. You're a lady of mystery."

Silence continued to seem like the best course, so Stella merely nodded, and picked at a loose thread at the edge of her shorts.

"Well, she took off after six months, but I didn't file the separation papers until I was sure she had a good job, one that could pay all her bills," Goat said. "Call me a sucker, but—"

"Sucker."

Goat stared at her for a minute, eyebrows raised, and then he laughed. Just a short laugh, but a heartfelt one, deep and rich and infectious, and Stella felt herself smiling for the first time in a long day.

"You know, Dusty," Goat drawled, giving her a long, leisurely once-over with those big old blue eyes. "That's what I just can't seem to get over, about you. The way you give me a hard time every chance you get. I haven't known too many women who are up for that particular challenge."

"Well—" Stella didn't know exactly quite what to say to that. "Huh."

It would have been nice if he'd said that's what he *liked* about her. Or what he couldn't *resist* about her. Or something like that.

But get over . . . measles was something you *got over*. Bad breakups. Hell, even shaving rashes.

"You know," she said as casually as she could, "that night, when we had the tornadoes—when you fixed me dinner—when Brandy showed up—"

"Yep." Goat sighed, and the smile melted out of his face. Oh—so not a particularly good memory, then.

But Stella soldiered on. "The thing is, I know it ended up—well, a little confusing, and all. But—see, I never got around to thanking you."

Goat shot her a glance—just a quick one, that met her gaze and then flashed away again. "Well, I don't know that you had much to thank me for," he said gruffly. "You barely got a glass of wine down—and as I recall, we managed to turn your dinner pretty much inedible—"

"It was delicious," Stella said hastily. "I mean, once I got the pepper scraped off."

"That's nice of you. But I didn't exactly show you the kind of time that . . . well, that I hoped to."

There was a silence then, and Stella noticed that they'd left the Wallachs' place far enough behind them that the dock was a mere smudge on the shore. She thought of and discarded a dozen different remarks. *Try me again,* was what she really wanted to say. *Just give me another try.*

It was dumb. It was pathetic. The woman she used to be, the one who was afraid to speak up, afraid to fight for what she wanted, that woman was dead—Stella'd buried that old self and replaced it with the new version, who said what needed saying and did what needed doing and slapped her own self on the back at the end of the day if there wasn't anyone else around to tell her she done good. This new self didn't sigh and whine when things needed to happen—she went out and *made* them happen.

And yet for all her grit, all her hard-won confidence, all her determination . . . here she was in a boat with the man who kept her up nights, and he couldn't get away even if he wanted to, and she couldn't seem to say the first thing about how much she wished he'd give them another chance.

Stella blinked hard and bit her bottom lip. Okay. No more. Time to be a big girl. She opened her eyes and drew a breath and fixed in her mind exactly what to say and said it—

"I'd like—"

"Would you—?"

And then they were laughing, both of them speaking at once, the tension of the moment released in the stumbled syllables, the fears and the hesitation lifting off them like dandelion fluffs carried away by the breeze.

"Go ahead," Goat said. "What were you going to say?"

"No, it's okay. You first."

And then there was a ringing from Goat's pocket, the shrill of a no-nonsense old-fashioned ringtone, and as Goat answered it, Stella thought *shit, shit, shit,* it figured cell phones worked just fine out here where only the ducks and the catfish were around to hear them, when she couldn't get a signal on half the country roads where a person could have an honest-to-God emergency.

Goat said a few words, asked for clarification, and said a terse good-bye.

"Well." He shouldered the oar again and got them turned around and headed back to the dock at an even faster clip than earlier. "Enough jawin' for one day, I guess. Got a suspect on the loose."

"They found out where Wil was?"

"Not hardly." Goat refused to look at her as he plowed the oar into the water with what Stella had to think was a little more force than was strictly necessary. "Your boy Neb's gone and busted out of jail."

TWENTY-ONE

. . . .

I t was probably not to her credit, Stella reflected later, that
her first thought had been *There goes any chance of getting laid
in this lifetime,* and her second was that the Donovans would
never be able to pay her now that Neb was on the lam.

At least it took Goat long enough to row them back to the
dock that she got most of the story out of him.

"Un-fucking-believable," he said, clearly disgusted, explaining that the HVAC system in the jail corridors had been making an annoying knocking sound, and when Neb heard the
staff complaining that maintenance wouldn't be in until Monday, he offered to track down the problem. Which worked
great, with Halpern and a few other corrections officers handing him tools as he stood on a desk with his head up in the
ceiling ductwork.

The problem came when Simmons heard about Neb's capable handiwork and figured she might as well have Neb take
a look at the phone problem, which had spread from the visitor booths to the line going into her office.

"'He was right there under the desk,'" Goat quoted Simmons saying. "Well, guess he wasn't, after all."

"You mean he just walked out of there?"

"Evidently. Though Simmons says she never left her office for a minute."

"Huh. I guess he must of went through the walls or something."

The stony expression on Goat's face conveyed his doubts, and they didn't speak again until he glided the rowboat into the dock. After dragging the boat up on the shore, he helped Stella out with a curt nod and a steadying hand at her waist, which gave her a passing thrill as he picked his kayak up off the dock and upended it over his shoulder as though it weighed next to nothing. At least Goat offered up a fine view of his hard-muscled back and biceps as he lashed the kayak on top of his truck, before muttering a distracted good-bye and driving off with his flasher on.

Stella had a long solo drive back to Prosper, stuck behind a cement truck, to wonder where Neb had got to after his bold prison break. Donna answered her cell phone after a couple of rings, only to explain in a breathless voice that she couldn't talk, because she had biscuits in the oven, an excuse so lame, Stella figured what her friend really had was a jailbird husband with an appetite for something special to take the edge off his prison experience.

Back in her own kitchen, Stella gave the four-layer dip—so sue her, she couldn't find any guacamole or olives or green onions in the fridge, and who really needed seven layers anyway—a final sprinkling of Tabasco and carried it into the living room, where Jelloman had already set out a big platter of fried chicken and buttermilk slaw. He and Noelle and Sabine had been cooking since their poker marathon ended with Todd taking the entire haul. Todd was now lying on the couch with his feet dangling over the end, looking at a Journeys catalog and trying to figure out which ridiculous pair of overpriced skate shoes he was going to spend her New York money on.

So that was the good part. That, and Tucker careening through the house with yet another pair of Stella's clogs—this one pistachio green, a fashion error, so she was thinking she'd just let him keep them—singing "lay-uh, lay-uh" at the top of his lungs. So what if he'd picked it up from Jelloman, who was a huge Clapton fan and had played that "Layla" tune once too often. Chrissy sang along, shimmying around the room, while Larry sat in Ollie's old La-Z-Boy staring at her across the room like he couldn't believe his luck.

Oh, and Sherilee had stopped by for a quick visit with her girls before they headed out for their special evening at the Fall Fest that was going on over at the Senior Center. That part was pretty good, too, when Jelloman bellowed, "Show her what I taught you, boy," and Todd executed a perfect riffle shuffle on a deck of cards and his mom's eyes went very wide and she looked like she was going to blow a gasket but instead she laughed, accepted a glass of wine, and quit admonishing the girls to stop climbing all over Mr. Nunn. Seeing as Mr. Nunn, a few Pabst Blue Ribbons into the evening, allowed as how he hoped his own daughter would provide him with a few grand-kids as fuckin' precious as these some day.

Stella paused in the entrance to the living room, dip balanced against her hip, and realized she wouldn't trade a single soul here for anything. It would be nice to have her parents here to see their granddaughter all grown up, to see all the friends Stella had found to build a family. She was doing okay, right here in Prosper, with her motley collection of loved ones.

And to hell with Wil.

Well. Maybe not all the way to hell, because Brandy said he was innocent, and—Stella was getting a little fuzzy on all the details, but if she understood Irene correctly from earlier, Brandy was on her way over to Iowa to stay with a friend from her waitress days, Goat having convinced Daphne that there wasn't really an upside to tossing his ex into the prison cell so recently vacated by Neb—she mostly believed the woman.

But she'd given the Wil hunt her best shot, at least from one thirty, when she polished off the last of a Personal Pan Pizza and a side of Buffalo Burnin' Hot wings from Pizza Hut in a Goat-mortification-fueled binge, until six thirty when she finally had to admit to herself that she was out of ideas, and came back home to discover that the party had started without her.

Jelloman lumbered over, chewing delicately at the end of a celery stalk, and settled himself on the couch next to her. That didn't leave a whole lot of leftover room, but the effect was cozy. Stella leaned on into the arm Jelloman flung around her. She breathed deep and detected a note of her dad's old favorite Brut cologne, and snuggled in a little farther.

"Where's Sabine?" she asked, yawning. The Crock-Pot was bubbling with the gal's famous coq au vin wieners.

"Aw, she just had to go tie up a few things," Jelloman said. "She'll be along."

Stella started to wonder if any of the things Sabine had to tie up included her side bets, the stable of younger guys who she kept around for amusement, but then her mind wandered back to her own closely held interests and she sighed.

"I spent the day runnin' around after a medium-bad guy," she murmured into Jelloman's flannel shirt. He'd left the vest slung over one of her kitchen chairs, the better to roll up his sleeves and cook. "Or maybe a mostly bad guy. I mean, we got us a dead body, that's got to be bad."

"I'd sure think so," Jelloman said. Mixed in with his cologne was a pleasant whiff of hemp smoke, like a top note of tobacco. "I don't cotton to killin'. There's got to be a better way. I mean, no offense, you did what you had to do and all."

Jelloman had never given Stella any trouble about the few murders she had under her belt, the news coverage of which was vague about just who shot and sliced up whom in the mess by the lake, but naturally everyone had heard a version of the truth by now.

She thought about sharing the remainder of her frustrations, how she and Chrissy had visited every known hangout they could connect with Wil. They'd cruised along the few streets where a person could pick up a fix as easy as ordering takeout lo mein, anything from prescription painkillers to the homegrown that competed with Jelloman's extra-fine custom hybrid weed. They'd contacted every motel and rooming house in Prosper, not to mention the neat little brick ranch where enterprising ladies entertained gentlemen callers for profit, in case their man Wil was cooling his heels locally while he threatened and stalked Brandy. They even checked in with the last few citizens who'd reported break-ins and thefts from their homes. But they came up empty-handed, and Stella just didn't feel like talking about it.

She also considered telling Jelloman what she knew about Laura Cassel. The picture that Goat had painted for her in the bar, of a loved and carefree young woman, which Stella now couldn't get out of her mind.

But it would all take so much explaining, and Stella couldn't quite come up with the energy to share it with her old friend. Jelloman threw an arm around Stella and pulled her in close, and if she pretended, for a few moments, that she was six again and it was Uncle Horace who held her and made her feel like everything really would be all right, well, she figured Jelloman wouldn't mind.

In the end, Stella spent a happy hour watching her daughter and Chrissy try to teach Melly and Glory how to do the Homey Twist, Sherilee getting in on the action and shaking her hips with a skill and style Stella would never have figured her for. *Find Sherilee a man,* Stella inscribed on her mental to-do list before letting her lids slide down until her world was reduced to a cozy cocoon that felt a little like having her daddy's arms around her, carrying her when she fell asleep on the way home from the fair.

Thank you, Big Guy, she remembered to think, sending the sentiment spinning heavenward just before she gave up and let the dream team in for the night.

TWENTY-TWO

. . . .

Stella had been down this particular path before, so she knew better than to fall for the lovely sensation of something cool and smooth prodding her in the temple.

It would be so easy to believe it was Goat, brushing her hair out of her face before he bent in for a firecrackin' kiss, and go back to sleep with that little extra embellishment sparkling up her dreams, but there was the matter of her breath, bouncing off her nest of sheets and reminding her how she'd spent the night before.

You shouldn't of had that last one, her breath announced, dry and cakey and just plain nasty as she inhaled it. And: *Johnnie's no substitute for six foot four inches of Sheriff Jones,* as if she had any illusions on the matter, waking up for the bazillionth time in a bed long since vacated by a worthless and incompetent man, left wide open for any attentive and good-loving man who just happened to fall out of the sky.

The thing—water pistol, wooden locomotive, crayon, who

the heck knew—jabbed a little harder against her cheek, and Stella rolled over in her bed.

"G'way, Tucker," she sighed. "Auntie Stella's very, very sleepy right now."

"Auntie Stella better get her ass out of bed," an unfamiliar voice whispered in her ear. "'Less she wants to spend the rest of the day splattered all over it."

That got her attention. Stella jerked awake, her heart rate lurching into overtime. Slowly, cautiously, she rolled over in the pale light of a late September dawn. She licked her lips a few times to get the crust off, then forced her eyes open. Crouched down next to the bed, his face inches from hers, was a man who bore more than a passing resemblance to a young Wayne Newton, dark hair slicked back over a broad forehead, eyes just a little too squinty and small, square white teeth showing in a grin that didn't look all too friendly.

Bad news come calling, and as her blood coursed hot through her veins, Stella got an eyeful of a second visitor standing behind him, someone she hadn't planned on ever seeing again—Brandy, dressed to the nines in a tight minty-green sweater with her hair restored to its fluffy glory.

"You must be Wil," Stella managed to croak out. "Well, go ahead. Might as well get it over with."

"I ain't shootin' you yet," the smooth-as-honey voice drawled. "We ain't even been properly introduced."

Wil gave Stella three minutes in the bathroom, enough time for her to brush her teeth while she was peeing and splash water on her face and generally try to get herself calmed down and under control.

When she came out of the bathroom, Noelle was standing in the hall in an old baseball shirt and shorts, and it was all Stella could do to keep from throwing herself on top of her baby girl to protect her.

"Good morning, Mama," Noelle said in a wobbly but brave voice. Stella could see the fear in her daughter's pretty violet eyes, but the girl kept her chin high and even managed a fleeting little smile.

"Oh, sugar," she said, gathering Noelle into a fierce hug.

Over her daughter's shoulder, Stella saw that Wil was pointing his stupid little .38—a match for the one Stella had taken off Brandy and, unfortunately, locked into the steel box bolted to the floor of her Jeep—at both of them, looking faintly amused.

"Your daughter's awfully cute," Brandy called from the kitchen. "She don't take after you much, though."

"What a bitch," Noelle muttered, easing past her into the bathroom. "I won't be but a minute. It's going to be okay, isn't it?"

"Of course it is," Stella promised.

When Noelle shut the door, Stella turned on Wil, nearly overcome with fury. "You fucking waste," she stammered. "You do *not* involve my daughter in your stupid-assed problems—do you understand?"

Wil merely chuckled. "Oh, calm down, Stella, ain't nothin' bad going to happen to no one if y'all behave. 'Sides, she's got sass. I like 'er."

Stella started to explain all the ways she'd make Wil pay for that comment, when she detected a lack of focus in his reddened eyes, a twitchiness in his movements, which made her think twice. She'd bet good money the man was hopped up on something, maybe PCP, and in her experience, an unpredictable and high person was not a person you wanted to go around threatening.

Noelle came out of the bathroom and Brandy handed each of them a package of Ho Hos and one of the juice boxes Stella kept in the fridge for Tucker.

"Eat up," she said. "Gotta start the day right."

Then she gathered up their purses, along with her own, and slung them all over an arm.

"Brandy, honey, what are you thinkin'?" Wil demanded.

"A girl's gotta have her things," Brandy said, and Stella's irritation with her slipped just a little. "I went through 'em, baby, there wasn't nothin' bad in there, just makeup and what-all."

"Well, you keep 'em with you. I'll drive," Wil said. Stella figured that went without saying when she looked out the kitchen window and saw his white van pulled up close to the garage door. Wil had picked out the signs that read CHEERY MAIDS—LET US CLEAN SO YOU DON'T HAVE TO! for the occasion. Stella had the fleeting thought that she'd be more than happy to let someone come clean—after all, it looked like she'd be out of the house for a while.

Wil handed the gun over to Brandy as they filed out to the driveway. He directed Stella and Noelle to take the seats in back, a pair of surprisingly comfortable captain's chairs.

"Buckle up," he ordered as he rummaged around on the floor between the front seats, coming up with a paper bag from which he pulled out two pairs of plastic restraints. As Brandy settled herself in the front passenger seat and touched up her lipstick in the vanity mirror, Wil knelt on the floor of the van in front of Stella and Noelle and told them to stick out their wrists, but he had a hard time getting the restraints secured in place.

"Guess you're just a beginner, huh," Noelle observed as he finally got the tab pulled through the slot. She had calmed down considerably as she got used to the idea of being held captive.

"Why'n't you watch your smart mouth," he shot back.

Stella gave her daughter a little head shake, which earned her a roll of the eyes. Same feisty Noelle as always, she didn't one bit like being told what to do. Stella was pleased that her daughter had some fighting spirit.

"I'm not entirely clear on the picture here," she said as Wil crawled back to the driver's seat and Brandy twisted around to wave the gun at them. "Yesterday you were trying to get me to kill this guy. Now you and him seem to have worked out your differences."

"Power of love, baby," Wil called out as he got himself settled and buckled in. He got the van started up and backed slowly down the drive onto the street, tapping along on the steering wheel with his thumbs, making *pfft-pfft* sounds with his teeth against his lips to keep the beat of whatever song was playing in the background of his high.

"I hate to say it, but I had this man all wrong," Brandy said with a dainty little sigh. At least she had the decency to blush. "After that horrible butch detective got her ass whupped and had to let me loose yesterday, I didn't know where to go, and

I was all desperate and whatnot, and then here's my cell phone ringin' and—well, it was *Wil*."

She beamed at her lover like a newlywed. Wil gave the steering wheel an extra special series of thumps and gave her a shotgun-style salute, which made her giggle even more. Wil lurched into a sloppy turn and tore down Stella's street and out onto Hickory doing nearly fifty. With any luck, they'd get pulled over for speeding, except Goat and his deputies had bigger fish to fry at the moment.

"He wasn't tryin' to kill me after all," Brandy continued. "He just didn't know how else to get that poor woman's shoes back. And when he realized it was too late to get the evidence off of Goat and all, he was like, if you can't beat 'em, join 'em, you know? He told me he wanted me back and then he told me the whole story."

"'Cause I didn't do it. I didn't kill no woman," Wil crowed, voice going thin and chortling. He was definitely on something, Stella thought, some little chemical enhancement that would render him even more unpredictable and dangerous. Great.

"Did you blow up her car?" Stella demanded.

Wil cast a guilty look at his sweetheart. "Aw, I didn't mean it to go like that," he said apologetically. "It's fuckin' hard to get that shit right. I didn't put hardly near as much of the junk in the tank as they said on the Internet. I thought it would, you know, just kind of be like a little bang."

"You could have killed her!"

"No—no, I made sure she was in the house. I only just wanted to make sure Brandy was taking my, you know, needs seriously. Since we'd been broke up and all. I mean, come on, Stella, I ain't stupid."

"Was that you trying to get in the window back of my house, too?"

"Well, yeah. I saw you over at the track talkin' to the law and them and I didn't know what-all you were fixin' to do."

"So you what, thought you'd break in and look for *clues*?" Stella leaned heavily on the sarcasm, but the truth was, she was at least a little bit impressed. Wil, hearing on the radio that the twister had taken out the snack shack, had to have hightailed it over to Prosper pretty quick. Idiot or not, managing to sneak all around a town that small without getting noticed was something.

"You know what I don't get about guys like you," she continued, "you could be doing just as well for yourself just going to work and punching the clock like a regular joe. I mean, come on, does the small-time crook thing really pay all that good? This ain't exactly a Maserati you're driving."

"Don't you talk that way," Brandy snapped as Stella gestured around the worn surfaces of the van. "Wil's doing *very well* for himself."

"Brandy," Stella said, exasperated, "even if he didn't kill Laura Cassel, which you only have *his* word on, you've gotta know about all that robbing he's been doing. He goes around measuring people's closets, or pretending to, most likely, checking out their silver and their jewelry and shit while he's there, and then he drives this here funmobile on over when they're out at work and helps himself."

"And then they get their *insurance*, Stella," Brandy shot back, "which they probably overexaggerated in the first place and they probably claim stuff while they're at it that weren't even missing. Everybody does it, you ask me, you're a damn fool if you don't—"

"Oh, so folks who do things by the rules are stupid?" Noelle broke in. "That's just about the biggest pile of crap I ever heard."

"They're goddamn victimless crimes!" Wil hollered, and swung his head around to give Stella a slightly unbalanced leer. "Takin' shit from rich folks, distributing a few recreational substances here and there—"

"So you're into drugs, too?" Stella wasn't surprised. She'd seen guys like this before, the ones who were motivated by the thrill of the underworld, for whom a dishonest buck would always spend way sweeter than an honest one.

"The point, Stella, is he ain't a murderer," Brandy said. "He didn't *do* it. He's innocent. And now we got everything worked out between us, we just want to clear his good name so's we can move on. And that's where you come in, to help us with the violence part, seein' as we're just not violent people."

"Just what are you saying, 'the violence part,'" Stella said. "What have you got in mind for me to do, anyway?"

"You're going to take care of a little job for us. Just like you do all the time, so don't go acting like it's any kind of hardship or nothing," Brandy said. "And Noelle's here for a little extra guarantee that you're going to do what you're told. We'll let her go as soon as we know you done the job."

Stella's heart sank. They were going to force her to kill someone—and the reason they were so sure of themselves was that they thought she killed folks all the time. It was safe to say that no amount of protesting would change their minds.

Still, she had to try. "You can't think this plan makes sense," she said to Brandy.

"Oh, but it does," Brandy interrupted. "Wil's thought it all through."

"You're willing to hang your future on—"

Stella gestured at the driver's seat, trying to communicate with the gesture *loser, idiot, smack-head,* but Brandy was staring at the man with adoration.

She finally tore her gaze away and fixed Stella with a peaceful smile. "I blame myself, really. I should have been there for Wil from the start. If I'd of only been a better communicator—if we'd just talked, you know, the way they do on Dr. Phil, why—"

"I can't stand Dr. Phil," Noelle cut in. "He's mean. Especially to women, like if they're a little heavy or something? I mean, say what you will about Oprah, she knows what it's like to be female, she *understands* women."

"I don't know," Brandy said doubtfully. "Thing about women is, they'll turn on you. You can't trust another woman like you can trust a man, 'cause a man don't want to compete with you, you know? Women are always *competing* with each other."

"You think *Oprah's* competing with other women?" Noelle demanded hotly. "So when she gets them little gals that got a couple of legs blown off in the service, or them women that quit being prostitutes so's they can start families and run companies, you figure Oprah's *competing* with them?"

"Noelle, sugar, let's save this conversation for later," Stella said gently. No sense getting Brandy any more riled than she already was.

"But, Mama, I don't even think Dr. Phil is a real doctor."

"Well, he's like a psychology doctor, a—"

"I mean he's always talking about this and that syndrome, shit that don't make no sense, and half the time I think he just goes and makes it up."

Something clicked in Stella's brain.

Something that had been struggling to make it to the surface for days.

"Noelle . . . ," she said slowly, "what did you just say?"

Noelle looked at her like she was crazy, and slowly and carefully repeated herself. "I think Dr. Phil makes shit up, Mama."

Like . . . what was it Dr. Herman had said in the office?

Some kind of medical syndrome. Groundbreaking research . . . memory loss . . . *like erasing digital files from a hard drive.*

That sure went against everything else Stella had heard about OxyContin. In her experience, it left folks crashed out and jittery, but they generally knew exactly where they'd been and what they'd done. What if Dr. Herman had made it all up?

Neb had said he'd bought his junk from "someone who'd surprise you," a respected member of the medical community. And naturally, when Stella found out Laura Cassel had been a drug rep, she'd tied the two together. But if he'd been getting his Oxy straight from the doctor . . .

And the doctor and Laura would have known each other. Picot was less than ten miles from Fairfax, where the hospital was—it had to be in her territory, so she'd have called on the medical offices there.

Maybe Laura had figured out the doctor was dealing. Threatened him with exposure.

Would that be enough to make him kill her?

Stella smacked her linked hands against her knees, cutting into the flesh of her wrists with the restraints.

"It's Dr. Herman!" she said. "I can't believe I didn't figure this out before. And the drugs, right. What did you do, get 'em from the doc and sell 'em to Neb?"

"I'd shut my mouth, I was you," Wil sputtered, turning to glare at Stella and then jerking the wheel after he drifted across the center line. "Ain't any reason for you to do all that figuring. You'll get your orders when it's time, and not a minute sooner."

Stella could so easily grab the gun if she could only use her hands. Hell, if she could get her seat belt unbuckled, she could probably push herself out of her seat and throw herself at Brandy, and the dumb bunny would no doubt drop the gun, she was so busy drooling over her crook boyfriend, but then Wil would probably wreck the car and she didn't feel like becoming part of a dumb-ass pileup.

Instead, she sat silently and fumed, thinking through her theory. If the doctor wanted to make some cash on the side, he'd do better with a partner—someone who moved in the low-life circles where customers were likely to be found. Using a middleman, the doc was less likely to draw attention to himself—he'd keep his hands more or less clean.

"Well, now, here we are," Wil said as they tore through the outskirts of Fairax and into a tired subdivision on the near end of town. He pulled into the tidy driveway of a rather ordinary white colonial. Black shutters shed splinters of paint on either side of square windows set in aluminum siding, but the house was in fairly good repair. The lawn was cut to a ruthless couple of inches of turf, but otherwise the landscaping was fairly in-different, a couple of shrubs hacked into spheres.

A bachelor's lawn. Stella's trained eye picked out a few other clues: the flyers jammed into the door handle, the empty ornamental urns.

"There's no Mrs. Doctor Herman, I take it."

"You think you're so smart, with this whole guessin' game," Wil said, cutting the ignition. "Okay. Fine, Miss Smarty Pants. Yes, it's Dr. Herman. And yes, his wife left him awhile back. Ding-ding-ding. Happy? Satisfied?"

"I still don't get why he killed Laura," Stella said.

"Well, not every love is like ours," Brandy said sorrowfully. "Ain't every couple can support each other through all the ups and the downs."

"Wait—you're saying Laura was his *girlfriend*?" Stella de-manded. She remembered what Goat said, that her parents thought she might be seeing an old boyfriend, someone she was embarrassed about. But if she was seeing a married man, she would have had a good reason to be evasive.

"Yeah, Sherlock. And he didn't mean to kill her, either—that was an accident." Now that the cat was out of the bag, Wil was warming to the subject. "She showed up at his place one morning all bent out of shape 'cause she'd got a gander at his numbers and put two and two together and figured out he was moving stock out the side. She got self-righteous on him—she said she was going to report him, how he was going to lose his license. I mean, that's not the kind of thing you spring on a guy before his coffee, you know?"

Brandy giggled as though he'd told a hilarious joke.

"So he just *killed* her?"

"No, he tried to talk her out of it, like for an hour or two, but she kept digging in her heels and wouldn't see no reason. Way he told me, he was just trying to keep her from leaving, he had a hold of her arm or something and she was trying to, I don't know, wiggle out or whatever and she slipped. Hit her head, something like that."

"Uh-huh." Now this was an area where Stella would wager she *did* have more experience than Wil—the sort of "accidents" that happen when a man and a woman have a domestic disagreement. "And let me guess . . . after she had this little *accident,* Dr. Herman panicked and called you, his one and only shady underworld friend?"

Wil's scowl deepened. "I'm a *problem*-solver, Stella, that's why he called me."

Dang if there wasn't a note of pride in the man's voice. Yeah, Stella thought with disgust, being summoned to dispose of the body had been, for all Wil's whining and complaining, a high point, a big day in his criminal career.

Another difference between them, then. When Stella's work met with success, what she felt was relief. Relief that another woman would be able to sleep easily that night, without fear of waking to the sound of curses and the impact of fists.

But she was never *proud* of hurting people, not even the wretched, hateful targets of her brand of justice. She was proud of turning her life around, certainly. Proud of running the sewing shop without Ollie, proud of picking up the pieces of their domestic life and making it run smoothly, paying the bills and figuring the taxes and negotiating with vendors.

She was definitely proud of the body she'd toned, of the hard muscle beneath her soft curves.

And she was proud of a few of the innovations she'd come up with. The bondage gear, for instance, that kept her targets incapacitated while Stella adjusted their attitudes. The gags that kept them quiet while she explained the new rules. The follow-up regimen that ensured none of them escaped her watchful eye afterwards.

But in the moment where she saw the defiance go out of a man's eyes, when he finally stopped cursing and started to look afraid, when she convinced herself he would never again be a threat to a woman—was it *pride* she felt?

No.

And seeing pride in Wil's eyes made her more than a little queasy.

"So why the track?" she demanded. It was the one piece of the puzzle she hadn't figured out yet.

"Oho," Wil chuckled. "That was pure dumb luck. I told the doc to go on back and finish up his rounds or whatever. Don't draw attention to himself, that's what I said. So who's his first appointment? Neb Donovan! In there to get a fifteen-thousand-mile checkup on that bum disk of his. Anyhow they're talking, and Neb's carrying on about this and that, how he's got to get a little help getting that foundation poured. How it's yea big and yea wide, so many cubic feet, and so on, and then the doc realizes how this might be the perfect opportunity."

"To pin a murder on an innocent man."

"Yeah, that's right. He got Neb to sign a blank piece of paper—hell, Neb was so messed up in those days, hitting the

Oxy around the clock, he never knew what he was signing. Then, after Neb left, the doc made out like it was a note from him so he could stick it on the body. He was thinking ahead, I'll give him that."

"So then what, the doctor finishes up his office hours, and the two of you all wait until dark and dragged that poor girl on out to the track in the middle of the night?"

Wil frowned. "The doc wasn't about to do that. Kinda pissed me off. He was all, *That's why I'm paying you, you figure it out.* Bastard. So I had to get her in the ground myself."

"What did he pay you, anyway?" Stella turned to Brandy. "And you're okay with this, Brandy? This man of yours putting someone's daughter in the ground for money?"

"It wasn't like he *wanted* to," Brandy retorted hotly. "He *had* to. The doctor said he'd turn Wil in if he didn't help. Believe me, that doctor's no good. I mean, he planted evidence on that poor girl to make it look like Wil done killed her."

"The shoes."

"The *patent leather* shoes," Brandy breathed, "that show every mark."

"So you want me to think the doctor went out and got shoes special and put 'em on the body just so—"

"No, I never said that. Only, when they took that body out to Wil's trunk, the doctor made Wil get the feet. Tell her, Wil."

A faint pink blush ticked the back of Wil's neck. Yeah, Stella thought, I guess I'd be embarrassed to be such a dumb-ass, too.

"He did" was all Wil said.

"And then he waited until the concrete was all hardened up to tell Wil about the prints," Brandy continued, clearly indignant, "so's he wouldn't get the idea to go fessing up any time."

"That rat bastard," Stella said sarcastically.

Brandy glanced at her suspiciously, but Stella flashed her a reassuring smile.

So that was the story, and now they were fast closing on the final chapter. Wil unbuckled his seat belt and leaned back to unfasten Stella's. She considered lurching forward, maybe knocking Wil out with a forehead butt to his nose, but that still left Brandy holding a gun on her.

"What-all are you going to make my mom do, anyway?" Noelle asked.

"Well, she's going to make the doc confess, what do you think?" Brandy said. "Wil got us a nice digital camcorder and one a those tripods? You know, where you set it up so you can talk into it and record a movie?"

"Wonder which Cozy Closet customer's missing that," Stella said—but she was vastly relieved the plan wasn't turning out to be a murder-for-hire after all. She glanced at Noelle, hoping fervently that Brandy would keep her mouth shut about the rest. All Noelle knew about her mother's leisure-time activities was that Stella seemed to have a lot of friends who were going through tough times that required lots of listening. She was pretty sure that her daughter, if she had her suspicions, preferred not to know exactly how far her mother's compassion went.

Brandy glared at her. "Ain't nobody as needs it worse than we do, anyway," she said.

"You oughtta *thank* us," Wil said. "We ain't askin' you to kill him. You won't have that on your conscience. All's you got to do is get him to make the tape."

"Why don't y'all just do it yourselves?" Noelle asked, disgusted.

Brandy sucked in a breath, looking amazed. "Noelle, don't you know what they say about your mama? She can make a man do *anything*. Why, if Wil and me tried to get the doc to talk, he might clam up and we could end up knocking him unconscious or something before he got the movie done. Your *mama,* though, she's like the best there is."

Noelle gave her mother a thoughtful look. To Stella's surprise, it was about 99 percent crafty curiosity, with not a trace of judgment. The thought that her daughter might actually approve of her avocation buoyed Stella's spirits considerably.

"So here's how this is gonna go," Wil said. "Brandy's gonna stay here with Noelle. That's like insurance, Stella. See, I know you don't want nothing bad to happen to your girl there, so's you're more likely to cooperate."

Stella gave Brandy her most withering stare. "Brandy, if you so much as look at Noelle cross-eyed, I'm gonna kick your ass all the way to Saint Louis."

Brandy turned away and stared out the van's passenger window at a bank of hostas lining the walk.

"I'd be more worried about the next hour if I was you, Stella," Wil said. He was aiming for a hard-ass tone, Stella knew, but he was making a miscalculation. She'd been around enough amateur bullies that he didn't scare her much. He wasn't one of the real ones, the mean ones. As stupid and naïve as Brandy was, there was a corner of Stella's heart that was grateful for Wil's basic makeup, which was plenty flawed, but with the wishy-washy sorts of failings that were unlikely to ever get taken out on his woman.

The two of them deserved each other. Neither one was likely to get nominated to sainthood in this lifetime, but neither was likely to upset the balance of the universe either. Their sins were relatively minor, and along the way they probably provided enough amusement and even occasional comfort to their fellow humans that they erased their cosmic debt.

Stella remembered the way Wil's neighbor had talked about him, admiringly, even affectionately. And Goat's bemusement when he shared his checkered history with Brandy—if even *he* couldn't manage to maintain a grudge against the gal, then how could she?

If she wanted, Stella was confident that she and Noelle could climb out of the van—which would be a little tricky, given the plastic restraints still on their wrists—and then walk down the street whistling and Brandy and Wil, for all their blustering and threatening and laying out of evil promises, would do no more than jump up and down in frustration. If Stella had had her doubts about Wil's innocence in Laura's death, they were laid to rest now.

But hell. She was here, and there was a *true* bad guy—a woman-killing, smug, unrepentant bastard not fifty feet away. And it wasn't like she had anything better to do today. And, for that matter, she hadn't had a single client since getting shot over the summer.

Her return to the job couldn't wait forever. Maybe it was time to dive back into the pool.

"All right," she said. "I'll do it. But I don't have my stuff."

"What stuff?" Wil demanded impatiently.

"You know—my gear. My restraints, my tools. I mean I know I look tough, but you can't expect me to go in there and tackle a six-foot-two guy and take him down on my own."

"Course not—that's why I'll be there."

Stella sighed. "No offense, but I'd really be more comfortable—"

"Quit stalling. Let's go."

He got out of the car and a second later the sliding door was yanked open and he extended a hand. Stella pointedly ignored it and jumped down carefully, taking the impact in her bum hip and barely staying on her feet. She held out her wrists expectantly.

Wil stared. "Oh. Um . . ."

Stella rolled her eyes. "Get my purse. There's scissors in there."

Wil snapped his mouth shut and got her purse. He rooted around for a few minutes until he came up with the little pink quilted case.

"This?" he demanded.

"They're sharper than they look," Stella sighed. "Can we get on with this? I like to be home in time for dinner on days I beat the shit out of someone. It's kind of a tradition."

Wil fumbled with the embroidery scissors, finally getting them out of the case. They *were* a lot sharper than they looked—an expensive pair of Ginghers with curved blades—and they sliced right through the restraints.

Stella rubbed at her wrists, massaging the tender spots where the plastic had cut into her flesh. Wil tossed the scissors back in the purse and handed it through the window to Brandy, then put his hand to Stella's back and gave her a little shove.

"So you're letting Brandy keep the gun, instead of bringing

it with us?" Stella asked, nodding in the direction of the van as Wil marched her down the street. "Think that's smart?"

"I was a wrestler in high school," Wil said. "I really don't think I'll have much trouble with a sixty-five-year-old man who takes blood pressure pills."

"How do you know what he's—?"

"Oh, the doc told me. It's, like, professional interest. Folks on Clonidine get a little extra kick from nembies and purple hearts—you know, downers. It's a nice little growth area for me."

Stella started to respond, then thought better of it. She wasn't about win a debate about the ethics of pushing prescription drugs today.

"Look," Stella said when they got to the front door. "Can I at least give you a little bit of advice? We might want to try to get in without drawing attention to ourselves."

"Come on, Stella," Wil said confidently. "As soon as we have the confession recorded, ain't nobody going to care about anything else. And when we're done, we just leave him here. That's the beauty of it—I can turn the tape in tomorrow or the next day, maybe mail it, give me and Brandy a little head start getting out of town, not that anyone's gonna come looking for us once they got the doc for it."

"I still think—"

"Man, you just have to run the show, don't you, Stella?" Wil shook his head and gave her a pitying look. "I don't mean to hurt your feelings here, but you ought to take a page out of Brandy's book, you know what I mean?"

Stella felt her hackles rising. "No, I have no idea what you're trying to say."

"Well, you know, being feminine? It's an art. There's more to it than just dressing classy and all. You got to let the man drive, see what I'm saying? A man wants to feel like he's in charge. That's where your real power is, you women, is if you let the man take the lead. Just a little something to think about, maybe get you a date one of these days."

Stella fumed silently as they approached the front door. "I'll think about it," she muttered through clenched teeth.

"Atta girl," Wil said.

An interesting thing happened after Wil pressed the buzzer. Stella glanced at him and noticed he was preening, building himself up for the encounter, and it occurred to her that she was witnessing the donning of the charm that Wil must go through for every call on a new customer, for every encounter with a neighbor. Here was the source of his charm. Here was the secret of his eluding the law. He stood a little taller, tugged his collar into place, and flashed his features through a quick calisthenic routine that included a grimace and a grin before it settled into pure, complacent confidence.

Another interesting thing happened when the door opened a fraction of an inch and Dr. Herman peered at them through the opening: a hand holding a gun snaked out and shot Wil Vines right in his handsome kisser.

TWENTY-THREE

. . . .

Maybe it was age, maybe it was nerves, maybe it was the burden of having already sent one fellow human being to an early death, but Dr. Herman was a terrible shot.

The bullet hit Wil in the cheek and traveled a path that, as far as Stella could tell at first glance, took a chunk out of his ear and possibly chipped his skull and most certainly dented his slick hairdo. He didn't fall down or anything, though. To Stella's shocked amusement, he actually said "Ow" and brought up a hand to his face, like he'd been bit by a mosquito, say, or run into a low-hanging branch.

Stella glanced back at the doctor in time to see that he'd opened the door a bit wider and now had the cheap little handgun trained on her. Perhaps it was a more stable stance, or the increased maneuverability he had with the door open, but he seemed more certain of his second shot, the gun pointed in the general direction of Stella's throat.

The thought that went through her head as she slammed her shoulder into the door with all her weight, as the door caught the doctor's chest and sent him staggering back into the room, was that she was so fucking *not* about to get herself shot again after the scars from the last round were still shiny and raw and she was painstakingly busting open a vitamin E capsule every damn night like Noelle told her, rubbing that shit on the tender tissue of her stomach and shoulder in hopes of getting the scars to fade enough so she could maybe someday wear a bathing suit again or even a tank top without scaring kids.

She was *not* about to let this old asshole shoot her. The last man who'd tried might have been out of shape, but he was at least roughly her age and had the advantage of years of building up his skills committing all kinds of crimes. The doctor, on the other hand, was a slack-necked white-collar-wearing soft-palmed nancy, and if Stella couldn't take him, then she didn't deserve to live.

Only, she didn't count on Wil.

As she threw herself at Dr. Herman, making a grunting kind of sound deep in her throat, Wil staggered forward and got in her way. He was waving one hand around in the air while with the other he tried to stop the blood pouring out of his face, and into his eyes. He somehow got one foot in front of Stella and the two of them went down together, Stella's elbow slamming hard against the tile floor of the doctor's entrance hall as she tried to disentangle from Wil.

The more she scrambled, the more she seemed to end up pinioned. When she finally worked one arm free and pushed herself up to a sitting position, there was the stupid doctor, squatting in front of her and waving his gun back and forth between them.

Wil, lying on his side with a blood-slicked hand on his

face, moaned. "How the fuck did you know we were coming?" he demanded.

"Careful preparation," Dr. Herman said, his voice smug. "Got a call a couple of nights ago from the folks in Fayette, wanting me to send over Neb's medical records. Now that got me to thinking—what's my old friend Wil going to do when his hard work gets unearthed, so to speak? I figured you'd probably be a little nervous. Frankly, I thought you would have called me by now."

"Why, so you could have you a last laugh, you cocksucker?"

"No, I figured you'd want me to bail you out. Or maybe hit me up for more cash, so you could run off to Mexico or wherever low-life scum like you go when the shit hits the fan."

Wil stopped pushing blood around on his face to blink, slack-jawed, at the doc. Even Stella worked up a little indignation on his behalf.

"Who's bailing *who* out?" he demanded. "Who covered up your sloppy-assed mistake? Who, I gotta ask you, was blubberin' like a girl when I got here and you'd done killed your girlfriend?"

"I was not—I was *not*—that was a state of shock, of emotional trauma," Dr. Herman protested. "Besides, I paid you handsomely."

"You paid me chickenshit!" Wil started to scramble to his feet, waving his hand around, still trying to get the blood wiped off his face, as Dr. Herman jerked the gun back and forth between him and Stella. "Twelve thousand bucks? It weren't worth it for the trouble. That ain't even enough to buy a ugly-ass used truck. That's not but a couple good weekends in Vegas. You busted up my *relationship,* you fucker—"

Stella sighed, a huge, impatient, world-weary sigh, the sigh of a kindergarden teacher breaking up yet another scuffle in the sandbox. Goddamn Y chromosome. Here they were at what any sane human being might consider an impasse, a time to quit shootin' and threatenin' and blamin' and start working toward a creative solution—and these two still couldn't stop slinging the shit.

"Just *shut* the fuck *uuuuup!*" she screamed, putting her fingers to her ears and lurching to her feet. She braced for the shot, but when it didn't come in the first seconds, she swung her bad leg back and then brought it forward with every last bit of momentum she could muster in a roundhouse kick to Dr. Herman's unprotected groin.

The twin sounds that filled the moment that followed—the second crack of the gun and Dr. Herman's high-pitched scream—echoed around in Stella's head as she got the hell out of the way, reckoning that if the two damn fools were bent on killing each other, she might as well let them do it without her.

TWENTY-FOUR

. . . .

Stella couldn't quite decide if she was disappointed that Dr. Herman's second shot lodged itself in the fleshy part of Wil's arm. The man was certainly carrying on like a stuck pig, but she could tell that not only would he live to tell the tale but that he'd also get out with nothing more than a few dollars' worth of gauze and bandages. Although if Dr. Herman's brethren had their say, it would probably cost a few thousand bucks, but that was the health care system for you.

Dr. Herman, on the other hand, might have inspired a little more sympathy if she wasn't just so disgusted with him. The shrill cry he let loose when her foot connected had diminished to a series of keening sobs, but he didn't even seem to notice when Stella carefully plucked his gun from his twitching hand.

Stella leaned back against a sofa and stared at the two of them for a minute, shaking her head and sighing. Worthless. God help a world that handed over the keys to every important organization—the United Nations, NASA, professional

sports—and in effect said, "Here, boys, go on ahead and drive."
When would women wake up and start running things?

"So, Doc," she said conversationally. "You ever think about
the fact if you'd just kept your dick in your pants, none a this
would have happened? Huh?"

The doc huffed a few shallow breaths before he rolled his
head to the side and glared at her. "Fu . . . fu . . . fuck you."

Stella shook her head. Typical. A man can't come up with an
answer to a perfectly legitimate question, he goes right on the
attack. "And selling drugs out of your office, I mean, isn't there
some kind of provision in that Hippocratic oath about that?
And how much money could you have *made,* anyway? Was it
really worth it?"

If it was possible for Dr. Herman's expression to turn any
more bitter, that last comment did the trick. "Everyone screws
over doctors," he panted. "Malpractice and the damn insurance companies—"

"And all those ex-wives, oh, yeah, blah blah blah," Stella
cut in. "My heart bleeds for you, buddy, it really does. I just got
to ask you, though. That shit you told me in your office, that
Kurtzoy syndrome—none of that was true, was it."

Dr. Herman managed to lift his head up off the floor an
inch or two so he could look at her. She was astonished to see
his face twist itself up into that self-important sneer he'd had
when he was sitting behind his big desk with all those diplo-
mas up on the wall behind his head.

"There *is* a Kurtzoy syndrome," he said, his voice assured
and arrogant as hell. "It has to do with spinal stenosis complicated by tortuosity of the nerve roots. I'm afraid it's prob-

ably a little too complicated to explain to a lay person like yourself."

Un-fucking-believable. There he was, a murderer, lying on the floor, felled by his own stupidity as much as by her determination, and he still felt like he could talk down to her just because he had a title in front of his name.

Stella gave the doctor one final disgusted kick in the testicles, just enough to keep him occupied for a few more minutes, and grabbed a tissue from a box before picking up his phone. Ignoring the renewed whimpering from the floor, she dialed her own cell phone number.

After a few rings, it was picked up.

"Wil—that you?"

"No, Brandy," Stella sighed. "It's not your lame-ass idiot boyfriend. Seriously, woman, you wake up to Wil every day and really think he's a better deal than you had with Goat?"

There was a long silence—so long, Stella began to wonder if Brandy had hung up on her.

Then Brandy hiccupped delicately in her ear. "Wil ain't a bad man," she whispered.

If Stella had a dollar for every time some confused female laid that line on her, she figured she could have already retired. Usually, when a woman resorted to that line, it was code for "this man of mine is so bad and such a disappointment and so far from what I dreamed of when I was a little girl that I've created an alternate reality in which my mind can relax and hallucinate while the rest of my self is being beat to hell."

But in some weird, confused way that Stella had never even imagined before meeting this woman, she kind of got it.

Wil wasn't a good man. He wasn't even a mediocre man. But he also wasn't exactly evil.

So his idea of a good time involved relieving folks of household goods they'd just as soon hang on to—was that any worse than some of these guys running for office who were selling off influence to the highest bidder and throwing their constituents under the bus every time the political winds changed directions?

Was he worse than men of the cloth carrying on in the pulpit on Sunday and getting their rocks off on Monday with some poor gal who had to put out to buy baby food?

Was he worse, come to think of it, than family physicians dealing drugs out of their offices just to make a few extra bucks?

Naw. The way Stella figured it, he wasn't even hardly much worse than average.

"Look here, Brandy. Your man's gonna live, but he's been shot a couple times. And I really don't appreciate you all sending me in there unarmed, 'cause it put me at a distinct disadvantage when I had to save Wil's ass *and* kick the doc's."

Brandy made a strangled sound. "Shot?" she squeaked. "Dr. Herman done shot Wil? With *what*?"

Oh, Lord in heaven. "A *gun,* Brandy. I guess it never occurred to your brilliant boyfriend that Dr. Herman might not like getting busted in on, huh? That he might have stored up a few precautions? Now, look, here's what we're gonna do. Drive that van on into the garage. Y'all come on in here and we'll get Wil into the van. Then you're gonna drop Noelle and him at the hospital, and you're going to go home and get me a few things I need."

"No, I wanna go with Wil. I *need* to be with him, Stella."

Stella gritted her teeth. Her patience was being taxed to the limit today. "Brandy, y'all had your chance, and excuse me for sayin' so, but you fucked it up good. Now we do it my way. Noelle goes with Wil, and that's like my insurance, see? 'Cause if you don't do exactly what I say, I call up my girl and tell her to let Goat in on exactly what you all done today. How you showed up at my private residence and stuck a gun in my ear. How you—"

"Okay, okay. But I got to go be with my man as soon as I'm done with your errands. What-all do you want me to get you?"

"Just drive that van in like I told you, girl. I'll make you a list."

Stella found a pad of paper in the doc's study that had *Darvocet* splashed across the top in bright curvy lettering. The irony struck her as one of the funnier notes in a mostly joyless and irritating day.

She went back out to the hall to write her list. Wil was sitting up looking glum, most of the blood wiped off his face except for a slow-moving trickle from his shot-up ear. Dr. Herman made a sound like a stepped-on cat when he saw her and covered his family jewels with shaking hands.

Not your finest work, she murmured to the Big Guy, *no offense intended.*

And then—quick, before the ladies arrived—she added her daily dose of gratitude:

Thank you for all the fine people who love me.

Thank you for meaningful work.

Thank you for saving my ass just now.

—and, while it didn't make the official list, Stella allowed herself a little flash of appreciation for that fine view of Goat's backside yesterday as he clambered out of the rowboat before pulling her to shore.

TWENTY-FIVE

. . . .

By the middle of October, all traces of the twisters had been erased. An early freeze had made short work of the impatiens and marigolds that had soldiered on through autumn, but pumpkins were shaping up on the vine and the oak trees that lined the streets of town were turning gold and the skies woke up every morning a glorious blue, which Stella figured was more than fair compensation.

The gal from Bernina came in and showed Stella and Chrissy all the fancy things their newest sewing machine could do. Chrissy got interested enough that she quit spending every spare minute doing geek things and set to work finishing the quilt she'd begun making for Tucker before he got kidnapped. What with all the computing and sewing, she decided she'd had enough of Larry—"Stella, he just couldn't stand to let me at the keyboard, he was always over my shoulder tellin' me what to do and I figure I don't much need that anymore"—and seemed content to be single.

The Donovans brought over a tall stack of cash and a strawberry cheesecake. Stella tried to give some of the money back, but Donna said they figured she'd more than earned it, seeing as she'd had to face down another gunfight so soon after her last one, and besides with Noelle there and Chrissy doing all the background work, it was like having extra folks on the payroll. Besides, Donna had money set aside for Neb's legal defense, which they turned out not to need—the dustup over his escape got cut short when the county commissioner stepped in to express his displeasure that the breach in the chain of command that resulted in the first jailbreak of the century in the state of Missouri had taken place on his watch.

"Kind of a 'don't ask, don't tell' situation," Donna explained it. "They didn't ask Neb what he was doing back home the next morning, and he ain't gonna tell everyone what a bunch of dumb-asses they got working over there."

A postcard arrived from Wil and Brandy, who were lying low while they waited for Wil's hearing on accessory charges. It featured a picture of a six-pack and a bug zapper and the caption GOOD TIMES IN VERSAILLES, MO. On the reverse, Brandy had written "Thanks I guess and tell Goat 'hi' from me." The *i*'s were dotted with little hearts.

Priscilla, who'd got a little time off work and didn't need it to defend her uncle, took Wil's case and oversaw the turning over of Dr. Herman's taped confession to Goat. She was arguing hard to get the charges reduced to next to nothing, given how helpful the tape turned out to be—Dr. Herman was cooling his heels in the state pen up in Jeff City and the state was going for second-degree murder.

Three weeks after the standoff at Dr. Herman's house, Stella asked everyone over for dinner. She was making Jelloman's favorite—barbecued ribs and corn bread—as a favor for all the house-sitting. She set the ribs to boil in beer after lunch, and cooked up a batch of barbecue sauce from a recipe Chrissy got off a website where the Johnnie Walker folks put up recipes.

She put her face over the pot and inhaled and figured the Johnnie was just the right touch, then left it to simmer.

An hour before the guests were due, Noelle drove up in her new Prius. The Donovans had been so thrilled with the outcome—Detective Simmons was in so much trouble for Neb's escape that he'd received an official apology on state stationery for his unfortunate and wrongful imprisonment, which Donna had framed in a cheery red frame with a berry-dotted mat and hung in the kitchen—that they'd thrown in a bonus for Noelle, seeing as she'd got dragged into the tail end of the excitement. Combined with all the new clients she had at the salon, Noelle figured it was time for her first new car.

After a whole lot of admiring and *ooh*ing, they left the car in the driveway and Noelle brought her makeup case inside.

"Mama, why do you let that dog in the kitchen?" Noelle demanded. Roxy had managed to get a purchase on the corner of a bag of buns and had tugged it onto the floor, where she was happily chomping her way through it, plastic and all.

"I'll beat her later," Stella promised, but Noelle bent down and gave her a huge hug. Roxy *was* pretty irresistible, recently bathed and sporting a bandanna Chrissy had whipped up out of fabric that featured skulls on a green background.

Roxy got bored when Noelle got busy beautifying her

mom, and wandered into the front room to bark at squirrels out the front window. Stella was using a chunk of the Donovans' money to fence the backyard and put in a doggy door.

Stella asked for something a little special, and Noelle got out the curling iron and did a whole retro-'80s thing. Stella wasn't sure she liked it, but Noelle carried on and worked up a smoky-eyed look that Stella figured made her look like the fairy godmother of Studio 54, but which Noelle swore made her look "hot for a mature woman."

They were folding Noelle's laundry together when the guests started to arrive. Chrissy brought Tucker, dressed in a little camp shirt made of the same skull fabric as Roxy's bandanna, and when the Donovans arrived, they took about a dozen pictures of the pair. Donna dragged Stella into the guest room and tugged her top this way and that and fussed with the buttons until she'd managed to get Stella's lace-edged camisole to peek out, showing a bit more freckly cleavage than Stella was accustomed to. "All good," Donna assured her, and dragged her back to the party.

Jelloman arrived with a big jug of his special tea and that dialed up the energy a bit. Somebody found Stella's party playlist, and soon Roxy was cavorting around the edges of a cluster of folks dancing while Todd sang and Tucker banged a spoon on the coffee table and howled with laughter.

Stella, however, sipped at a can of Fresca—she was too nervous to get into the Johnnie Walker Black just yet—and tried not to look at the clock.

She hadn't seen Goat since Laura Cassel's interment. She'd been standing at the back of the sad cluster of folks, listening to a pastor murmur those words from the Twenty-third Psalm that always made her think of the first funeral she ever attended, when they'd said good-bye to Uncle Horace and Stella understood for the first time that there was a kind of gone that stayed gone and went on hurting your heart your whole life, even while you found a way to go on and build a life around the hurt.

Stella didn't think Laura's parents noticed her at the back of the small throng of mourners at the cemetery. It was a windy, blustery day, clouds spitting out splatters of rain occasionally, and Stella had her coat collar turned up and was holding it against her raw cheeks when someone slipped an arm around her and pulled her against his tall, strong frame. And she hadn't fought it, she'd let Goat fold her against him and buried her face into his coat for a moment and let him shield her from the wind and the rain and the grief on the faces of a family saying good-bye to their daughter for the last time.

It called to mind another day, another funeral, when she'd hidden in the folds of her mother's good wool coat and cried hard as her father tossed the first handful of dirt down on top of Uncle Horace's casket.

But there were days for grieving and days for gratitude and days for just wading into all the goodness that the Big Guy saw fit to rain down on the world. And when there was a knock on the door, Stella was the only one to hear it because everyone else was in the kitchen filling up their plates and hollering over the music and each other's conversation.

Stella set her pop can down on a coaster and gave her hair a quick pat and opened the door, and there he was, Sheriff Jones in his off-hour duds, soft chamois shirt tucked into a pair of jeans so old and faded, they were frayed along the seams. He brought with him a faint scent of woodsmoke and spice and he was grinning that crooked grin where one corner of his mouth went a little bit up and the other didn't, and Stella thought to herself how, come to think of it, he gave that particular smile only to her.

"You fixin' to invite me in?" he asked. "Or do you just want to bring me a plate and I'll set out here and eat it?"

Stella stumbled backwards into the house and Goat came right along with her, his hand under her elbow so she wouldn't trip over the dog, who'd come bounding out to see who'd come calling.

And when he brushed his lips against hers, she was only barely aware of Roxy pushing her snout between them, of the raucous laughter from the other room, of the night breeze blowing leaves into the room, and she closed her eyes and figured she just might as well fix this moment in her memory so she could take it out and cherish it the next time she needed to remember that all the hard times made the good ones so much sweeter.

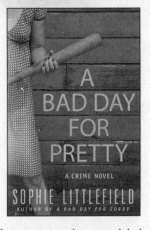
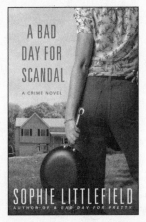